DOCTRINE OF THE HOLLOW

YOU'LL REMEMBER EVERYTHING- JUST NOT AS YOURSELF

MURTAZA VAPIWALA

Made with ♥ on the Notion Press Platform
www.notionpress.com

To the ones who forgot who they were — and to the few who remembered anyway

Contents

Contents

Foreword

Some stories are born from imagination. Others are born from questions we dare not ask. This one is both.

When I first stumbled upon the idea that became Doctrine of the Hollow, I wasn't trying to write a novel. I was trying to understand a feeling — the silence that creeps into places meant to be loud, the unease behind smiling faces, and the weight of truths buried deep under systems we blindly trust.

This story was written not to answer questions, but to raise them. To peel back the skin of institutions and see what bleeds beneath. And perhaps, somewhere along the way, remind us that obedience without understanding is the quietest kind of horror.

If you're holding this book, thank you — not just for reading, but for being willing to listen.

— Murtaza Vapiwala

Preface

This novel began as a whisper — a passing thought in the midst of exams, routines, and responsibilities. But like all persistent whispers, it grew louder until I had no choice but to sit down and let it speak.

Doctrine of the Hollow is not just a psychological thriller; it's a reflection of what happens when power collides with identity, when silence becomes a weapon, and when people begin to question what they've always been told.

Though the setting is fictional, the emotions — fear, paranoia, defiance — are drawn from the world around us. In many ways, writing this book was an act of rebellion against the comfort of normalcy.

This preface is not a warning. It's an invitation.

Acknowledgements

First and foremost, I thank *Khuda* — for the strength to write, the courage to finish, and the clarity to begin again.

To my parents, who gave me the freedom to dream, even when the dreams didn't make sense at first — thank you for your endless support.

To the readers who believed in this story before it was even finished — your encouragement turned silence into words.

To the friends who read early drafts, gave brutally honest feedback, or simply asked, "How's the book going?" — you kept me going.

And to every writer struggling with self-doubt: keep writing. The world needs your voice, especially when it tries to silence you.

Prologue

They say silence is the absence of sound.

But in Blackstone, silence was never empty. It was filled with glances that lasted too long, rules that no one questioned, and memories that didn't quite line up. It wasn't silence that haunted the campus. It was what came with it.

The train that arrived each year brought more than just students. It brought the illusion of choice. Of freedom. Of escape.

Aaron boarded that train like many before him — unaware, uncertain, hopeful. But what waited beyond the gates of Blackstone Academy of Law wasn't just education. It was something older. Something hidden. Something hollow.

And once you entered, you weren't allowed to leave the same.

CHAPTER ONE

BEFORE THE STORM

Ten days ago, a *news report* made the country gasp. Today, I was still boarding the train.

The rain poured in thick sheets, hammering against the metal roof of the station. The night sky rumbled, the occasional flicker of lightning cutting through the darkness. The air smelled of wet concrete, rusting metal, and something faintly greasy from the nearby food stalls.

I stepped onto the train, hesitating for just a second. I glanced back—at what, I wasn't sure. *Home? The past? The life I was leaving behind?* A mix of all three. But before I could unpack the feeling, the doors slid shut.

Just before they did, my eyes caught someone standing near the platform edge—a teenager, perhaps my age, maybe younger. His face was partially shadowed under the dim station lights, but there was something unsettling about the way he looked at me. Not with curiosity. Not with disinterest. But something else. *A warning, maybe. Or a knowing.*

And then he was gone, swallowed by the storm as the train pulled away. Inside, the air was thick with the scent of polished wood and faint traces of industrial cleaner. My cabin was small but comfortable, a first-class AC compartment meant for long journeys. A cushioned seat, a small table, a window blurred by the relentless downpour outside. The soft hum of the train moving along the tracks vibrated beneath my feet, a reminder that I was already far from home.

I placed my bag on the seat beside me and exhaled slowly. My fingers absently traced the ridges of the zipper, my thoughts pulling in different directions.

Blackstone Academy of Law. That was where I was headed. One of the country's most prestigious law schools, the kind that produced top corporate attorneys—the kind that made money. That was my dream. Not my father's.

I leaned back, running a hand through my damp hair. The fight replayed in my head, just like it had a dozen times since I left Vapi.

"You're throwing away the legacy. The empire I built. Do you even understand what you're doing?" my father's voice had been steady, but there was something underneath. Something dangerously close to desperation.

I had stood there, gripping the letter of acceptance, feeling both powerful and small at the same time. *"I'm not throwing anything away. I'm choosing something for myself. For once."*

"For yourself?" He scoffed. *"You think this is about you? Do you know how many people depend on this business? How many families are fed because of what I built? And you—you're walking away. Just like that."*

I didn't answer immediately. I knew arguing would get me nowhere.

My mother had been standing nearby, eyes darting between us like she wanted to step in but knew it wouldn't change anything. Her hands were clenched in the fabric of her clothes, knuckles white.

"I'm not walking away," I finally said. *"I'm just... choosing a different path."*

His silence was worse than any shouting match could have been. When he finally spoke again, his voice was quiet but sharp. *"Then don't expect to come back."*

That was it. The final line between us, drawn in ink too thick to erase.

I turned away, still clutching the letter. And I left.

Now, as the train rumbled forward, I shook off the memory and reached into my bag. I pulled out a small, worn photo album. I hadn't meant to bring it, but at the last second, I'd slipped it in. Maybe some part of me wasn't ready to let go.

The first few photos were from school—classroom pranks, festival celebrations, blurry shots of teachers' mid-lecture. Then, the farewell night. A snapshot of my friends and me, arms slung over each other's shoulders, pretending nothing was changing. The dinner after—laughter frozen in time, Bhavya cracking one of his usual jokes, the cola glasses raised like toasts at a real party.

Bhavya had ordered way too much food that night. *"One last feast before he becomes serious future lawyer,"* he had joked, stuffing an extra slice of pizza onto my plate. *"Or before you disappear into Blackstone's library forever."*

I had rolled my eyes. *"That's not happening."*

"We'll see," he'd grinned. *"Just don't turn into one of those guys who only talks in legal jargon."*

I traced a finger over the edge of the photo, my chest tightening. I wondered what Bhavya would think now, knowing I was already questioning everything before I'd even arrived.

Just as I was flipping through the pages, lost in the memories, a sudden knock on the door jolted me back to reality. I looked up, and standing there in the dim light of the corridor was the train conductor.

I looked up. The train conductor stood at the entrance of my cabin, his uniform slightly damp from the humidity. His eyes carried the exhaustion of someone who had spent too many years walking up and down the same train aisles.

"Ticket?" he asked, voice rough.

I handed it over. He examined it for a moment before nodding. *"Heading to Nagpur?"*

"Yeah," I said.

"Where in Nagpur?" he asked, flipping the ticket back to me.

"Blackstone Academy of Law."

His hand froze mid-air.

For a second, he just stood there. The rain outside pounded harder. The storm raged on. But inside the cabin, the silence grew thicker. And it wasn't the good kind.

His throat bobbed as he swallowed. *"My son... he studied there."*

Something about the way he said it made my stomach tighten. *"Studied?"*

The conductor exhaled sharply, his grip tightening around the ticket. His next words came slower, quieter—like they carried a weight too heavy to bear.

And then I understood.

He wasn't just saying his son studied there.

He was saying his son never came back.

Outside, another crack of thunder split the sky. The train's rhythm stayed steady, but the atmosphere inside had shifted. The cabin felt smaller, the air denser.

I opened my mouth, then closed it. What was I supposed to say? *Sorry? Ask what had happened? Offer some empty reassurance?*

Instead, I just nodded. A small, almost imperceptible movement. But he saw it.

The conductor lingered for a moment, as if expecting something more. Then, with a tired sigh, he straightened up, muttered a quiet, *"Good night,"* and stepped out of the cabin.

The door slid shut behind him.

I stared at the ticket still in my hand, my pulse steady but offbeat. My gaze flickered to the window, where raindrops raced down the glass, merging into one another before vanishing into the dark.

The train kept moving. But suddenly, I wasn't sure if I wanted to reach my destination anymore.

CHAPTER TWO

YOU SHOULDN'T HAVE COME

Sleep didn't come easy.

Even with the train rocking gently, even with the rhythmic clatter of wheels on tracks, my mind refused to settle. The conductor's words sat heavy in my chest, an anchor I couldn't shake. I shifted, exhaled, tried to push it away. But the more I tried, the more I felt it creeping in.

Eventually, exhaustion won. My thoughts blurred, my breathing slowed, and before I knew it—I slipped under.

And I was back. Ten days ago.

The floor of my room was a mess, scattered with papers, documents, and a half-packed suitcase. I was running through my checklist, making sure I had everything I needed—*admission papers, ID cards, travel tickets*. The fan overhead hummed softly, the only sound apart from the occasional honk from the street outside. Everything felt normal.

Until my phone buzzed.

Saatvik.

I frowned. It was late for a call.

I picked up. *"Yeah?"*

His voice came sharp, urgent. *"Open the news. Right now."*

I hesitated. *"What? Why?"*

"Just do it," he snapped. *"Check The Daily Post."*

I grabbed my laptop, fingers unsteady as I typed. The homepage loaded sluggishly, my Wi-Fi acting up like always. At first, everything looked normal—just some regular stuff, the stock market, politics, and celeb gossip. But when the article finally appeared, my stomach dropped.

? *"The Nagpur Enigma: A Disturbing Pattern at India's Most Elite Institution"*

News Report: In a shocking revelation, investigative journalist Rohan Mehta has uncovered a bizarre and deeply unsettling pattern linked to one of India's most prestigious institutions in Nagpur. According to leaked internal reports, at least one student from every batch in the past five years has vanished under mysterious circumstances.

? Same time of year.

? Same group of students involved.

? Same eerie silence from the institution.

What makes this even more troubling is that each of these students, weeks before their disappearance, had either:

• Attempted to access restricted areas on campus,

• Filed unusual requests for archived documents, or

• Contacted faculty members who are no longer listed as staff.

Their final communications hint at something alarming—messages cut off mid-sentence, draft emails never sent, and in one particular case from last year, a chilling text:

"If something happens to me, don't believe what they tell you. It was never an accident."

Despite the gravity of these findings, the institution has dismissed the claims as "coincidences" and "irresponsible fearmongering." Officials have refused to release full student records, citing privacy laws. Attempts to contact the families of the deceased have also led to dead ends—either they refuse to comment, or they simply cannot be found.

But the most unsettling part of this story? Rohan Mehta himself has not been seen or heard from since publishing this report.

The full truth remains buried. But as a new batch of students arrives in Nagpur—including some already en route—one question lingers:

Will history repeat itself?

I stared at the screen, my pulse hammering in my ears.

Saatvik's voice broke through the silence. *"Are you still going?"*

I swallowed, but my throat was dry. My mind spun in circles, looking for logic, looking for an answer that made sense.

But I had none.

"I... I don't know."

"Well, what are you going to do now?"

I opened my mouth, but nothing came out.

And then—

Darkness.

The world around me shifted.

I was no longer in the train. I was back at the station. The same one I had left from.

The night was still dark. The rain still poured hard, drumming against the metal roof. But the station was empty. Silent. Completely devoid of life.

Except for him.

The boy.

He stood at the far end of the platform, half-hidden by the mist and the falling rain. Motionless. Watching me.

A shiver crawled down my spine. I tried to move, to speak, but something held me in place. The weight of the moment pressed against my chest.

Then, in the eerie silence, he finally spoke.

A deep, painful whisper.

"You shouldn't have come."

The words cut through the air, heavy with something unspoken. A warning. A plea.

The mist thickened. The rain blurred everything.

And just as suddenly as it had begun—

I woke up.

My hands were shaking. My breath uneven. My throat dry.

I grabbed the bottle of water beside me, gulping it down in desperate swallows. The cold liquid grounded me, but the heaviness in my chest refused to fade. I wiped my face, ran a hand through my hair.

The clock read *5:00 AM.*

An hour to go.

I exhaled, trying to piece my thoughts together. Trying to make sense of what was happening. I needed answers. But where would I even start?

My eyes flickered toward the aisle. A few rows away, the TC stood by the window, his silhouette barely illuminated by the early morning light. He looked lost in thought, his fingers idly tapping against his knee.

I hesitated.

Then, finally, I made up my mind.

I shifted in my seat, gathering my thoughts. And then, slowly, I stood up and walked toward him.

The TC stood there, arms crossed, watching me with that same knowing look.

He exhaled, staring out the window at the darkness beyond. *"You're up early."*

I nodded. *"Couldn't sleep."*

The TC gave a knowing hum, folding his arms. *"Not many can, on this route."*

I hesitated for a moment, then decided to go for it. *"You've been on this train for a long time, haven't you?"*

"Long enough."

"Then maybe you can tell me something." I leaned in slightly. *"The academy... the one I'm going to. There's been talk about it. About students disappearing. Strange incidents."*

The TC didn't flinch, but I caught the way his grip on his wrist tightened slightly. *"Talk is talk."*

I shook my head. *"No, this is different. People have vanished."*

He let out a slow breath. *"I know."*

That threw me off. *"You know?"*

He finally turned to me, his gaze steady but distant, as if recalling something buried deep in time. *"Things happen in places like that. Places with history. With shadows."* He paused. *"But you won't find answers in newspaper stories."*

"Then where will I find them?"

He studied me for a long moment, his face unreadable. *"Some things aren't meant to be found."*

A silence stretched between us, thick and heavy.

I clenched my fists. *"Is that what happened to your son?"*

For the first time, his expression shifted. Just slightly.

The muscles in his jaw tensed. A long, exhausted sigh left his lips.

"Some questions don't have good answers," he murmured.

I didn't push. Something in his voice told me it wouldn't matter if I did. The rhythmic clatter of the train filled the space between us. The darkness outside had begun to fade into a muted grey. The first light of dawn crept over the horizon.

A quiet announcement crackled over the speakers.

"Next station... Nagpur Junction."

I turned back to the TC, my thoughts tangled in everything left unsaid.

"What's your name?" I asked.

He looked at me for a moment, then gave the faintest trace of a smile.

"Ravindra Sharma."

The name settled in my mind, weighty with meaning I didn't understand yet.

The train shuddered slightly as it began to slow. The city loomed ahead, washed in the soft glow of morning.

I exhaled.
I had arrived.
But I wasn't sure I wanted to be here anymore.

CHAPTER THREE

SPEAK AT YOUR OWN RISK

The ride from the station to *Blackstone Academy of Law* was a blur. The city passed by in fleeting glimpses—streets bustling with early morning life, vendors setting up stalls, the occasional student on a bike, probably heading to the same place as me. But my mind was elsewhere. The weight of my father's last words still clung to me like a shadow.

If you leave now, don't expect to come back.

I clenched my fists. I had made my choice. Blackstone was one of the best law schools in the country. If I had to carve out my future on my own, so be it.

The cab pulled up to the university gates, and for a moment, I just stared. The sheer scale of the place was overwhelming. The campus stretched far and wide, a perfect blend of modern architecture and tradition. The towering administrative building stood at the centre, flanked by massive academic blocks. Beyond them, I could see glimpses of the sports complex and a sprawling green field.

I paid the driver, hoisted my bag onto my shoulder, and stepped in.

The hostel formalities were straightforward. I signed a few documents, collected my room key, and checked the name of my roommate—*Raghav.* The warden informed me he had arrived a few days earlier.

I made my way to the dorm, the corridors alive with new students settling in. Just as I reached my room, the door swung open, and a sharp-featured guy stepped out. He had an easy confidence about him, his neatly combed hair and casual T-shirt suggesting he had already made himself at home.

"Aaron?" he asked, looking me up and down.

I nodded. *"Yeah. You must be Raghav."*

He grinned. *"Welcome to boredom."*

I let out a short laugh. *"That bad?"*

"You'll see. Come on, let's take a look around. Might as well know where to run when classes start crushing your soul."

We spent the next hour walking through the campus. The sports complex was impressive—basketball and lawn tennis courts, a well-equipped gym, and a massive cricket ground. The library, with its towering bookshelves and glass-walled study areas, was quieter than I expected. The whole place felt prestigious, structured, disciplined.

"So, where are you from?" Raghav asked as we walked past the gymnasium.

"Mumbai," he replied. *"You?"*

"Vapi."

We talked about our cities for a while—about how his school life was filled with cricket matches and last-minute exam cramming, about how I spent most of my time locked in debates and essays. It felt like a conversation we were supposed to have on the first day of university. Light, harmless.

Then, without thinking, I asked, *"Have you seen the article about the university?"*

It happened in a blur.

Before I could react, Raghav's hand clamped over my mouth, fingers pressing hard against my skin. His other hand grabbed my arm, pulling me a step closer. His grip wasn't just firm—it was almost desperate.

His breathing had changed, shallow and rapid. His eyes darted around the open space, scanning everything—the trees, the benches, the students passing by. My pulse spiked.

His voice was a whisper, but it carried a sharp, almost panicked edge.

"Are you crazy? Think twice before you speak."

I tensed under his grip, my breath catching in my throat. It wasn't just fear in his eyes. It was something worse—something like warning.

For a second, neither of us moved.

Then, with a final glance over his shoulder, he let go of me.

"Don't say a word," he muttered. *"Just follow me."*

The entire walk back to the dorm felt suffocating. The campus no longer looked so normal. The hallways felt too long. The walls too high. I could hear my own heartbeat in my ears.

When we entered our room, I dropped my bag onto the bed. *"What the hell was that?"*

Raghav sighed, running a hand through his hair. *"Look, I'm sorry. I didn't mean to freak you out. But you can't just talk about... that in the open."*

I crossed my arms. *"Talk about what exactly?"*

He exhaled. *"The news. It's... not entirely false."*

Something cold settled in my stomach. *"What do you mean?"*

Raghav sat down on his bed, his posture stiff.

"A third-year student disappeared last year," he said. *"One night, he just... vanished. No goodbyes, no trace. It was as if he was erased from existence."*

I swallowed. *"What happened to him?"*

Raghav hesitated. Then he leaned forward slightly, his voice quieter now.

"People say he went into a restricted area of the campus."

I frowned. *"Restricted area? You mean like a faculty zone or something?"*

"No," he said, shaking his head. *"Something worse. No one knows where it is. No one's even seen it."*

I blinked. *"What do you mean? It has to be somewhere on the map."*

"There's no record of it," Raghav said. *"No maps, no documents. Nothing online. No professor talks about it. It's like it doesn't exist at all."*

A chill crept up my spine.

"And the student..." I said slowly. *"Are you saying he found it?"*

Raghav didn't answer right away. His fingers tapped against his knee, his gaze flickering toward the door.

"All I know is that no one has seen him since that night," he muttered. *"And his parents? They demanded answers. The university gave them nothing. A few days later, they left. And no one has heard from them ever since."*

I felt something cold settle in my chest.

"There's no official record of missing students," Raghav continued. *"No numbers, no names. But everyone knows there's more than one."*

The conversation in the dorm took a heavier tone as Raghav hesitated. *"Look, this is just what I've heard. Even I don't know for sure if it's true. No one does. It's all just whispers and rumours passed down. But there's no denying that something is off about this place."*

I stared at him, the weight of his words pressing down on me. If even Raghav, who had been here longer, wasn't sure of what was real and what wasn't, then what did that mean for me?

A chill ran down my spine as I spoke, my voice barely above a whisper.

"What if it's true?" I asked. *"And worse... what if we become its next victims?"*

Silence.

I had wanted answers.

But now, I wasn't sure I wanted to know more.

CHAPTER FOUR

THE WRONG TURN

As the weight of our conversation settled in the room, a heavy silence lingered between us. I was still trying to process everything Raghav had told me, my mind racing with possibilities—some rational, others terrifying.

Raghav sighed, rubbing his temples as if pushing the tension away. Then, all of a sudden, he clapped his hands together and turned to me with a smirk.

"You know what? Enough of this heavy stuff," he said. *"There's something way more important we need to talk about."*

I looked at him, puzzled. *"What?"*

He grinned. *"The freshers' party. It's tonight at 8:30. The seniors from the Business Administration department are hosting it, and trust me, it's going to be huge."*

I blinked, caught off guard by the sudden shift in topic. *"A party? After... everything we just talked about?"*

"That's exactly why we should go!" Raghav said, leaning forward. *"Look, I get it, man. All this—"* he gestured vaguely *"—it's a lot. But if we keep thinking about it, we'll drive ourselves insane. A party is the perfect distraction."*

I wasn't entirely convinced. *"I don't know... I'm not really in the mood."*

"That's the whole point! You need to be in a place with loud music, a bunch of people, and free food. And who knows? Maybe you'll actually have fun." His grin widened. *"Besides, you should see the way some of the seniors throw parties here. It's next level."*

I sighed, leaning back against the chair. The idea of a party did feel strange after what we had just talked about, but at the same time, maybe he was right. Maybe stepping away from all the paranoia, even for a few hours, wasn't such a bad idea.

"Alright," I said finally. *"Let's go."*

Raghav pumped his fist in the air. *"That's the spirit! Get ready, my friend.*

Tonight, we forget about everything else."
As the evening arrived, Raghav rummaged through his suitcase, tossing clothes in every direction like a man on a mission.
"Alright, bro. Freshers' party means we go all in. No boring casuals. We gotta pull up like rich uncles at a family wedding."
I raised an eyebrow, holding up a simple button-up shirt. *"You mean... a suit?"*
"Exactly." He yanked out a crisp navy-blue blazer and held it up. *"Old money vibes, bro. We gotta make an impression."*
I hesitated. *"We're law students, not British Royals."*
Raghav smirked. *"Speak for yourself. I'm going for 'mysterious businessman with a questionable past.'"*
After some back-and-forth, I gave in and changed into a charcoal-black suit, paired with a white shirt. Raghav, of course, had gone full *'CEO of Dubai'* mode, styling his hair like he had just walked out of a luxury watch commercial.

We stepped out of the dorm and walked toward the party ground. The place was unrecognizable. Fairy lights hung from the trees, music thumped through the speakers, and colourful food stalls lined the sides, offering everything from gourmet pizza to fresh brownies. The freshers were scattered in groups—some dancing, some laughing, some nervously standing by the food, deciding if they should eat first or socialize.
"This," Raghav said, inhaling deeply, *"smells like free food and terrible decisions."*
We made a beeline for the dessert stall, where a chef was serving sizzling hot brownies with vanilla ice cream. Raghav grabbed a plate and handed me one. As I took a bite, he leaned in.
"Bro, tell me why this tastes like childhood trauma but in a good way?"
I nearly choked. *"What does that even mean?"*
"You know when you'd cry over math homework, and your mom would bring you dessert to shut you up? This is that, but fancy."
We moved to another stall, where a guy was struggling with a massive chocolate-covered waffle. The chocolate sauce dripped all over his white shirt, and he froze like he had just committed a crime.
Raghav sighed dramatically. *"Gone too soon. He was a brave soldier."*
I shook my head, laughing. *"You're impossible."*
"Hey, at least I have my priorities straight—first, food, then trauma, then law school."

I couldn't argue with that. For the first time since I arrived, everything felt normal. The tension from earlier had melted into the background, buried under music, laughter, and the taste of overpriced campus desserts.

The music pulsed in the background, blending with the chatter and laughter of students scattered across the lawn. The night felt lighter than the day had been, and for the first time since I'd arrived, I wasn't thinking about mysterious disappearances or eerie news reports.

We had found ourselves with a group of freshers—*Aryan, Siddharth,* and a couple of others whose names I hadn't quite caught in the chaos. We clinked our plastic cups of cola together in a toast.

"To new beginnings!" Aryan grinned, taking a sip.

"To surviving law school," Siddharth added dramatically.

We all laughed. The weight of the past few hours felt distant, like a bad dream fading with the morning sun.

Just as I was about to grab another bite of my brownie, I noticed Raghav's phone screen light up beside him. The glow reflected on his face, and I saw the way his relaxed expression stiffened, his fingers pausing mid-air before swiping across the screen.

I only caught a glimpse of the message before he tilted the screen away:

"Behind the main campus. Right now!"

A sudden, heavy silence settled over him. His throat bobbed slightly, and I could see the gears turning in his head.

"You good?" I asked, nudging him lightly.

Raghav forced a small chuckle, but it was offbeat, unconvincing. *"Yeah. Yeah, just—uh, I need to check on something."* He grabbed his phone and stood up a little too quickly. *"I'll be back in a bit."*

"Wait, where are you—"

"Just—enjoy the party," he cut in before I could finish, already moving away from the group.

I watched him weave through the crowd, his shoulders slightly tense, his pace a little too brisk for someone who was "checking on something."

And just like that, the lightness of the evening had started to crack.

I slipped away from the crowd, careful to keep my distance. Raghav walked with purpose, his posture stiff, his pace steady but urgent. The party's noise faded behind me—laughter and music swallowed by the cool night air. The path ahead was dim, the glow from the old-fashioned lampposts barely piercing the darkness. A faint mist clung to the ground, and the trees lining the walkway swayed gently, their shadows stretching long and distorted.

The campus at night had a strange, almost unreal feel to it. The main building loomed in the distance, its towering form barely visible against the night sky. My footsteps felt too loud, crunching softly against the gravel. The only other sound was the occasional rustle of leaves, a whisper in the stillness.

I stuck to the edges of the path, making sure to stay hidden whenever Raghav glanced back. My heart pounded. Who had messaged him? Why was he in such a hurry?

He took a sharp turn near the faculty block, heading toward the back of the main campus. I slowed down, pressing myself against a tree. My breath came out in short, measured exhales. For a second, doubt crept in—should I really be doing this?

Raghav turned again, disappearing behind an old, ivy-covered wall. I crept forward, peering around the corner. The moment I stepped past the wall—

Baam!

A force slammed me against a tree, my back hitting the rough bark. A hand gripped my collar, pulling me forward before shoving me back again. I barely had time to react before a voice growled, inches from my face.

"So you're the one involved, huh?"

A boy, slightly taller than me, eyes burning with suspicion. His grip tightened, and his fist drew back, ready to swing.

Instinct kicked in. I twisted my body, breaking his hold, and shoved him back. His punch barely grazed my shoulder as I stepped to the side. My adrenaline spiked—I wasn't about to get beaten up in the middle of nowhere.

Before either of us could move again, Raghav's voice cut through the tension.

"No! He isn't the guy, Shiraz! He's my friend—Aaron."

Shiraz froze, still breathing hard, his fists clenched. I exhaled sharply, my pulse still racing.

What the hell had I just walked into?

Still catching my breath from the sudden confrontation, I turned toward Raghav, but before I could say anything, my eyes landed on another figure standing just behind Shiraz. He looked our age, watching me with an unreadable expression, arms crossed like he'd been part of this from the beginning.

"Who's he?" I asked, my voice still uneven.

Raghav exhaled, rubbing his temple as if debating what to say. *"He's*

Daniyal," he finally answered.

There was a pause, thick with something unspoken. Then Raghav stepped closer, lowering his voice just enough that only I could hear.

"Listen," he said, his usual ease replaced by something heavier. *"You should have never followed me."*

Something about the way he said it—calm, almost regretful—sent a chill down my spine.

Shiraz's grip on my collar didn't loosen, but his expression shifted ever so slightly. His eyes darted toward Raghav, then back to me, as if calculating something. Then, almost like an afterthought, he muttered, *"If you're here, you might already be part of it."*

His words sent a ripple of unease down my spine. *Part of what?* I wanted to ask, but my throat felt dry.

Raghav put a firm hand on Shiraz's shoulder. *"He doesn't know anything."* His voice was sharp, like he was warning him as much as reassuring me.

Shiraz let go of my collar, stepping back with an unreadable expression.

I inhaled deeply, but the air suddenly felt heavier. *What the hell is going on?* A million questions started racing through my mind. *Who are these guys? What is Raghav involved in? And why did he keep this from me?*

I looked at Raghav, hoping for an explanation—something, anything—but his face gave nothing away. Just a calm, practiced expression that I was starting to hate.

Now it will be hard enough to trust anyone.

CHAPTER FIVE

Secrets in the Rain

The air was thick with tension. My thoughts raced, trying to make sense of everything that had just happened. I took a step forward, my voice sharp and demanding.

"What the hell is going on, Raghav? Who are these guys?" I asked, my patience wearing thin.

Raghav didn't respond immediately. Instead, he turned his head towards Daniyal and then Shiraz, as if silently asking for their permission. The two exchanged a glance, their expressions unreadable. Then, almost in sync, they both gave a slight shake of their heads. A firm no.

My stomach twisted. *What the hell was this?* Why was Raghav, my friend, seeking permission from them? Why couldn't he just tell me what was happening?

"Raghav?" My voice was quieter this time, but no less insistent.

He finally looked back at me, his face unreadable. *"Not now,"* he muttered.

Not now? After all that? That was all I was getting?

I clenched my fists, frustration bubbling to the surface. *"Not now? Are you serious? First, you get a cryptic message. Then you sneak out like you're in some goddamn spy movie. And now, I get jumped by this guy—"*

I shot a glare at Shiraz, who remained unfazed. *"And after all that, you're telling me 'not now'?"*

Raghav exhaled sharply but still didn't answer.

Daniyal, who had been watching in silence, finally stepped forward. His presence was commanding, and for a moment, I felt like a cornered animal.

"You don't know what you're asking for," Daniyal said in a tone that sent a chill down my spine. *"Some things are better left unknown."*

I scoffed. *"Oh, come on. That's the most clichéd bullshit I've ever heard. If there's something happening here, I deserve to know."*

Shiraz let out a low chuckle, shaking his head. *"He's got guts,"* he murmured. Daniyal didn't smile. He didn't even blink. Instead, he leaned in just slightly, his eyes locking onto mine.

A cold shiver ran down my spine. My mind flooded with questions. *What is 'it'? Who are these guys? Why is Raghav hiding this from me?*

A slow, burning frustration spread through my chest. Enough of this game. Enough of the vague warnings, the unspoken threats. I clenched my jaw and stepped forward toward Daniyal, my voice cold and unwavering.

"If I'm already part of it," I said, staring straight into his eyes, *"then keeping secrets won't help you. So either talk, or we drop the act. And trust me—I can fight too."*

Daniyal didn't flinch. His gaze met mine, unwavering, calculating. A tense silence stretched between us, thick as the night air. The kind of silence that could tip in any direction—toward an answer, or toward something much worse.

Then, finally, he let out a slow breath, tilting his head slightly. A smirk flickered at the edge of his lips, but it wasn't amusement. It was a test.

"Alright," he murmured, voice edged with something unreadable. *"You want answers? Fine. But here's the deal, tough guy."*

I kept my stance firm, waiting.

"You prove yourself first." He folded his arms, his tone sharpening. *"Tell us something about this place that we don't know. Something that forces us to tell you what's really going on."*

His eyes flicked toward Shiraz and Raghav. There was no hesitation. Both of them gave a slow, approving nod.

I exhaled. So that was it. They wanted proof.

I had to give them something real—something that shook them just enough to force their hand.

I took a few steps back, forcing myself to breathe, to think. If they wanted proof, I had to give them something real—something that would knock them off balance. My mind raced through every interaction, every detail Raghav had told me since I arrived. Maybe there was something they had overlooked, a crack I could slip through.

But nothing came.

It was useless. I was new to all of this. They had been here longer, they knew more. I was scrambling in the dark while they stood steady, waiting for me to fail.

Shiraz let out a scoff, shaking his head. *"Forget it, bro. There's nothing you can tell us that we wouldn't already know. You're wasting your time here."*

He turned, Daniyal following, and Raghav hesitated for a second before stepping back as well. They were leaving, brushing me off like I was just another clueless freshman who had wandered too far.

Panic flickered through me. If they walked away now, I might never get my answers.

And then, it hit me.

I exhaled, my mind racing. Was this the right move? If I told them this, I'd be stepping deeper into something I barely understood. Maybe it would be safer to just walk away—pretend none of this ever happened.

But then I thought about everything. The news report. The warning. The way they looked at me, like I was standing at the edge of something massive. If I backed off now, I'd never get the truth.

"What if I tell you about a victim of this university?"

They stopped.

Slowly, they turned back toward me.

I had their attention.

Silence stretched between us like a taut rope, each side pulling, waiting to see who would snap first. By now, I had pieced it together—this was linked to the news report. And these guys... they were connected to it in some way. I took a slow step forward, my voice steady, deliberate. *"Alright. Here's the deal."* I let my words settle, watching their faces, their guarded expressions. *"If I'm right about all this—if that news report wasn't just some random conspiracy—then there's something I need to tell you."*

Shiraz narrowed his eyes. Daniyal crossed his arms. The air between us had thickened, weighted with unspoken tension.

I exhaled. *"The parents of the victims aren't disappearing from the chaos. They're being silenced. Shut down. Isolated."* I let the words land, saw the way their postures stiffened. Then I dropped the final blow.

"And I know the name of one of them."

Then I said it. *"Ravindra Sharma. A TC on the Ahmedabad-Nagpur train."*

A crack of wind tore through the trees, bending branches, sending leaves scattering in a frantic rustle. The sky darkened, heavy clouds crawling over the moon. A distant rumble of thunder echoed in the background, low, warning.

And just as the words left my lips, the rain began to pour.

The night had decided—it would not be silent anymore.

Because now, there was no denying it.

Tonight was a night of truths.
And they owed me one.

CHAPTER SIX

NO WAY BACK

The rain poured relentlessly, drenching everything in sight. Thunder rumbled in the distance, and the wind howled like it carried secrets of its own. Water dripped from my hair, clothes stuck to my skin—but none of that mattered.

I had them.

Daniyal's eyes narrowed at me. *"How do we even know you're telling the truth?"*

I met his stare, unblinking.

"I mean it," he went on. *"This whole thing—your story, the ticket collector, the message on the train—it could all be made up. You expect us to just believe you?"*

I didn't flinch. I didn't defend myself. I just stood there, letting the rain hit me, cold and steady.

"If you really doubt me," I said quietly, *"check for yourself."*

Daniyal frowned. *"Check what?"*

"Go on the railway government website," I replied. *"Search for him. Ravindra Sharma.*

If I'm lying, you'll know."

For a beat, no one moved.

Then Shiraz, still holding his phone, gave me a long look and started typing.

The rain kept falling. Thunder grumbled in the distance like it was waiting.

We stood there, drenched, watching him scroll. I could hear the taps of his fingers on the screen, sharp and deliberate.

After a moment, Shiraz stopped. His thumb hovered over something.

"Ravindra Sharma," he read aloud. *"Posted in Western Railways. Ticket Collector. Service started in July. Two years ago."*

He looked up at me slowly, expression unreadable.

Shiraz was still frozen, eyes locked on his phone. Daniyal's jaw was tight, unreadable. Raghav looked... tense. Like he'd rather be anywhere but here. For a moment, no one spoke. Only the hammering of rain filled the air, a reminder of the weight between us. Then Shiraz let out a sharp breath, locked his phone, and shoved it into his pocket.

"Shit," he muttered.

Daniyal ran a hand through his wet hair, exhaling. His usual composure had cracks—not many, but enough.

"This changes things," he said finally.

"Yeah, no kidding," I snapped. *"Now are you ready to start talking, or do I have to drag the truth out of you?"*

Daniyal's eyes flicked toward me—dark, unreadable. But before he could speak, Raghav stepped in.

"This isn't the place for this," he said firmly, shaking his head. *"We're standing in the middle of a storm, yelling at each other. We need to go. Now."*

Shiraz scoffed, but didn't argue. Daniyal nodded.

"Where?" I asked.

Raghav looked at me. *"Our dorm."*

Something in the way he said it—the silent agreement between them—made me feel like I'd just stepped deeper into something I couldn't escape.

But maybe I didn't want to escape anymore.

"Lead the way."

We moved. The rain didn't let up. It drenched us as we hurried toward the dorms. None of us complained. The silence between us? Heavier than the storm.

Whatever came next wouldn't be easy.

And for the first time, I wasn't sure I was ready to hear the truth.

The walk was quiet—just rain, and thoughts. My clothes clung to me, shoes squelching with every step. By the time we reached the dorm, the rain had slowed. But the pressure in my chest hadn't.

Raghav pulled open the door. We stepped inside. Warmth greeted us. Damp wood. Old books. Faint traces of earlier-brewed tea.

Raghav tossed a towel to Shiraz. I handed one to Daniyal. He took it without a word. The room was dim, shadows flickering on the walls. The storm still growled outside.

We sat—Raghav and I on one bed, Daniyal and Shiraz on the other. Beds creaked. No one rushed to speak.

Finally, Daniyal broke the silence.

"Okay, Aaron." His voice was calm, deliberate. *"It seems we owe you a truth."*

I didn't move. Just listened.

"But before we go ahead," he continued, leaning forward, *"you still have a chance to back out. Walk away. Pretend this night didn't happen. If you choose that, we won't stop you."*

A pause.

"But if you dig deeper..." his voice lowered, *"...there's no going back."*

I swallowed. The words hung heavy in the air. The lamp flickered.

No arrogance in his face now. Just seriousness.

I considered it. Could I walk away? Pretend this was just a weird night at Blackstone?

No. That was a lie. I'd seen too much.

I looked up. *"There's no way I'm backing out. If I walk away from this now, I'll regret it for the rest of my life."*

Silence. Then glances passed between the three of them. Some silent understanding. Daniyal nodded.

"Alright," he said. *"Here it is."*

He took a breath. Fingers tapping against his knee.

"I came to this university a week ago. Everything seemed normal. Then—my first night, around 2:30 AM—I got a message."

He hesitated.

"It said: They're watching. Be careful. You're about to see something that will change everything."

Wind rattled the window. The room shrunk in that moment.

"And what does this have to do with Shiraz?" I asked.

Daniyal glanced at Shiraz.

Shiraz leaned forward.

"I'm his best friend," he said. *"We came here together. Known each other since we were kids. We're roommates."*

A simple fact. But his voice carried layers. This wasn't just friendship—it was history.

I leaned in, trying to ground myself.

"Okay," I said. *"So Shiraz fits. But why Raghav? How does he fit into this?"*

Again, silence. Daniyal and Shiraz exchanged a look, then turned to Raghav.

Raghav sighed. Ran a hand through his hair.

"I suppose I should start from the beginning."

He leaned back. Looked at the ceiling.

"My cousin studied here. Three, maybe four years ago. Dropped out in his second year. Gave some vague excuse. Went to London."

Rain drummed harder.

"I visited his house a few months later. Found something in his room—an old journal. Pages worn. I expected college nonsense. It wasn't."

The air shifted. Daniyal and Shiraz sat up.

"It talked about students disappearing. Professors acting weird. Like some students were being watched. My cousin thought he was one of them."

Raghav exhaled. *"That's why he left. He was scared. He never said it, but I could tell."*

The room felt colder. The storm outside seemed to press in.

"At first, I thought it was paranoia," Raghav said. *"But then the news broke. And I realized—he wasn't crazy. But by then, my admission here was finalized."*

He looked at Daniyal and Shiraz.

"When I arrived, they were the first ones I met. At first, it was normal. Then... I noticed things. The way we avoided certain topics. The way we tiptoed around some truths. It was like we weren't hiding from each other. We were hiding from something else."

The storm outside wasn't just weather anymore. It was a warning.

"This journal..." I asked. *"Did it say anything else?"*

Raghav nodded.

"Yeah. One last entry. It said: I am ending it here. I'm leaving this behind. I don't want these memories to follow me. But if anyone finds this, and if you plan to attend this so-called prestigious institution—my advice is simple."

His eyes met mine.

"Don't make the same mistake I did. Just blend in."

Goosebumps traced my arms.

No one said a word. Only the rain and distant thunder remained.

And that's when it hit me—everyone in this room was connected to this nightmare.

Everyone except me.

A coincidence, I told myself.

But I knew better. And as I looked at them, the weight of it all settled in—this wasn't just their nightmare anymore.

It was mine too.

CHAPTER SEVEN

IT WAS ONLY A MATTER OF TIME

The weight of everything I had just learned pressed down on me like an iron grip. My mind was reeling, trying to piece it all together, to make sense of the madness that had unravelled before me. I turned to the clock—past midnight. The world outside continued as if nothing had changed, but within these walls, reality had shifted irreversibly.

Yet, there was one thing that still didn't sit right with me.

I looked up, my voice quieter than before, but laced with genuine concern. *"Why don't you tell this to the authorities? This isn't something that can just be ignored. Someone needs to know. They need to investigate this."*

Daniyal exhaled sharply, shaking his head, almost as if he had been waiting for me to ask this exact question. He studied me for a moment before speaking. *"You've read the article about the university, right? The one that got everyone talking?"*

"Of course, I have," I answered immediately.

Daniyal leaned forward slightly, his expression unreadable. *"Do me a favor. Take out your phone. Go online. Search for it again. Read it."*

I frowned but did as he said. My fingers moved fast, typing in the keywords, expecting to find the article in an instant. But the moment the search results loaded; my breath hitched.

Nothing.

I scrolled down. Still nothing. No mention of the report. No warnings. No allegations. It was as if it had never existed.

The room felt smaller. The air, heavier. The only sound was the soft hum of the rain outside, punctuated by the occasional rumble of thunder. My chest tightened as I kept searching, desperately hoping I had just missed it. But the more I scrolled, the more horrifying it became.

It was gone. Erased. Wiped clean from existence.

A slow chill crept up my spine as I looked up at them, my voice barely above a whisper. *"This is impossible. How can this be?"*

Shiraz, who had been silent up until now, finally spoke, his voice low. *"Now you understand. Now you see why we haven't gone to the authorities."*

Silence draped over the room, thick and suffocating.

I swallowed, my throat dry. This was bigger than I had imagined. The more we dug, the deeper and more twisted it became. Every revelation led to another unanswered question, another piece of the puzzle that refused to fit.

I took a deep breath, steadying myself before speaking again. *"Alright... then answer this. In all these days, have you ever thought about why they sent that message to you, Daniyal? Why you? Of all the students here, why were you the one who got that text?"*

Daniyal's jaw tightened. He met my gaze with an intensity that made my skin prickle. It was almost like he had been expecting me to ask that.

He turned slightly, looking at Shiraz.

Shiraz hesitated before nodding, his voice careful. *"Perhaps... it's time he knows everything."*

Daniyal exhaled deeply, like he had been holding onto something heavy for too long. Finally, he spoke. *"There weren't just two of us."* He paused. *"There were three. Me, Shiraz... and Ishaan."*

Ishaan.

A name unfamiliar to me, but from the way Daniyal said it, I could tell he meant something.

Daniyal continued, his voice distant, lost in a memory. *"The three of us... we grew up together. We were inseparable. All three of us wanted the same thing—to be legal corporate stalwarts. When Ishaan got accepted into this university a year before us, it was bittersweet. We were sad, but proud. I still remember his words before he left. He said, 'Don't worry, you both will also come next year. We'll meet soon.' He was so sure of it. We all were."*

A tense pause settled between us.

"But then... eight months after he left, we got a message from him. A single text. No context. No follow-up. Just this: 'If something happens to me, don't believe what they tell you. It was never an accident.'"

A cold, unnatural silence filled the room.

"That was the last message we ever received from him. After that... he vanished."

I leaned forward slightly, my voice steady but firm. *"Didn't you try to call him?"*

Shiraz and Daniyal, who had been lost in their own thoughts, looked up at me.

I repeated it. *"When you got the message from Ishaan... did you try to call him?"*

Daniyal let out a breath through his nose, his jaw tightening. He didn't answer right away. Instead, he looked at Shiraz.

Shiraz's fingers drummed lightly against his knee before he ran a hand through his hair, exhaling sharply. *"Of course we did."* His voice was quieter now. *"We called him over and over again."*

I sat up straighter. *"And?"*

Shiraz's lips pressed into a thin line. He exchanged another glance with Daniyal, and for a second, I could see it—the hesitation. The thing they weren't sure they wanted to say out loud.

Daniyal leaned back, crossing his arms. *"The first time we called, it rang. For a long time."*

A chill ran down my spine.

"We thought he would pick up," Shiraz added. *"He always did. Always. But he didn't. It just kept ringing. No voicemail. Nothing."*

I swallowed. *"And after that?"*

Daniyal's voice dropped lower. *"The second time, it didn't ring at all."*

The silence that followed was suffocating.

Shiraz's fingers curled into a fist. *"Number not in service."*

The storm outside groaned, a deep rumble vibrating through the walls.

I blinked. *"Not in service?"*

Daniyal nodded slowly. *"Like it never existed."*

I didn't realize I was gripping the edge of my bed until my knuckles ached.

My thoughts spiralled, trying to make sense of it. Ishaan had sent a message. But the moment they tried to reach him—he was already gone.

Or worse... someone had made sure he couldn't be reached.

A shiver ran down my spine. The storm outside wasn't letting up. If anything, it was getting closer.

I stared at them, my heartbeat thundering in my ears.

My voice came out barely audible. *"And you think... you're connected to Ishaan? That they know you're the only ones who received that message? So, they're targeting you now, just like they targeted him? And all the students who went missing—they were all somehow linked to the ones who disappeared before them?"*

Daniyal met my gaze and nodded.

Shiraz did too.

A shiver ran down my spine. I exhaled slowly, my hands tightening into fists.

But there was still something missing. One last question, lingering in the air like an unspoken curse.

I turned my attention to Raghav, then back to the others. *"Then tell me something,"* I said, my voice steady but tense. *"If this is how they operate... then why hasn't Raghav received a text yet? He's connected to his cousin, isn't he? Isn't that considered a link? Or do they not know about it?"*

A heavy silence filled the room. The three of them exchanged glances, a flicker of uncertainty flashing between them.

Raghav exhaled. *"This is exactly the thing that doesn't fit,"* he admitted. *"We've been thinking about it too. Maybe you're right—maybe the university doesn't know that I'm connected to a past student. But that doesn't make sense either, does it?"*

Daniyal ran a hand through his hair, his frustration evident. *"We've been going over it for the past two, three days, trying to figure it out. And tonight—when we finally wanted to talk about it—we sent you that message. The one you saw."*

Shiraz leaned back against the chair. *"For now, we can't be sure of anything. This is the only pattern we have, but we need to be open to other possibilities. This is just the beginning. There's a lot more to uncover."*

Raghav sighed, rubbing his temples before glancing at the clock. *"It's past two already,"* he muttered. *"We should get some sleep. The first day of lectures. The boredom starts in six hours."*

Daniyal and Shiraz muttered their agreement, stretching as they got up. I walked them to the door, my mind still spiralling through everything. The unanswered questions. The missing pieces. The feeling that we were standing on the edge of something much, much bigger than we realized.

I was about to turn back when—

"Umm... guys?"

Raghav's voice was quiet. Too quiet.

I turned around. So did Daniyal and Shiraz.

Raghav was still at his desk, phone in his hand, but something was wrong. His fingers were tight around the device, knuckles pale, his breathing shallow. His eyes flickered between us and the screen, unfocused, disbelieving.

The rain outside grew harsher, as if the storm itself was reacting to whatever he had just seen. A flash of lightning illuminated his face—eyes wide, lips slightly parted, completely frozen.

Shiraz took a step closer. *"Raghav?"*

Raghav swallowed hard. He didn't look up, just slowly turned the phone toward us.

A message. An unknown number.

The text was brief. But it was enough.

"You were never supposed to be forgotten."

"It was only a matter of time."

Daniyal stiffened. Shiraz rubbed his forehead, muttering something I couldn't make out.

I felt my stomach drop.

The storm outside roared. The windows shuddered.

No one spoke.

No one breathed.

This wasn't supposed to happen.

But it was happening.

CHAPTER EIGHT

Silent Agreements

The moment the message appeared, the air in the room shifted. Just minutes ago, we had been talking about this exact thing, trying to make sense of Ishaan's warning. And now—this?

My mind raced. *This can't be a coincidence. Who sent this? How did they know?*

Shiraz was the first to speak, his voice tense. *"Are they spying on us? Are they monitoring us?"*

No one answered right away. The only sound was the muffled rain outside, the occasional distant rumble of thunder.

Daniyal exhaled sharply. *"Whatever this is, now is not the time to talk about it. We'll deal with this in the morning. Until then—act like nothing happened."*

A silent agreement passed between us. Without another word, Shiraz and Daniyal left, their footsteps fading down the corridor.

I shut the door, my fingers lingering on the lock for a second longer than necessary. I turned to Raghav. Neither of us spoke as we turned off the lights.

Darkness swallowed the room, but tonight, it felt heavier—like something unseen was watching from the shadows.

I lay in bed, staring at the ceiling. My thoughts swirled, but exhaustion weighed me down. My last thought before sleep finally claimed me was a quiet whisper in my own mind:

What if it's already too late?

And then, after a few hours—

The blaring sound of my alarm jolted me awake. I reached out, fumbling for my phone, and turned it off. The screen read *7:30 AM.*

With a sigh, I sat up, rubbing my eyes. The room was quiet except for the soft hum of the ceiling fan. Raghav was still asleep, his blanket pulled over his head, his slow breathing the only indication that he was still in deep sleep.

I didn't disturb him. Instead, I got up and walked towards the window. The rain had stopped, but the sky was still covered in thick clouds—a reminder that the monsoon wasn't done yet. The air smelled fresh, carrying the scent of damp earth and wet leaves.

I stood there for a moment, gathering my thoughts. Last night still lingered at the back of my mind—the message, the timing, the unsettling feeling that someone was watching us. But I pushed it aside. Right now, I had bigger problems—like surviving four back-to-back lectures without collapsing.

Turning back, I walked over to Raghav's bed and tapped his shoulder. *"Wake up, sunshine,"* I said, shaking him lightly. *"Classes start in an hour, and we need to grab breakfast first."*

Raghav groaned, burying his face deeper into the pillow. *"Five more minutes…"*

I yanked his blanket off. *"Five minutes will turn into fifty. Get up before I start playing motivational speeches on full volume."*

He shot up immediately, eyes half-closed. *"You're a menace."*

I grinned. *"And you're going to be late if you don't move."*

After getting ready, we made our way to the canteen. The usual morning chaos was in full swing, students rushing in and out, some still yawning, others already buried in books. The smell of eggs, toast, and coffee filled the air. We grabbed our trays and found an empty table.

Raghav picked up a piece of toast and held it up. *"You know, I think I've cracked the secret to surviving law school."*

"Oh? Enlighten me."

"Eat whatever they serve, sleep whenever you can, and pretend you know what's going on."

I smirked. *"Solid advice. I assume you mastered step two last night?"*

He nodded proudly. *"Absolutely. And let me tell you, ignorance is bliss. I woke up with zero stress."*

"Well, enjoy it while it lasts. We have four lectures today."

Raghav groaned. *"Four? That's criminal."*

"Welcome to law school."

We continued eating, talking about everything and nothing at the same time—complaining about assignments, making fun of a guy who had somehow managed to spill coffee on himself twice, and debating whether the canteen's aloo paratha was actually edible or a potential lawsuit in the making.

Eventually, we finished breakfast and headed toward our first lecture.

The first class was *Constitutional Law*—one of those subjects that could either be deeply interesting or painfully dry, depending on the professor's mood. Today, unfortunately, it was the latter. The professor spent the entire lecture droning on about fundamental rights in the most uninspiring way possible.

Raghav leaned over and whispered, *"If I don't make it, please inform my parents."*

I stifled a laugh. *"Will do."*

The second lecture was *Contract Law*, which wasn't much better. The professor threw around legal jargon like confetti, and half the class was just nodding along, pretending to understand.

At one point, Raghav scribbled on his notebook and slid it over to me.

Consideration, acceptance, and frustration... same as my love life.

I bit my lip to keep from laughing and scribbled back: *Sounds like a breach of trust to me.*

He rolled his eyes, shaking his head.

By the time the third lecture, *Criminal Law*, started, I was running on sheer willpower. The only saving grace was that this professor had a dramatic flair—he made every case sound like a blockbuster thriller. He even slammed his book on the table at one point to emphasize *actus reus*.

Raghav nudged me. *"I swear, he's auditioning for a Netflix show."*

"I'd watch it."

Finally, we reached the fourth and final lecture—*Legal Methods*. At this point, I could feel my brain melting. The professor assigned readings that I was too tired to process.

Just as I was about to completely zone out, my phone buzzed.

I glanced down at the screen. A message from Daniyal:

Meet us at the cafeteria for lunch.

I nudged Raghav and tilted my phone toward him. He read the message and raised an eyebrow. *"Finally, things are getting interesting."*

The lecture dragged on for a few more minutes, but the second the professor dismissed us, we grabbed our bags and headed straight for the cafeteria.

The cafeteria buzzed with chatter and the clatter of trays as we made our way to the table where Daniyal and Shiraz were already seated. Shiraz leaned back in his chair, arms crossed, while Daniyal was absentmindedly stirring his juice with a spoon.

"First day down," Shiraz said as we sat. "So, what's the verdict? Professors scary enough?"

"Honestly, could've been worse," I said, stretching my arms. "The first two lectures were fine, but that third one nearly put me in a coma."

Raghav chuckled. "Yeah, man, that Contract Law professor? Guy could make an action scene sound like a bedtime story."

"At least he wasn't the Economics professor," Daniyal said, shaking his head. "I swear he spent an hour explaining supply and demand, and I still don't know what the hell he was talking about."

Shiraz smirked. "I'll tell you what's in demand—some actual sleep after those four lectures."

"Library or gym after this?" I asked, taking a bite of my food. "Or straight to the dorms?"

"Gym?" Shiraz scoffed. "Bro, I just survived four lectures. I'm not lifting anything heavier than this spoon."

We laughed, the conversation light and natural. It felt normal. Just four students talking about an exhausting first day—no tension, no paranoia.

But then Daniyal's posture changed. He leaned forward slightly, his voice dropping to a sharp, crisp tone.

"Listen," he said. "I don't think it's safe to have any discussions in the dorm room."

The shift in mood was immediate. I felt the weight of his words settle over the table.

"Yeah, right," I said, keeping my voice low but firm. "Last night might've been a coincidence, but we can't afford to take any risks."

"Exactly," Shiraz muttered, his usual easy-going demeanour replaced with quiet seriousness.

Raghav tapped his fingers against the table in thought. "What about the back of the campus?" he suggested. "Where you called me for the discussion last night? No one goes there. It's covered with trees, so if someone is keeping an eye on us, it'll be harder for them."

I considered it for a moment before nodding. "Sounds good."

Shiraz adjusted his watch, then looked up. "Alright then. Finish up, and we'll meet there."

We returned to our meals, but the food didn't taste the same anymore.

We ate in silence, but the truth was clear—after lunch, we weren't just going to have a conversation.

We were stepping deeper into something we couldn't walk away from.

36

THE FOUR STAGES

Raghav and I walked towards *The Grove*, the damp earth soft beneath our shoes. The morning sun was hidden behind thick, stubborn clouds, casting a dull light over the campus. The air smelled of wet leaves and distant rain, and the occasional drip from the treetops hit my shoulder as we passed under them. There was no one around—just the rustling branches swaying slightly in the breeze.

The path curved slightly, leading us into the secluded area. Shiraz and Daniyal were already there, standing with their hands in their pockets, their faces unreadable.

Daniyal's eyes flicked past us for a second before he spoke.

"You're sure no one followed you?" His voice was quiet but sharp.

I glanced at Raghav, then back at him. *"Yeah. We made sure."*

Shiraz gave a slow exhale, his fingers tapping against his arm. *"Good. So by now, it's getting clearer that the pattern we suspected is real."* His tone was steady, but the way his jaw tensed gave him away. *"For now, it seems like the only explanation."*

A silence settled between us, thick with unspoken thoughts.

"If this is how they operate," I said, *"you both need to be extra careful."* My gaze shifted between Daniyal and Raghav. *"You're the ones who received the message. That puts you at the centre of this."*

Daniyal nodded slowly. *"Which also means we have to be ready for whatever their next move is."*

"But how do we do that?" Shiraz muttered. *"We don't know their pattern. If we want to stay ahead of them... we need to predict what's coming next."*

A pause. The wind stirred the trees around us, and I could hear the faint chirp of birds somewhere deeper in the grove. We all stood there, each lost in thought, the same question hanging in the air.

Then Raghav spoke.

"Maybe... there's something that can help." His voice was lower now, more deliberate. *"And I think now is the time to take it out."*

I turned to him as he reached into his bag.

Slowly, he pulled out a worn, leather-bound diary. The cover was scratched, the edges frayed, as if it had been opened and closed too many times.

Daniyal and Shiraz exchanged glances, then turned their eyes to Raghav, their expressions unreadable.

I swallowed. *"Is that—?"*

"My brother's diary," Raghav said, gripping it tightly.

A heavy silence followed. The trees swayed slightly, their shadows stretching across the ground. And in that moment, it felt like everything was about to change.

"You never told us you brought the diary here," I said, my voice steady but sharp. The weight of the revelation settled in my chest, pressing down like a stone. *"Why keep it a secret?"*

Raghav's fingers curled slightly around the edges of the diary. He let out a slow breath. *"I was waiting for the right moment."* His gaze flickered between the three of us. *"I was going to tell you both last night, but then everything changed. I didn't expect things to take such a huge turn. And I didn't want to overwhelm any of you—"* His voice carried an unusual seriousness, a rare kind of concern.

I studied him for a second. *"You thought you could handle this on your own?"*

Raghav shook his head. *"Not alone. Just... without making things worse for you guys."*

Daniyal exhaled sharply. *"And what about last night? When we were all in your dorm? You brought up the diary then—you could've told us."*

"I could have," Raghav admitted, *"but it didn't feel right. We were already dealing with too much. Too many questions, too much uncertainty. If I threw this in at that moment, it would've made things worse."*

Daniyal and Shiraz exchanged a glance, their expressions shifting. I let out a slow breath. As much as we hated being kept in the dark, I understood why Raghav did it.

"So," I said, nodding toward the diary, *"what more is left to uncover?"*

Raghav tightened his grip on the book. *"Something that might help us. But it's not written the way you'd expect. My brother didn't just lay things out—he left pieces, fragments, like he was scared to even put everything into words."*

Silence settled over us. The air felt heavier, the wind colder. Even with nothing but the swaying trees and distant murmurs of campus life, it felt like we were being watched. Like whatever secrets were inside that diary were just as dangerous as the people trying to keep them buried.

The pages felt heavier than they should have—more than just paper, they carried something unseen, something unsettling.

"There are only ten pages used in the diary," Raghav said, his voice measured. *"Most of them are fragmented—almost impossible to make sense of."*

Daniyal frowned. *"And the rest?"*

"Three pages." Raghav hesitated. *"They aren't straightforward, but they can be understood."*

A flicker of relief passed between us. *"That's some good news,"* I said. *"Open them."*

Raghav didn't move.

"But..."

The word hung in the air, his tone warning. A strange chill crept through me.

I narrowed my eyes. *"But what? Is something wrong?"*

Raghav exhaled slowly, gripping the diary tighter. For a few seconds, he said nothing. Then, in a voice barely above a whisper, he murmured, *"They aren't normal."* His fingers traced the worn edges of the diary. *"They tell something that... perhaps no one would want to know."*

A gust of wind rustled the leaves overhead, the sky thick with the promise of rain.

"Something worse than a nightmare, a reality."

Silence wrapped around us. Daniyal, Shiraz, and I exchanged uneasy glances. No one spoke. No one could.

The diary sat between us, waiting.

Raghav hesitated for a moment before opening the diary. The pages were old, slightly worn, as if they had been turned over too many times in anxious hands. He carefully flipped through until he reached one of the three pages he had mentioned.

"This one," he said, his voice quiet but firm. *"This is the one we need to see first."*

I, Shiraz, and Daniyal leaned in as Raghav tilted the diary slightly, revealing the ink-stained words. The handwriting was hurried, uneven—written by someone who either had no time or was too shaken to write clearly.

August 4, 2022 – 2:37 AM

I knew it! I knew it!

There is a pattern to all of this. This isn't random. This is terrifying. Unnatural. And worst of all—unstoppable.

I don't know how much time I have. Maybe days. Maybe hours. Maybe I'm already out of time, and I just don't know it yet. But I have to write this down. I have to leave something behind. Because if I disappear—when I disappear—someone needs to know.

As far as I understand, there are four stages to this:

Stage 1: Observation.

Stage 2: Interaction.

Stage 3: Involvement.

Stage 4: Disappearance.

I don't know which stage I'm in. It happens so smoothly, so quietly, that by the time you realize where you are, it's already too late.

I've tried everything. I ignored it, pretended it wasn't real. I convinced myself it was in my head. But it wasn't. It never was. They were always there, watching, waiting. Letting me think I had control.

I don't.

The worst part is, I don't even know when it truly started. When I became part of this. It's like waking up in a nightmare and realizing you've been dreaming for years. Maybe I was already in Stage 2 when I thought I was still in Stage 1. Maybe I was in Stage 3 when I was still trying to convince myself there was no pattern at all.

And now? Now, I think I'm too far in.

I should burn this diary. Rip these pages apart and pretend none of this ever existed. But a part of me knows that won't change anything.

So, if you're reading this—whoever you are—then that means you've started to notice it too.

I'm sorry.

Because this doesn't happen in any university.

This doesn't happen anywhere.

A heavy silence followed. No one spoke immediately. The air felt heavier, as if the words themselves had altered the very atmosphere around us.

"What the hell does this mean?" Shiraz finally broke the silence, his voice lower than usual.

"I don't know," Daniyal murmured, eyes still locked on the page. "But it doesn't sound good."

I exhaled slowly. "And this is just one of the three?"

Raghav nodded. "Yes. And believe me, the other two... are worse." The wind

stirred, carrying a faint, distant whisper through the trees.
For the first time, it felt like we had a direction.
A thread to follow.
But the question was—did we really want to know where it led?

CHAPTER TEN

THE HUNT BEGINS

The sky had darkened considerably, thick clouds rolling overhead like a shifting mass of uncertainty. The air was heavier now, damp with the scent of approaching rain. In the distance, faint rumbles of thunder echoed across the sky, low and drawn out, as if the storm itself was waiting for something. None of us had spoken in the last minute—not since we read that page. The words had settled over us like an invisible weight, pressing down on our thoughts, making it harder to breathe.

Raghav, who had been watching us closely, finally exhaled. *"There are still two more pages,"* he said, his voice quieter than before. *"But they're... completely different from this one. And trust me, you don't want to read them now. It's better if you leave them for later and just focus on this one."*

I turned to Shiraz and Daniyal. None of us wanted to admit it, but he was right. Something about the way Raghav said it, the way his fingers held the edge of the diary like it carried something far worse than words, made me uneasy.

Then, without another word, Raghav shut the diary and slid it into his bag, as if sealing something dangerous inside.

For a moment, no one spoke. The distant thunder hummed again, closer this time. We weren't just trying to gather our thoughts—we were trying to convince ourselves that we hadn't just uncovered something terrifying.

Daniyal was the first to break the silence. He straightened up, clapping his hands together once as if to shake off the tension. *"Alright. Enough with self-absorption. Let's try to make sense of this and connect it to what's happening here."* His eyes flicked between us, sharp and certain. *"As far as I can tell, one thing is confirmed—the university is making these students disappear. The diary said it—Stage Four is disappearance. That means if we line up the stages with what's been happening, there's only one explanation."* He leaned forward. *"The students who vanish are somehow linked to the ones who were targeted before them, and this happens in four stages. It's a chain."*

No one responded immediately. Instead, we exchanged a look—one that spoke louder than words.

We wanted to deny it. We wanted to believe there was another answer, something that made more sense.

But deep down, we all knew Daniyal might be right.

And that was the scariest part.

I swallowed hard, my mind racing through the implications. A thought was forming—something that connected with Daniyal's theory. I hesitated, my pulse quickening. Should I say it? Should I even think it?

But there was no time for hesitation.

"If the theory is true," I finally spoke, my voice steady despite the storm brewing inside me, *"and if the diary entry is anything to go by... then Raghav's brother wasn't able to tell which stage he was on. And after this entry, he wrote two more."* I exhaled, my mind clicking the pieces into place. *"That means, based on the timeline, he must have been at the end of stage two when he wrote this entry. Which means..."* I trailed off, the conclusion sending a chill down my spine.

"He interacted with someone," Daniyal finished, his voice lower than before.

A faint gust of wind rushed through, swaying the trees, making the moment feel even heavier. The storm was closing in.

We were still settling into what I had just said when Raghav finally spoke. His voice was measured, but there was an unmistakable strain beneath it. *"If my brother was at the end of stage two when he wrote this,"* he said, *"and if we connect it to the timeline of when Daniyal and I received the message, then that means—"*

"It means," Shiraz suddenly cut in, his voice tense, *"we are at the end of stage one. Observation."*

A crack of thunder rolled across the sky.

"And if stage two is interaction," Shiraz continued, glancing at Raghav and Daniyal, *"that means any day now... both of you will come face-to-face with someone you don't know."*

Silence. A silence so deep it felt like the storm itself was waiting for us to acknowledge it. The wind howled, the leaves rustled violently, and the sky seemed moments away from breaking open.

None of us spoke. But we all understood.

It had already begun.

A heavy silence hung between us, the weight of our conversation pressing down like the thick clouds above. Then—*click*. A sharp snap of a twig near the tree branch.

All four of us turned at once, breath caught, hesitation at its peak, terrified and confused. My heartbeat quickened as I scanned the shadows, bracing for the worst.

Then, I saw it.

A squirrel, darting across the damp earth, clutching a nut before scurrying up the tree trunk.

We exhaled almost in unison, a quiet relief settling over us for a moment. But the tension never fully left.

My mind was racing, pieces of our discussion clicking into place. And then—something struck me. A question so obvious that I couldn't believe I hadn't thought of it before.

I hesitated at first, but then reminded myself—there was no time for hesitation anymore.

"Raghav... didn't you tell us your brother quit in his second year and went to London for studies?"

The moment I spoke, I saw it in their eyes—the realization, slow and creeping, sinking into all of us at once. We had spent so much time thinking about what had happened to him that we never asked how he got out.

Daniyal turned to Raghav, frowning. *"Did he ever mention anything about how he got out?"*

Raghav shook his head. *"No... nothing. Not a word about escaping."*

Silence. A different kind of tension now.

Shiraz exhaled sharply and cleared his throat. *"Look, we can keep thinking about this and get lost in theories, or we can focus on what we do know. Right now, we need to talk about the interaction. That's coming up, and we have to be prepared."*

He was right. As much as this question about Raghav's brother haunted me, it wouldn't help us survive what was coming next.

"Great," Shiraz continued. *"Now that we know interaction is the second stage, we have to keep our distance from unknown people as much as possible. If we want to get ahead of them, we need to start investigating. That's the key to uncovering this—and getting out before it's too late. Any ideas?"*

I took a breath. I had one.

"What if we look for records of the missing students?"

Daniyal frowned. *"It's not that easy. If they're missing, do you really think the university would keep their records alongside the rest of the students?"*

"I know that," I said, my voice steady. "And that's exactly why I think I know where we might find them."

All three of them turned to me at once.

"Where?" Shiraz asked.

I met their gazes. "The hidden area of the campus. If that place is off the grid, away from records, then there's a high chance we'll find something there."

Raghav exhaled sharply. "But no one knows where that is. It's called hidden for a reason, bro."

"Maybe," Daniyal spoke up, "but that doesn't mean we can't find it. There must be a record of the university's blueprints—old ones and new ones. If we can get our hands on both, we can compare them. Look for areas that existed before but don't show up anymore. If there's a space missing, that's where we need to go."

A moment of realization passed between us. This was the first real plan we had. A step forward.

Then, suddenly—

A loud crack of thunder ripped through the air, and the skies finally gave way. Rain poured down in heavy sheets, drenching the ground almost instantly.

"Okay," Shiraz shouted over the downpour, "now is not the time to discuss this in detail! We'll talk tomorrow—somewhere dry!"

None of us argued. Without another word, we started walking. The rain had started to fall in heavy sheets by the time we wrapped up our discussion. We walked through the downpour, our minds weighed down by the unsettling realization of what lay ahead.

As we walked back through the downpour, a single thought refused to leave my mind—

if the university had erased places from its records, what else had it erased?

CHAPTER ELEVEN

EYES IN THE DARK

The day had passed in a blur of lectures, hurried meals, and half-hearted note-taking. The usual monotony of classes had felt even more unbearable today—not because of the subjects, but because my mind was elsewhere. Every free moment, my thoughts circled back to our next move. Even during lunch, as conversations flowed around me, I found myself absentmindedly tracing patterns on the table, thinking about where the university might keep something as critical as its blueprints.

By the time evening rolled around, I was more exhausted than I should have been. But there was no time to rest.

The sky was a blend of burnt orange and deep violet, streaked with heavy clouds that refused to clear. The sun was half-sunk behind the distant tree line, casting long, shifting shadows across the campus. A breeze moved through the branches above, shaking loose a few dried leaves that spiralled lazily to the ground.

I adjusted the strap of my bag and kept walking. By the time I reached *the Grove*, the others were already there—Daniyal leaning against a tree, Shiraz flipping through his notes, and Raghav sitting cross-legged on a fallen log, absentmindedly tapping a pen against his knee.

"You're late," Shiraz said without looking up.

"Yeah, I know," I exhaled, rubbing the back of my neck. *"Professor Anand went off on one of his tangents again. Took forever to wrap up class."*

Shiraz gave a knowing smirk. *"Classic Anand."*

I dropped my bag beside the log and sat down. *"Let's get to it. Where do we even start?"*

Raghav exhaled, tossing his pen in the air and catching it. *"We need to think about where the university would keep something like that. Floor plans, blueprints—any of it."*

"Facilities Management Office?" Daniyal suggested.

Shiraz shook his head immediately. *"No chance. Places like that mostly deal with repairs, maintenance records, and renovation approvals. They don't need access to full blueprints—just references for structural audits."*

I nodded. That made sense.

"What about the storage room?" I said.

"That's mostly old assignments, projects, and student paperwork," Raghav countered. *"They wouldn't dump something this important in a place where any faculty member could rummage through."*

A silence settled in. The wind picked up slightly, rustling the leaves above us. The light had dimmed, and the clouds, still lingering, made it feel later than it actually was.

"Archives," Shiraz said suddenly.

We all turned to him.

"The Records Room. It's a repository for everything about this university—documents, reports, maybe even architectural plans. If the blueprints are anywhere, it's there."

Daniyal frowned. *"Wouldn't that be too obvious?"*

"Not necessarily," I said, thinking it through. *"It's not just a room—it's an entire restricted floor under the admin building. It's not the kind of place students can just walk into."*

There was a brief silence as the weight of that sank in.

"So even if the blueprints are there," Raghav said, his voice quieter now, *"how do we get in?"*

No one had an answer.

The conversation came to a halt the moment we heard footsteps crunching on the gravel behind us. Instinctively, we froze. My pulse spiked. It was late, and no one was supposed to be here—not even us.

Daniyal and Shiraz exchanged quick glances. Raghav's fingers curled into a fist. My mind raced through the possibilities—another student? A professor? Someone spying on us?

Then, from the shadows, a tall figure stepped into the dim light filtering through the trees.

The warden.

Relief washed over me, but only just. He wasn't someone to be taken lightly. His sharp eyes scanned each of us in turn, lingering on me a fraction longer than I liked.

"You students shouldn't be here," he said, his voice calm but firm. *"It's not*

allowed."

For a moment, none of us spoke. Then I nodded quickly, trying to sound casual. *"We were just getting some air after classes, sir."*

The warden's gaze didn't waver. His posture was rigid, his uniform crisp despite the humidity of the evening. A heavy keychain hung from his belt, clinking slightly as he shifted his stance.

"You should head back," he finally said. *"I don't want to see you here again."*

He turned and walked away, his boots crunching against the ground, leaving behind a thick silence.

As soon as he was out of earshot, I exhaled, rubbing my hands together. *"That was close."*

I nodded. *"The warden must have access to the records room. If we track his movements, we can figure out when and how he gets in."*

Daniyal frowned. *"And then what? Even if we know when he goes there, we can't just follow him in."*

Raghav crossed his arms. *"Maybe we don't need to. If we know where he keeps his keys..."*

"That's risky," Shiraz muttered. *"You really think we can steal from a warden? Even if we put them back, one wrong move and we're done for."*

"Okay, then we find another way," I said, thinking fast. *"What if we get him to open it without realizing?"*

Daniyal scoffed. *"What, like ask him nicely? 'Excuse me, sir, mind unlocking the records room for us?'"*

Raghav chuckled, but I was already shaking my head. *"No, not like that. But maybe we create a situation where he has to open it. Something that makes him go inside while we watch."*

Shiraz looked intrigued. *"That could work. We just need to figure out what would make him do that."*

We fell into silence again, each of us lost in thought. The warden had just given us our first real lead, but following it wasn't going to be easy.

The silence stretched between us, broken only by the distant hum of the campus. I stared at the ground, my mind running through everything we knew so far. The warden. The restricted areas. The fact that the blueprints had to be somewhere only a select few could access.

And then it hit me.

"Financial documentation," I muttered.

The others turned to me. Daniyal frowned. *"What?"*

I lifted my head. *"Financial records. Payrolls, salaries, budgets—these aren't kept in just any office. They're sensitive, and they have to be updated at the end of every month."* I looked at them, my thoughts gaining momentum. *"They need to be stored in a secure place. A place only a handful of people can access."*

Shiraz leaned forward. *"You're saying the warden—"*

"—might be in charge of handling those records," I finished. *"He could be the one taking them out at the end of every month, handing them over to someone who updates them, and then putting them back."*

Raghav rubbed his chin. *"Okay, but that still doesn't confirm they're kept in the same place as the blueprints."*

"True," I admitted. *"But think about it—if there's one room meant for secure storage, wouldn't it make sense to keep all restricted documents there? Financial records, confidential files... maybe even old structural plans."*

Shiraz nodded slowly. *"I mean, it's more logical than anything else we've thought of."*

Daniyal exhaled sharply. *"Even if we assume this, we can't just wait around hoping to get lucky. What if we're wrong?"*

Raghav shook his head. *"We don't have time to chase wild theories anymore. The month ends in a few days.*

If Aaron's right, the warden will have to access that room soon. We just have to wait and watch."

A slow, determined grin spread across Shiraz's face. *"Then I guess it's settled."*

I glanced toward the darkened campus. Just a few more days, and we'd finally have a lead.

If we were right.

We started walking back toward the campus, the discussion still lingering in the air. For the first time in days, it felt like we had a plan—something tangible to work with. Four more days. All we had to do was wait and watch.

Then Daniyal's phone buzzed.

He pulled it out absentmindedly but stopped mid-step. His eyebrows furrowed as he read the screen.

"You don't have four days. Move faster."

A second later, the message disappeared.

Daniyal blinked. *"What the—"*

We crowded around him. *"What happened?"* I asked.

He hesitated, then turned his phone toward us. The message was gone. The chat was empty.

"There was a message," he said, his voice lower now. *"It said we don't have*

four days... that we need to move faster."
A cold weight settled in my stomach.
"Who sent it?" Shiraz asked.
Daniyal shook his head. *"There's no sender. No number. Just... gone."*
Silence. The four of us stood there, the distant hum of the campus barely audible.
"This means someone's watching us," Raghav muttered. *"And they want us to hurry."*
Or they were warning us.
I looked around, suddenly hyper-aware of our surroundings. The trees loomed taller in the dimming light, the sky a deep shade of bruised purple. The evening air carried a chill I hadn't noticed before.
For the first time since this began, I felt it—the weight of unseen eyes.
I exhaled, forcing myself to shake it off. *"We stick to the plan,"* I said, though my voice felt distant, like it belonged to someone else. *"But we stay sharp. If someone's trying to rush us... it means we're running out of time."*
No one argued.
We picked up our pace.
Behind us, the wind stirred the branches, whispering through the trees.

CHAPTER TWELVE

A SHIFT IN THE GAME

The rain hadn't stopped since morning, turning the campus into a blur of grey and silver. Water streaked down the balcony door, the wind occasionally hurling droplets against the glass. The trees bent under the storm, their branches thrashing. Somewhere in the distance, thunder rumbled.

I stood by the railing, watching the downpour swallow the world. Inside, the air was heavy with the scent of damp clothes and cheap hostel coffee. The clock on the wall ticked steadily. *3:00 PM.*

No one spoke.

Daniyal sat on the bed, arms crossed, tapping his foot. Shiraz leaned against the desk, staring at his phone. Raghav was by the door, shifting his weight between his feet, glancing at the window every now and then.

We were all here, trapped inside, waiting. For what exactly, none of us could say.

Daniyal was the first to break the silence. His voice was edged with frustration.

"I told you we shouldn't have waited this long. This was a stupid idea."

Everyone turned to look at him. I exhaled, trying to keep my voice steady.

"Oh yeah? The plan was to stay sharp, to be on alert. But instead, you walked straight into the trap."

Daniyal let out a dry laugh, shaking his head. *"Right. Because you guys have been so brilliant at staying sharp. Confident words from someone who's just as stuck as the rest of us."*

I clenched my jaw, but before I could fire back, Shiraz cut in. *"Enough. Both of you."* His tone was sharper than usual. *"Cut some slack, okay?"*

Raghav, who had been quiet, finally spoke up. *"He's right. This—"* he gestured between us, *"this is exactly what they want. The more we fight, the*

weaker we get. We break apart, and it becomes easier for them to get to us."
A silence followed, heavier than before.
Shiraz leaned back, running a hand through his hair. *"We can't let that happen."*
No one spoke for a moment. I turned back to the window, watching the relentless downpour. The rain blurred everything outside, and for a second, I wished it could blur out the tension in this room too.
Behind me, I heard Daniyal exhale sharply, lost in thought.
I turned away from the window, forcing my thoughts back to the room. *"Alright,"* I said, my voice even. *"Before this gets any worse, would you mind telling us what exactly happened to you guys yesterday?"*
I looked at both Daniyal and Shiraz as I finished my sentence.
They exchanged a glance—brief, but enough to say they were thinking the same thing. Daniyal let out a slow breath and finally spoke.
It was late evening when Shiraz and I were walking back to the dorms. The sky had that dusky orange glow, and the ground was still wet from the afternoon rain. We weren't talking about anything important—just the usual stuff. Classes, assignments, some nonsense Shiraz was complaining about.
Then, out of nowhere, someone called my name.
"Hey! Wait up!"
We turned around. A guy—probably another student—was jogging toward us, slightly out of breath. He had dark, slightly messy hair, and his uniform was a bit damp, like he'd been out for a while.
He stopped in front of us, catching his breath before speaking.
"I think this belongs to you."
I frowned as he held out a notebook.
I shook my head. *"Thanks, but I don't think I left any notebook behind."*
The guy tilted his head, his expression unreadable. *"Oh? I could've sworn it was yours. But just to be sure, why don't you check inside? Make sure it's not something you lost."*
Something about the way he said it felt... off.
I hesitated, but then took the notebook and started flipping through the pages, giving them a quick glance. It looked empty—just an ordinary notebook.
Until I reached the last page.
There, in small but firm handwriting, was a single line:
"Up until now, we were going easy on you. But don't expect that to continue."
My grip tightened on the notebook.

Before I could react, the guy swiftly reached out and took it from my hands. *"Ah. Looks like this isn't yours after all,"* he said with a slight smile. *"I'll take it back."*

Then, just like that, he turned and walked away.

Shiraz and I stood there for a moment, frozen.

We didn't say anything. We just knew—whatever this was, it wasn't random.

A heavy silence settled over the room as Raghav, and I processed what we had just heard.

Then, Raghav finally spoke, his voice quieter than usual. *"In my brother's diary... he mentioned an interaction. A first contact. Could this be what he was talking about?"*

We all exchanged uneasy glances.

Shiraz shook his head. *"But that doesn't make sense. Everything we know—the way they operate—it takes months, years, for them to pull things off. Why would they move this fast with us?"*

No one answered immediately. The only sound was the rain hammering against the balcony railing.

After a few seconds, I broke the silence. *"Who says they have to follow the same timeline for everyone?"* I said, thinking aloud. *"What if they keep a close watch on every student and act based on how they behave? Maybe their approach isn't fixed. Maybe it's adaptive."*

A slow, unsettling realization sank into all of us.

Daniyal exhaled sharply, then turned to me and Raghav. *"Alright... now what about you two? What happened with you guys?"*

Raghav and I looked at each other.

Then, without breaking eye contact with me, Raghav muttered, *"What we have to say... isn't going to make this any better."*

CHAPTER THIRTEEN

THE NAMES HAVE POWER

The night air was cool, carrying the scent of damp earth. A few puddles glistened under the dim yellow glow of the campus streetlights. The rain had stopped, but the ground still held the memory of it.

Raghav and I walked side by side, our footsteps muffled against the wet pavement. After everything that had happened, neither of us wanted to stay locked inside our rooms. A walk seemed like the easiest way to shake off the weight pressing on our chests.

We talked about home—about the streets we grew up on, the food we missed, the people we hadn't thought about in a while.

"Man, I could kill for a plate of Keshav's Chinese bhel right now," Raghav sighed, shaking his head. *"I swear, no place here even comes close."*

I chuckled. *"You and your street food. You realize this is the fifth time you've brought them up this week?"*

"Because they deserve it," he said, grinning. *"You just don't understand—"*

A voice cut through the night.

"Hey, sorry—uh, do you know where the library is?"

We both stopped.

A guy stood a few feet ahead, his face half-hidden in shadow. He looked about our age, dressed in the usual uniform, though his shirt was slightly damp, like he'd been out longer than necessary. His hair stuck to his forehead, dark strands curling at the ends.

Raghav answered without thinking. *"Yeah, just go straight and take the first left."*

The guy nodded. *"Oh, thanks. Sorry, I'm new here, so..."* His voice was casual, easy-going. Then he glanced at Raghav, tilting his head slightly. *"By the way, what's your name?"*

There was a brief hesitation, but then Raghav answered. *"Raghav."*

The guy smiled. *"Oh, Raghav. Nice name."*

Something about the way he said it made my stomach twist.

Raghav must've felt it too, because his posture stiffened slightly. We turned to leave, but before we could take a step, the guy reached out.

His hand landed lightly on Raghav's shoulder.

I saw Raghav freeze.

The guy leaned in, just enough that his voice barely carried past the space between them.

"You should be more careful while speaking your name around here."

The words weren't threatening. But they weren't friendly either.

And then, as if nothing had happened, he pulled away and walked off.

Neither of us moved.

I felt my pulse hammering, the night suddenly colder than before.

Raghav swallowed, his shoulders still tense. I could tell he wanted to say something, but he didn't.

Neither did I.

We just stood there, staring after the stranger as he disappeared into the darkness.

The rain hadn't let up. If anything, it was coming down harder, drumming against the balcony railing like an unrelenting force. The room felt smaller, the air heavier. No one spoke for a long time.

Then, Daniyal finally broke the silence.

"Is it possible," he said slowly, *"that you guys encountered the same guy we did?"*

I leaned back against the wall, arms crossed. *"Perhaps,"* I said. *"But what difference does it make? The important thing is that you both were encountered by someone. And despite me and Shiraz being there, we still screwed up."*

Daniyal's brow furrowed as if something had just clicked in his mind. His gaze sharpened as he looked between me and Shiraz.

"Wait," he muttered. *"Why weren't you two encountered?"*

The question hung in the air, charged.

Raghav was the one to answer. *"Maybe because they only target the ones who received the text."*

Daniyal nodded at first, but his expression darkened. *"Yeah... but think about it. If the university is this systematic, this precise—then how come they don't know that these two are with us?"*

The room fell silent again. Outside, thunder rumbled.

And inside, an unease settled over us that was impossible to ignore.

Shiraz exhaled sharply, running a hand down his face. *"Look, either we sit here debating why we two weren't encountered, or we focus on what we need to do next. Be serious, guys. The interaction has happened."* He paused, his voice lowering. *"More importantly, Daniyal received that text three days ago. It told him not to wait four days."*

Something clicked in all of us.

Shiraz straightened. *"Wait a minute. Daniyal got a message telling him not to wait. Does that mean—"*

Daniyal cut in, his voice suddenly tense. *"It means that whoever sent me that text knew something like this would happen during this gap. They were trying to warn us."* His expression darkened. *"But the question is—who?"*

A heavy silence settled over the room.

The rain outside didn't stop. Neither did the weight of that question.

We all sat there, trying to piece it together, but nothing came to mind.

Then Raghav spoke, his voice steady but resigned. *"Look, I don't know who that guy was, and I don't know how to contact him. But I do know that it's too late now. We don't have any other option but to stick to the plan."* He glanced around the room. *"Right now, there's nothing we can do but wait for tomorrow."*

Daniyal and Shiraz let out quiet sighs, the exhaustion creeping into their faces. Daniyal pushed himself up from the bed and turned to me.

"You better be right tomorrow, Aaron," he said, his tone firm. *"Or else we'll be way behind the eight ball on everything."*

With that, he and Shiraz left, heading back to their dorms.

The door shut behind them.

The rain kept falling.

And the weight of tomorrow settled over me like a storm that hadn't yet arrived.

CHAPTER FOURTEEN

BURIED BELOW

Lunch hour had finally arrived, and *Raghav* and I made our way to the *cafeteria*, the usual hum of conversation filling the air. The morning had passed in a blur of lectures, the kind where my mind kept drifting back to more pressing concerns—like the *warden*. While we sat through classes, *Shiraz* and *Daniyal* had been keeping an eye on him, watching for any movement toward the room.

A few minutes after we sat down with our food, they joined us. *Raghav* leaned forward, lowering his voice. *"So, any luck?"*

Shiraz shook his head. *"Nope. Nothing."*

Daniyal scoffed. *"Dude's been eating chips and staring at his monitor all day long. I think he might actually be part of the furniture at this point."*

Raghav and I let out a chuckle. I turned to *Shiraz*. *"Where is he now?"*

Shiraz jerked his chin slightly. *"Why don't you look to your right?"*

I did—and there he was, standing at the counter, ordering food.

Raghav smirked. *"Looks like the chips didn't make up for lunch."*

Everyone chuckled lightly, but the tension still hung between us. I glanced at *Daniyal*. *"Why don't you guys take a break? We don't have any more lectures, so we'll take over. If something happens, we'll call you."*

Shiraz exhaled. *"Sounds like a plan."*

Daniyal pointed a finger at me as he stood up. *"If something happens, call us immediately."*

I nodded, watching as they left. Then, *Raghav* and I settled in, eyes discreetly fixed on the *warden*, waiting for him to make his move.

As soon as the *warden* finished his lunch, he started moving. *Raghav* and I exchanged a glance before casually falling into step behind him, careful to keep our distance. To anyone watching, we were just two students strolling down the path, lost in conversation.

For a few minutes, he walked with purpose, but then, as if nothing was out of the ordinary, he stepped into his *cabin*. We positioned ourselves nearby, making sure we had a good view without looking suspicious.

And then—nothing.

The *warden* sat at his desk, eyes fixed on his monitor. Occasionally, he scrolled through his phone. Minutes stretched into an hour, then two. At some point, he leaned back, arms crossed, and let his eyes drift shut.

We had been watching the *warden* for hours now. The *cafeteria*, his *cabin*, the endless staring at his monitor—nothing. I was starting to feel ridiculous. I leaned back on the bench outside the *admin building*, exhaling. *"We were wrong,"* I muttered. *"He's got nothing to do with this."*

Raghav shot me a look, frowning. *"Aaron, it's not your fault—"*

"Isn't it?" I cut him off. *"I convinced all of you. I was so sure. We wasted an entire day on this, and now we're back to square one."*

Before *Raghav* could respond, his phone buzzed.

Daniyal.

"Any movement?" his voice came through, low and expectant.

Raghav shook his head. *"Nothing. We were wrong. We need a different approach."*

Silence on the other end for a moment, then *Daniyal* sighed. *"Alright. We tried. Let's regroup after dinner. Meet us at the grove at ten."*

"Got it."

The call ended.

I stared up at the sky. The campus lights flickered against the dark clouds, and a sharp gust of wind rustled the trees. I wanted to believe we were onto something, but maybe this was all in my head.

Dinner was quiet. No one talked much. The disappointment sat between us like a wall. By the time *Raghav* and I reached the *grove*, only *Daniyal* was there, leaning against a tree, scrolling through his phone.

"Where's Shiraz?" I asked.

Daniyal slipped his phone into his pocket. *"Running a bit late. We should start."*

I hesitated. *"Listen, guys... I'm sorry. If it weren't for me, we might actually have a lead by now."*

Daniyal shook his head. *"What's done is done. No one was sure about this. It could've gone either way."*

Raghav nodded. *"Yeah, don't beat yourself up over it."*

I sighed. *"I just wish something—anything—would happen to give us a break."*

As if the universe had been waiting for me to say that, *Daniyal's* phone buzzed.

A message.

From *Shiraz.*

Library entrance. Now.

Daniyal looked up, eyes sharp. *"Let's go."*

We ran.

Shiraz stood near a pillar, looking like he was just another student waiting around. But the way his fingers tapped impatiently against his arm told me something was up.

I barely caught my breath before asking, *"What's going on?"*

"Wait a minute," he said, eyes fixed on something ahead. *"You'll see for yourself."*

Seconds later, the *library* doors swung open.

The *warden* stepped out.

Two files in his hands.

Daniyal frowned. *"Where the hell is he going with those?"*

Shiraz kept his voice low. *"I saw him come in with those files. He didn't check anything out. He's up to something."*

We followed him.

The night swallowed our footsteps as we kept a safe distance. The *warden* moved with purpose, heading toward the *admin building.* As we approached, we saw the elevator doors slide open.

He stepped inside.

The display screen above flickered as the numbers changed.

L1 → G → B1 → R.

We exchanged glances.

"Level R?" I whispered.

Daniyal's eyes gleamed. *"Records Room."*

We didn't hesitate. *Shiraz* pointed to the fire exit. We slipped inside, taking the stairs down. Heart pounding, I peeked around the corner.

The *warden* stood in front of a door labelled *Records Room.*

He pulled out a card, swiped it against the scanner. A beep. The door unlocked. He stepped inside.

Seconds later, he walked out.

Empty-handed.

I swallowed hard.

Daniyal leaned in. *"Well, Aaron,"* he murmured, a hint of amusement in his voice. *"Looks like you got your wish."*

This wasn't over. Not even close.

CHAPTER FIFTEEN

THE PLAN

The *grove* felt different in the early morning—a little colder, a little quieter. When *Raghav* and I arrived, *Daniyal* and *Shiraz* were already there, standing beneath the trees like shadows.

Raghav yawned and stretched. *"I really like our grove discussions, but not enough to have them at six in the morning."*

Shiraz smirked. *"It's important. We can't afford to waste time now. The sooner we act, the better."*

I nodded. *"Right. So, what's the plan? Do you guys have anything?"*

Daniyal exhaled, rubbing his temples. *"Well... as of now, nothing. The key stays in his cabin, which means the only way to get it is to break in and take it."*

Shiraz added, *"And he keeps his cabin locked. So before we even think about getting the key, we have to figure out how to unlock the cabin. Either way, if we somehow pull this off, we'll still get caught. There are security cameras everywhere."*

A brief silence followed. The weight of what we were about to attempt was sinking in.

I cleared my throat. *"Does anyone know what his cabin keys look like?"*

Raghav frowned. *"What difference does it make?"*

"It makes a difference if his keys are physical. If they have cuts and a pattern, we can duplicate them. We wouldn't even need to steal them—just a clear picture should be enough."

Shiraz's eyes lit up. *"That's actually a great idea. But how do we get the picture? He has the keys with him all the time, which means our only chance is when they're inside the cabin and he's not around."*

Daniyal tapped his fingers against his arm. Then, as if a switch flipped in his mind, he said, *"If we create a quick distraction, it's doable."*

Raghav crossed his arms. *"And how do we do that?"*

Daniyal smirked. *"Easy. The university has a zero-tolerance policy for smoking. One of us tells him someone's smoking near the main building, and he'll run to catch them. Meanwhile, someone else sneaks into the cabin, takes the picture, and gets out before he returns."*

I thought for a moment, then shook my head. *"That's only half the problem. Even if we manage to get a duplicate key, when do we use it? He's around all the time. The only time he steps out is for his evening walk, and even then, we can't just waltz into the records room while the cameras record us."*

Another silence. This one heavier than the last.

Then, after a few seconds, *Raghav* spoke up. *"I have an idea. But it's risky."*

Daniyal turned to him. *"What is it?"*

Raghav hesitated. *"If we cut the main power supply... including the backup generator, it might give us enough time."*

Shiraz raised an eyebrow. *"But none of us know how to do that."*

"I do." *Raghav's* voice was calm, confident. *"My dad runs a business dealing with generators and circuits. I know my way around them. Most of the time, the main circuit and the generator are close to each other. If we do this right, the entire admin building will go dark."*

I exhaled. *"That's too risky. There's a high chance we'll get caught."*

"That's why we have to do it at night," *Raghav* said. *"Late. When it's dark. Preferably when there's heavy rain to cover us."*

The group fell silent. The wind rustled the trees above us, the morning light filtering through the branches. The sky was overcast—heavy with clouds.

Daniyal finally spoke. *"It doesn't seem like we have much of a choice. If we start over, we'll be too late. If we move ahead, escaping the cameras is only possible with what Raghav suggested."*

One by one, we nodded. The air around us felt heavier now, like we had crossed some invisible line.

Raghav rolled his shoulders. *"Alright. But I'll need help. Someone has to come with me."*

Shiraz stepped forward. *"I'll go."*

I ran a hand through my hair. *"Okay. Then I'll go and check what kind of key he has."*

Daniyal looked at me. *"I'm coming with you."*

I gave him a nod of approval.

Daniyal exhaled. *"Alright. We meet back here in the evening to confirm the status. No delays."*

Everyone murmured their agreement.

As we parted ways, I glanced up at the sky. The clouds looked darker than before. Something told me the rain wasn't far away.
And we were running out of time.

CHAPTER SIXTEEN

THE NIGHT WE CHOSE

The sun was beginning to set, casting long shadows through the trees as *Daniyal* and I stood near the *grove*, waiting. The air was cooler now, the usual hum of campus life fading as students returned to their hostels.

A few minutes later, we spotted *Raghav* and *Shiraz* making their way toward us.

"Well?" Shiraz asked the moment they reached us. *"How did it go?"*

Daniyal and I exchanged a knowing look before he smirked.

"We got the picture," Daniyal said, pulling out his phone.

"Smooth as butter," I added. *"I went to the warden, told him some student was smoking near the main building. He got all worked up and stormed off with me while Daniyal slipped inside and got the shot."*

Daniyal shook his head. *"Yeah, but man, that place? It smelled like a mix of expired milk and dead rats. I swear, if hell had a waiting room, that would be it."*

Raghav let out a short laugh. *"I'd say that's the least of his crimes."*

Shiraz leaned in as *Daniyal* held up his phone, displaying a clear image of the warden's key lying on his cluttered desk.

"It's a physical key," I pointed out. *"Which means we can get it duplicated. We just need to head into the city, find a locksmith, and we'll have our way in."*

A brief silence followed. This wasn't just some vague idea anymore. The pieces were falling into place. The next step would be crossing a line we couldn't come back from.

"So?" I asked, searching their expressions. *"How did it go with you guys? Everything good?"*

A pause.

Shiraz and *Raghav* exchanged a look. Not a casual one—one that carried weight, hesitation. Something was off.

The easy atmosphere from before vanished in an instant.

Daniyal noticed too. *"Why do you guys look like that?"* he asked, frowning. *"What happened?"*

Shiraz looked down for a second, exhaling, while *Raghav* rubbed the back of his neck. The hesitation stretched long enough to make me uneasy.

Finally, *Raghav* spoke.

"Actually... no. Not everything is good."

I tensed.

"We found the main circuit and the generator," he continued.

"Well, that's good, right?" I asked, trying to hold onto some hope.

Raghav sighed. *"Yeah. But the issue is..."* He hesitated again before looking at me directly. *"They've gone all out with security. I mean, really gone out of their way. Advanced systems. Equipment I didn't expect."*

Daniyal's expression darkened. *"Explain."*

Raghav nodded. *"See, if I break the main circuit, the power will go off—but not for long. If I manually manipulate it, I can delay the reset, but there's a problem."* He looked at *Shiraz*, who took over. *"The system is designed to detect when there's no load on the circuit.*

If that happens, it automatically resets itself."

I clenched my jaw. *"So even if you break it—"*

"It'll fix itself," *Raghav* confirmed.

Daniyal exhaled sharply. *"Shit."*

"And that's not the worst part," Shiraz added. *"The generator is designed the same way. Even if we disable the starter mechanism, the system is smart enough to restart itself. So even if Raghav messes with it, we're on a timer."*

The weight of their words settled in.

I ran a hand through my hair. *"So, what does that mean? Are we screwed?"*

Raghav and *Shiraz* exchanged another glance.

"Not exactly," *Raghav* said. *"I can mess with it long enough to buy time. The power will go out, but..."* He hesitated. *"We won't have as much time as we hoped."*

I narrowed my eyes. *"How much?"*

Another silent exchange between them. *Shiraz* spoke this time.

"Fifteen, twenty minutes. Max."

I felt a pit in my stomach.

Daniyal and I reacted at the same time. *"That's it?"*

The wind howled through the trees. A low, distant rumble of thunder echoed across the sky.

"Yeah," *Raghav* confirmed. *"And there's more. I've explained everything to*

Shiraz—he needs to be there with me when I pull this off."
I inhaled slowly. *"Which means Daniyal and I are going in alone."*
No one spoke.
A sharp gust of wind blew through the *grove*, rustling the leaves violently. The air felt heavier now, like the storm brewing above was waiting for us to make a decision.
Daniyal ran a hand over his face, muttering something under his breath. Then, finally, he looked up.
"Well," he said, his voice quieter but firm, *"I guess that's that, then."*
I nodded. There was no turning back now.
The storm was coming. And so were we.
The silence lingered for a few seconds before *Raghav* spoke again.
"Uh... guys," he said, hesitating. *"There's one more thing."*
I turned to him, my stomach already sinking. *"More?"*
Raghav sighed. *"Yeah. I'm afraid so."* He looked between us, his expression grim. *"See, when I cut the power, there's a chance the security guards will notice. If that happens, they might start checking the area."*
Daniyal exhaled sharply. *"Great."*
"So once it's done," Raghav continued, *"we'll have to run straight back to the dorms—no waiting, no stopping. The problem is..."* He hesitated, then met our eyes. *"As soon as we're out of there, we won't be able to tell you exactly how much time you'll have left before the power comes back. You two will have to keep track yourselves."*
Daniyal and I exchanged a look. Neither of us said anything, but we nodded almost at the same time—like we'd already anticipated this.
I took a breath. *"There's one more thing."*
Raghav and *Shiraz* looked at me.
"There's a high chance it'll rain heavily tonight," I said, glancing up at the dark sky. The storm hadn't hit yet, but the air felt thick, electric. *"That means we have to do this tonight—no pushing it."*
Shiraz nodded. *"Yeah, makes sense. But what's the issue?"*
I straightened. *"The issue is the rain itself. If we don't wear raincoats and gumboots, we'll leave water trails inside the building—footprints, puddles, something that could lead them straight to the Records Room."*
Daniyal's brows lifted slightly, as if impressed. *"Good thinking."*
"So," I continued, *"we wear them until we reach the admin building, and just before we go inside, we toss them aside. That way, we don't drag any water in with us."*

Shiraz crossed his arms, nodding. *"Yeah, that actually makes a lot of sense."*
Daniyal clapped his hands together. *"Alright. Then here's the plan. Shiraz and I go to the city right now, find a locksmith, and get the key made."*
I nodded. *"Meanwhile, Raghav and I will start preparing everything we need for tonight."*
Daniyal adjusted his watch. *"After 11:30, we meet back here. Same spot."*
No more words were needed.
We all nodded, and just like that, we split up—each of us heading toward our next task, while the storm loomed heavier above.

CHAPTER SEVENTEEN

WHEN SHADOWS MOVE

The rain was relentless. Thick, heavy sheets hammered the ground, turning the dirt into slush. The wind howled through the trees, bending their branches like they were made of rubber. It was almost *11:30*, and the storm showed no signs of letting up. If anything, it was getting worse.

I stood under the cover of a large tree with *Raghav*, both of us watching the path ahead. My hoodie was already damp, the cold creeping through the fabric, but I barely noticed. My eyes flicked toward my watch. Any second now.

Then, from the darkness, two figures emerged, running.

Daniyal and *Shiraz*.

They skidded to a stop in front of us, drenched and breathless. *Shiraz* pushed back his hood and exhaled sharply.

"Sorry we're late."

I shook my head. *"It's fine. You got the keys?"*

Daniyal gave a sharp nod, reaching into his pocket. The keys glistened under the dim glow of a distant lamppost. *"Right here."*

"Perfect," Raghav said. *"Here's how this is going to go. You two head to the warden's cabin, unlock it, and grab the keycard. The second you have it, message us. That's our signal to cut the power."*

His tone was firm, calculated. He was already in execution mode.

"Once the power is out," he continued, *"you'll have twenty minutes—tops. You go in, find the blueprints, take pictures, put the keycard back in the warden's cabin, and head straight for the dorms. No delays, no detours. Understood?"*

Daniyal and I exchanged a glance. We both knew what was at stake.

"Understood."

"Alright then," Shiraz said, *"set your timers."*
I flicked my wrist and tapped my watch screen. The timer blinked to life. *Twenty minutes.* That was all we had.
Raghav took a deep breath. *"Good luck, guys."*
Daniyal smirked. *"You too. Try not to electrocute yourselves."*
I huffed a quiet laugh, gave a small nod, and then—we split.
The rain hadn't let up. If anything, it was getting worse. Sheets of water crashed against the ground, the wind howling through the campus like it wanted to tear the trees out from their roots. My hoodie was soaked through, sticking to my skin, but that was the least of my worries.
Daniyal and I moved quickly, keeping close to the shadows as we made our way to the *warden's cabin.* The storm masked our footsteps, but I still felt every nerve in my body on high alert. If we got caught now... No. We wouldn't. We couldn't.
Reaching the door, *Daniyal* fished into his pocket and pulled out the keys, his fingers slick with rainwater.
I swallowed. *"This better work."*
Daniyal didn't answer. He slid the key into the lock and twisted. For a second, nothing happened—then *click.* The door creaked open.
Daniyal exhaled. *"Perfect."*
We slipped inside, shutting the door behind us. The room was pitch dark, the only sound the muffled roar of the storm outside. I pulled out my phone and flicked on the torch. The faint beam illuminated the small, cluttered office.
We worked fast, checking the desk first, then the key holders on the wall. Nothing. My pulse was hammering against my ribs. I yanked open the drawers, shuffling past files and loose papers until—there.
"Got 'em." I held up the keycard.
Daniyal leaned in, his face barely visible in the dim light. *"Great. I'll message them."* He tapped on his phone, muttering, *"We got it. Yeah."*
We closed the cabin door behind us and sprinted toward the *admin building.* The rain made it harder to see, but we knew where we had to go. Just as we neared our entry point, I skidded to a stop—two security guards.
Daniyal grabbed my arm, yanking me back. We ducked behind a bush, breathing hard.
"Damn it," I hissed.
The guards were talking, their voices barely audible over the rain.
Daniyal wiped his wet face. *"Maybe when the power cuts, they'll run to check*

what's wrong. That'll be our cue."

I checked my watch. *"Why is it taking them so long?"* My voice was barely above a whisper.

Then—a flashlight beam cut through the darkness.

"Hey! Who's there?" one of the guards called out.

My stomach clenched. The second guard turned. *"What is it?"*

"I think I saw something."

Daniyal's grip on my arm tightened. *"Shit, shit, shit."*

The guards started walking toward us.

I could feel my heartbeat in my throat. *"No. Not now. Come on, guys... cut the power. It's now or never."*

Then—everything went dark.

The entire campus plunged into complete blackness. The guards froze.

"Hey! What the hell?" one of them muttered.

The other cursed.

And just like that—they ran off toward the power source.

Daniyal didn't wait. *"Now!"*

We bolted for the *admin building.* Rain pounded against us as we yanked off our coats and boots, tossing them aside just before reaching the entrance. My fingers were ice-cold as I pushed open the door.

We slipped inside.

I tapped my watch. Timer started.

20 minutes.

Daniyal and I switched on our flashlights, the beams cutting through the darkness as we moved quickly toward the fire exit. The rain outside hammered against the building, but in here, it was eerily silent. Each step echoed in the empty corridor.

We reached *Level R.* The door to the *records room* stood in front of us, a dull, metallic grey.

I glanced at *Daniyal. "You ready for this?"*

He smirked. *"I was born ready."*

I rolled my eyes. *"Of course, James Bond."*

Taking a breath, I slid the keycard into the slot. For a second, nothing happened—then a small green light blinked on. The lock released with a soft click.

We slipped inside and shut the door behind us.

The air smelled of old paper and dust. Our flashlights swept across the room—three shelves, two cupboards. The space wasn't large, but it was cluttered enough to be a problem.

"I'll take the cupboards," Daniyal whispered. *"You check the shelves."*

I nodded. *"Got it."*

We split up, wasting no time.

I worked quickly, flipping through folders, prying open boxes, running my fingers along faded labels. Each carton held something different—student records, legal documents, faculty reports.

None of it was what we needed.

A glance at my watch. 7 minutes gone.

Shit.

I moved to the last shelf, scanning frantically. Then—I saw it.

A box labelled *"FLOOR PLANS."*

Heart pounding, I yanked it out and pulled off the lid. Inside—blueprints. Floor plans. Exactly what we came for.

"Daniyal!"

He was at my side in seconds. *"You found them?"*

I nodded, already flipping through the papers. *Daniyal* held the flashlight steady as I pulled out my phone and started snapping photos—one blueprint after another, making sure nothing was blurred.

Timer: *15 minutes down.*

"We need to go. Now." Daniyal's voice was sharp.

We stacked the papers back in order, returned the box to the shelf, and gave the room one last sweep. Satisfied, we slipped out, locking the door behind us.

But as we turned toward the exit—we froze.

Two security guards.

They stood right outside the building, facing the front entrance.

Daniyal yanked me back behind a pillar. *"Shit."*

I checked my watch. *4 minutes left.*

We were running out of time. The guards weren't moving. If they didn't leave soon, we were screwed.

We needed a distraction. But how?

I racked my brain. Nothing. *Daniyal* looked just as stuck. *2 minutes left.*

And then—one of the guards suddenly shouted.

"Hey! Who's there?!"

My stomach clenched. Had they seen us? Were we caught?

But then—they ran.

"Hey! Stop!"

Something—or someone—had drawn their attention. And just like that, they were gone.

Daniyal didn't hesitate. *"Go. Now!"*

We bolted for the exit, sprinting through the rain. My coat and boots were exactly where I had left them, but there was no time to fully gear up. I shoved my coat on, grabbed my boots, and ran barefoot across the muddy ground.

Then—the lights came back on.

We had just escaped in time.

We dashed toward the *warden's cabin*, threw the key back inside, and didn't stop running until we reached our *dorm*.

My heart was still racing.

We had done it.

But something about the way the guards ran... the way the power came back so conveniently right after we escaped...

We burst into the dorm room, dripping wet, barely catching our breath. The air inside felt unnaturally still, the only sound our ragged breathing. I ran a hand through my soaked hair, but before I could say anything, I noticed them.

Raghav and *Shiraz* were already inside, standing near the window. They turned as we entered, eyes scanning us.

"You guys okay?" *Raghav* asked, concern laced in his voice.

Daniyal and I locked eyes. Then, almost instinctively, we let out a breathless laugh—part exhaustion, part disbelief. We had done it. We had actually pulled it off.

Shiraz and *Raghav* exchanged glances, understanding our reaction without needing an explanation. *Shiraz* exhaled deeply. *"Damn... So it went fine?"*

"Not without obstacles," *Daniyal* admitted, shaking his head. *"But yeah. We got what we needed."*

I peeled off my soaked coat and dropped it onto the chair. *"And the power outage? Perfectly timed. Exactly twenty minutes."*

Shiraz smirked. *"Don't thank me. Thank him."* He nodded toward *Raghav*.

Raghav shrugged, feigning modesty. *"Well, can't take all the credit. My father's business had its... benefits."*

For a moment, there was silence. Relief settled in, a fragile sense of victory. Then *Daniyal* spoke. *"Oh, and hey—nice move with the distraction at the admin building. If those guards hadn't run off, we would've been trapped."*

I nodded. *"Seriously. You guys nailed the timing."*

Shiraz frowned. *"What distraction?"*

I blinked. *"The guards. At the entrance. Someone lured them away right when we were about to be caught."*

Raghav and *Shiraz* exchanged puzzled looks.

"We didn't do that," Raghav said slowly. *"After we cut the power, we came straight back here."*

Daniyal and I went still.

I swallowed. *"Then who—"*

A sudden knock cut through the room.

Three sharp raps.

A voice followed. Low, steady.

"Open up. I know you're in there."

We all froze.

Outside, the rain hadn't let up. If anything, it was coming down harder now, hammering against the glass like a warning.

CHAPTER EIGHTEEN

UNSEEN, UNSPOKEN

The rain was still falling, a steady rhythm against the window, filling the silence between us. We all looked at each other, frozen in place.

Daniyal shot a glance at *Raghav*, a silent command. *Check the door.*

Raghav hesitated for a second before walking over, his footsteps barely audible over the rain. He peered through the peephole, then turned to us and whispered, *"It's a student."*

Daniyal and I exchanged a glance. *A student?*

I nodded at *Raghav*, and he unlatched the door. The second it opened, a figure stepped inside, rain-soaked and breathless. He was taller than us, older-looking, and his sharp gaze flickered over each of us before locking onto *Raghav*. *"Close the door."*

Raghav hesitated but did as he was told.

Then, in a voice as crisp as the night air outside, the stranger spoke. *"What makes you all think you can do this without getting caught?"*

A heavy silence followed. The only sound was the rain, as if the entire room was holding its breath.

Daniyal straightened. *"We're still waiting."*

The stranger turned to him, expression unreadable.

Daniyal crossed his arms. *"For your name, that is."*

The guy exhaled sharply. *"Agasthya."* Then, his next words sent a chill down my spine. *"Ishaan's friend."*

Shiraz and *Daniyal* stiffened. I felt it too—that drop in my stomach, the sudden weight in the room. Outside, the rain poured harder, justifying the silence that followed.

Shiraz was the first to speak. *"You knew Ishaan?"*

Agasthya's eyes darkened. *"I knew him. He was a great friend."*

Daniyal narrowed his eyes. *"Was?"*

Agasthya didn't answer at first. Then, after a moment, he said quietly, *"He went missing a long time ago."*

Shiraz exhaled sharply. *"We know that."*

Agasthya studied him for a second before his gaze flicked to *Daniyal.* *"Then I guess you must be Shiraz. And you,"* he turned to *Daniyal,* *"must be Daniyal."*

Daniyal's posture tensed. *"How do you know us?"*

Agasthya shrugged. *"Ishaan told me about you two. How you were always together. Like brothers."*

Something about the way he said it made my stomach twist. The way he said *were.*

I swallowed and spoke up. *"Then you must also know what happened to him."* The question hung in the air.

Agasthya's expression didn't change. He just stood there, unmoving. *"Unfortunately, no."*

I clenched my jaw.

"All I know is that, for about a month before he disappeared, he started acting strange. Like something was wrong."

His voice was steady, but I caught something behind it. Something unsettled.

"He became... secretive. He'd leave at odd hours, come back late, barely say a word. I asked him about it, but he always brushed it off. A week before he disappeared, I even tried following him, but no matter what I did, I lost him. Every time. Like he was never there."

Shiraz shifted uncomfortably.

"At the time, I thought maybe school was getting to him. Stress, exams, whatever. But then, the night before he vanished, he finally spoke to me."

Agasthya's voice dropped slightly.

"He just said, 'Don't ever try to go deep inside. Just behave normally and act like nothing happened.'"

My skin prickled.

"I asked him if everything was okay." *Agasthya's* jaw clenched. "He said, 'Yeah, it's fine.'"

A pause.

"That was the last time I ever saw him."

Agasthya exhaled sharply and shook his head, as if shaking off the weight of the past. Then, his eyes hardened again. *"Enough about this."*

His tone was sharper now, more controlled. *"I know you guys know what's happening here. And by now, you must've figured out that the same applies to* me."

Then, his gaze landed on me and *Raghav*. *"Now tell me, who's Raghav?"*

I tensed.

Raghav inhaled. *"That would be me."*

Agasthya nodded slightly. *"You guys got the text, right?"* His gaze flicked to *Daniyal* and *Raghav*.

Daniyal narrowed his eyes. *"How do you know that?"*

Agasthya smirked. *"I know all your conversations from the grove. You thought it was just the squirrel, didn't you?"*

My pulse spiked.

I shot a look at *Daniyal*. *"I told you something was wrong."*

Raghav scoffed. *"Yeah, right."*

Daniyal ignored him. *"So you were the one who created the distraction?"*

Agasthya nodded. *"Yeah. That was me."*

I exhaled, my mind racing.

"*Then you must be the one who texted Daniyal, 'You don't have four days.'*"

A slow smirk crept onto *Agasthya's* face. *"You guys are not as dumb as I thought."*

Shiraz scoffed. *"Tough words from someone who follows us like a lunatic."*

Agasthya didn't seem bothered. *"Hey, if it weren't for me, these two wouldn't be standing here."* He gestured at *Daniyal* and me.

Raghav frowned. *"If you knew about us, why didn't you just contact us?"*

Agasthya's smirk faded.

"*Because I got the text too.*"

The room fell into stunned silence.

"*I'm on their radar, just like you. If I talked to you directly, whoever's keeping tabs on us would get suspicious. Maybe we wouldn't even be standing here now.*"

No one had an argument for that.

Daniyal ran a hand through his damp hair. *"So after this, you're just gonna be with us like nothing happened?"*

Agasthya shook his head. *"No."*

The finality in his voice was clear.

"*I'll still be around. I'll text you when necessary. But we can't let them know we know each other.*"

Shiraz frowned. *"Then how do we contact you?"*

Agasthya smirked. *"Don't worry. I'll be there when you need me."*

Then, before we could say anything else, he turned and pulled open the door.

The rain was still coming down hard.

He glanced back once. *"Be more careful next time."*

And then, he was gone.

The door clicked shut.

Silence.

Shiraz ran a hand down his face. *"What the hell just happened?"*

No one answered. Because the truth was—none of us knew. And outside, the storm raged on.

CHAPTER NINETEEN

THE SECOND PAGE

The *grove* was eerily silent, the only sound being the occasional rustling of leaves. It was *4:30 AM*. Last night had been intense—more than any of them could have anticipated—but something told me that it wasn't over yet. The rain had stopped, yet the sky remained dark and heavy, as if morning had yet to arrive.

As thoughts raced through my mind, I heard footsteps approaching. *Shiraz* and *Daniyal* had arrived. *Shiraz*, rubbing his eyes, didn't waste a second before snapping, *"Okay, now tell me—why the heck did you call us at 4:30 in the morning?"*

I exhaled sharply. *"I don't know. I'm as clueless as you guys."* Then I turned to *Raghav*. *"Now that everyone is here, can you tell us what this is about?"*

Raghav didn't answer. Without a word, he reached into his bag and pulled out an old, worn-out diary. The moment I saw it, my breath hitched. It was his brother's diary.

For a second, no one spoke. The wind stirred, making the trees shift and sway as if they, too, were listening.

Daniyal broke the silence. *"Haven't seen this thing in a while."* His voice was quiet, uneasy.

Raghav ran a hand over the diary's cover, his fingers lingering on its edges. Then, finally, he spoke. *"Before we move forward... I think it's time we see the second page."*

We all exchanged glances. As eager as we were, none of us were sure if we should.

Shiraz let out a dry laugh, though there was no humour in it. *"Last time I read that thing, I didn't sleep for two or three days."* He shook his head. *"I don't think I want to look at it again."*

I swallowed hard. If *Shiraz*—who rarely let anything get to him—was hesitant, what did that say about whatever was on that page?

Still, I turned to *Raghav*. *"If you think it's the right time..."* My voice was steady, but even I wasn't sure if I believed that.

Raghav gave a small nod, then carefully flipped through the pages of the diary. The worn paper rustled under his fingers as he stopped at a particular page. He looked up at us, his expression unreadable.

"You guys ready?"

No one spoke. We just turned our eyes toward the open page.

September 4th, 2022 – 12:57 AM

I didn't think I'd last long enough to write a second entry.

If you're reading this, I need you to listen carefully.

Never share this with anyone.

Never ask questions.

Never, under any circumstances, think about coming here.

But if you do—

Just go to class. Write your exams. Take your degree.

And leave. And never come back.

I'm writing this because someone needs to know. But if you repeat what I'm about to say...

They won't recover from it.

A week ago, I got in. I don't know where I found the courage, but I did. And I was right. They track everything.

I saw the reports.

At first, I didn't understand what I was looking at. Pages upon pages of files, each one containing details—family, friends, hometowns. But the names... I had never heard of any of them.

I tried searching for them online. Nothing.

It was as if they had never existed.

But that wasn't the worst part.

At the bottom of each report, there was a single word.

Some reports said: "Connected."

Others said: "Not Connected."

At first, I thought they had simply disappeared. But now, I'm not even sure they were ever alive to begin with.

even now, when I am writing this, I feel someone's watching me.

I feel sick. I feel regret.

If I ever make it out of here—which, honestly, I don't think I will—I swear, I will never speak of this to anyone. Not a single word.

We were still standing there, silent, weighed down by what they had just read. No one knew what to say.

Then, finally, I spoke. *"In the entry, he said, 'I got in.' What does that mean? Did he find the room?"*

Daniyal, leaning against a tree, exhaled sharply. *"That's... that's a great question."*

Shiraz crossed his arms. *"And what about 'connected' and 'not connected'? What does that even mean?"*

"Another great question." I glanced at the others, but no one had an answer.

Then, without warning, the wind stilled. The rustling trees went silent, as if the world itself had been listening—and had nothing to say.

Raghav finally spoke. His voice was quiet but firm. *"This is exactly why I wanted to show you guys. We keep moving forward, but... do we really know what we're getting into? What if we go looking for answers and... we never come back?"*

The weight of his words settled like a boulder on my chest. The others must have felt it too.

Daniyal broke the silence. *"But what's the guarantee that if we stop now, they'll leave us alone? How sure are we about that?"* He gestured toward the diary. *"From the way it was written, I don't think stopping is an option anymore."*

I took a deep breath. *"If that's true... then we move forward. At least that way, we might get some answers. And maybe—just maybe—we'll find a way out."*

Shiraz let out a dry chuckle. *"Guess we don't have a choice, do we?"*

No one responded. Instead, we just stood there for a moment, looking at each other. Then, as if on cue, the wind picked up again, rustling the trees, breaking the unnatural stillness.

Without another word, we turned and left.

But even as I walked, a thought gnawed at me. I know what I just said... but truth be told, I'm not sure I believe it myself.

CHAPTER TWENTY

PLANS WITHIN PLANS

Night had settled over the campus, and for once, we weren't huddled in *Raghav* and my room. Too many things had happened there—too many unsettling conversations, too many moments where the walls felt like they were listening. This time, we had gathered in *Daniyal* and *Shiraz's* room. The atmosphere was still tense, but at least it was different.

Daniyal leaned against the wall, legs crossed, looking half like he was deep in thought and half like he was about to take a nap. *Raghav* sat on the bed, arms crossed, his face unreadable. Meanwhile, *Shiraz* and I were at the computer, transferring the photos we had taken onto everyone's laptops.

"Alright," I finally said, breaking the silence. "*The photos are transferred to everyone's laptop.*"

Shiraz nodded, clicking through the files. "*And I've segregated the different areas into four folders.*"

"*The admin building, the main building, the library, and other areas,*" I added. "*The problem is, they aren't sorted by year. We didn't exactly have time for a proper filing system while sneaking around and—*"

"*Risking our lives,*" *Daniyal* added.

"*Yes, that,*" I sighed. "*So, we'll have to go through each photo carefully.*"

Raghav raised an eyebrow. "*How many photos per folder?*"

"*Forty.*"

Raghav exhaled sharply. "*That's a lot.*"

"*Yeah, well,*" I shrugged. "*If Tony Stark could build an Iron Man suit in a cave with a box of scraps, we can sort through some blueprints.*"

"*Difference is,*" *Daniyal* muttered, "*he had a genius IQ, and we have Shiraz, who once forgot his own password and had to reset it four times in a day.*"

Shiraz shot him a glare. "*That was one time—*"

"*And then you locked yourself out of your email,*" *Raghav* reminded him.

"Okay, fine. Maybe twice."

I shook my head. *"Look, the point is, this is going to take a while. So let's focus, compare every photo, and find something useful. And for the love of all things holy, if anyone finds a hidden chamber or a secret tunnel, don't keep it to yourself."*

Shiraz sighed dramatically. *"So no 'I am inevitable' moment?"*

"Not unless you want to be snapped out of existence," I said.

Everyone chuckled, but soon, the laughter faded as we got to work. The room fell silent except for the occasional clicks of keyboards and the hum of the laptop fans.

For now, all we had were old floor plans and fading blueprints. But somewhere in these files, there had to be something—something that told us what we were up against.

We had been staring at screens for what felt like an eternity, eyes scanning every blueprint, every floor plan, every tiny, meaningless line that might hold a clue. The clock on the wall read nearly midnight—we had been at this for an hour and a half.

A few moments later, *Raghav* let out a deep sigh and leaned back. *"Okay, I'm done. Who needs coffee?"*

I glanced at my watch and smirked. *"If this is your condition after just an hour and a half, may God have mercy on you during exams."*

Raghav shot me a look. *"Excuse me? I have a GPA of 9.2. I think I'm doing just fine."*

I raised an eyebrow. *"I have a 9.4."*

Shiraz grinned. *"Same here."*

Daniyal, who had been unusually quiet, finally spoke. *"9.5."*

There was a moment of silence before I turned to *Raghav*, grinning. *"Looks like you're the weak link."*

Raghav folded his arms. *"Yeah? Well, I got you guys into the admin building, so shut up."*

That earned a round of laughter.

Daniyal stretched, rolling his shoulders. *"I guess a break wouldn't hurt. Let's grab a coffee—this is gonna take a while."*

No one argued. We closed our laptops, stood up, and grabbed our cups, the warmth of the coffee almost comforting in the quiet of the night.

As we settled back down, *Raghav* spoke again. *"Guys, exams are in five days."*

There was a collective pause before I groaned. *"Damn. We've been so caught up in this mess, we haven't studied at all."*

Shiraz stared at him incredulously. *"How are you even thinking about exams right now? We're literally uncovering something that could get us killed."*
Daniyal shrugged. *"I actually agree with him. If we survive this, I don't want to face my father's belt, so we better start studying."*
That got a laugh out of everyone.
I exhaled, shaking my head. *"For a while now, things are going so well that I forgot we were actually in a mess."*
The weight of those words lingered in the air.
After a long pause, *Raghav* said quietly, *"What if we never got ourselves into this? What if we just lived normal lives, like the other students? Is this how it would've been?"*
I stared at my coffee. *"Maybe it would've been better."*
Shiraz let out a low *"Yeah."*
Daniyal took a sip of his coffee and leaned forward. *"Maybe. But for now, this is what we've got. So let's finish up and get back to work."*
That was the push we needed. We came back to our senses, finished our drinks, and reopened our laptops.
No more distractions. Just the blueprints, the mystery, and whatever lay ahead.
Another hour passed in silence. The only sounds were the occasional clicks of laptop keys and the faint hum of the night outside. No one spoke—everyone was too focused, their eyes scanning floor plans, searching for something, anything.
Then, suddenly—
"Guys, quick! I think I got something," *Daniyal* said, breaking the silence like a gunshot.
We all snapped our heads up, pushing our laptops aside and crowding around him in a semi-circle. My heart pounded a little faster.
"What is it?" I asked.
Daniyal pointed at his screen. *"Look at this. There's another opening—another room—right beside the Records Room."*
I leaned in closer, my brows furrowing. *"Another room?"*
"Yeah," *Daniyal* said, his voice tense. *"I don't remember seeing any other opening when we were down there. Do you?"* He looked directly at me.
I shook my head. *"Not that I recall. Which year is this blueprint from?"*
Daniyal squinted at the timestamp. *"Before 2020."*
Shiraz, who had been silent until now, rubbed his chin. *"After 2020, the institution went through a renovation. I remember hearing about that."*

I turned back to *Daniyal*. *"Check the images from after 2020. Let's see if that room is still there."*

Daniyal clicked through the files rapidly. We all waited in tense silence, eyes locked on the screen.

One image. Nothing.

Next image. Nothing.

Another. Still nothing.

The room had vanished.

Raghav exhaled. *"Okay, so there's a decent chance that the room still exists and was just... removed from the blueprints."*

No one spoke. But we were all thinking the same thing.

"So that means," I finally said, *"we have to go back in there again."*

A collective sigh of exhaustion filled the room.

Daniyal leaned back in his chair, rubbing his temples. *"This time, I think we should wait. If we lay low for now, maybe whoever's keeping tabs on us will slow down too. That way, we buy ourselves some time."*

Raghav frowned. *"And for how long do we put this off?"*

We all thought for a moment. Then, an idea struck me.

"Navratri."

Shiraz blinked. *"What?"*

I turned to them. *"Navratri is coming up in twenty days. The last five days, until Dussehra, the university gives a holiday. Most of the students will go home. If we stay back, we can pull this off when there are barely any people around."*

Raghav nodded slowly. *"That's... actually a great plan."*

"Perfect," *Daniyal* said. *"For now, we stay low, focus on exams, and then carry out the plan during the break."*

We all agreed. The decision had been made.

Raghav and I grabbed our stuff, heading back to our room. But as we walked through the dark corridors, a thought clung to my mind, cold and unshakable.

Someone erased that room from the records. Someone who didn't want it to be found.

And if they knew we were looking for it...

They'd make sure we never found anything ever again.

CHAPTER TWENTY-ONE

NO RAIN TO HIDE

The past twenty days had been a blur of textbooks, late-night cramming, and a sleep schedule that barely qualified as human. Every morning, I'd drag myself to the *library*, flip through the same notes I barely understood, eat whatever I could grab, and repeat the cycle until exhaustion knocked me out.

And today was the final day.

Legal Theory.

The single most mind-numbing, soul-draining subject ever created.

See, with other subjects, you at least feel like you're learning something. *Contract Law?* It tells you what to do if someone scams you. *Criminal Law?* Helps you avoid or commit the perfect crime. *Torts?* Well... at least you can sue someone.

But *Legal Theory?* It's just a hundred different ways of saying the same thing. Philosophers arguing for centuries over what law is, why it exists, and whether we should follow it—only for every professor to end the discussion with *"Well, there's no right answer."*

Then why am I writing a three-hour paper about it?

Just as I finished that thought, the bell rang.

A collective sigh of relief rippled through the *exam hall*. Pens clattered onto desks as invigilators rushed to snatch up our answer sheets like they were top-secret government files. I flexed my fingers, trying to shake out the stiffness, and glanced over at *Raghav*, who looked half-dead.

We grabbed our stuff and walked out, stepping into the sunlit corridor.

"Can't believe I survived that," Raghav muttered, rubbing his eyes.

"You know what? Me too," I said, running a hand through my hair.

He let out a dramatic groan. *"I can't think of anything but going back to my room and passing out for—oh, I don't know—ten to twelve hours."*

Before I could respond, a familiar voice chimed in from behind us.

"Well, we can't expect anything else from you, can we, Raghav?"

We turned around to see *Shiraz* and *Daniyal* approaching, looking just as exhausted—but somehow still smirking.

"Hey guys," I said, adjusting my bag.

Shiraz slung his arm around me. *"So? How was the exam?"*

Raghav scoffed. *"Well, we both walked out alive, so I'd say pretty good."*

We all laughed, shaking off the last remnants of exam stress.

Daniyal cracked his knuckles. *"Alright, now that this torture is over—shall we get back to work?"*

The energy in the air shifted. *Raghav* and I exchanged glances.

"I think it's time we start planning," I said.

Shiraz grinned. *"Perfect. Drop your stuff in your rooms and meet us at the grove in half an hour."*

With a collective nod, we split up. As I walked back toward my room, I couldn't shake the feeling that these past twenty days had been the calm before the storm.

I dumped my bag on the bed, barely resisting the urge to collapse beside it. The room felt weirdly empty now that exams were over—no scattered notes, no last-minute revision panic, just... silence.

Raghav reappeared from his side of the room, stretching his arms over his head. *"Alright, let's go before Shiraz decides to hunt us down."*

We stepped out into the cool evening air, walking side by side through the winding paths of the campus. The trees around us had started to shift from lush green to deep orange, the first real sign that monsoon had ended early, and autumn was creeping in. A light breeze rustled the branches, carrying with it the scent of damp earth and distant woodsmoke.

"Feels weird, doesn't it?" *Raghav* said, kicking a stray pebble.

"What?"

"The weather. Usually, the rains would still be around, clinging on like an unwanted guest. But this year? It's like someone hit the fast-forward button. Straight from drowning in humidity to the crisp air of October."

I nodded, glancing up at the sky. The clouds had cleared, leaving a dull pinkish hue bleeding into the blue.

"Maybe nature decided to spare us the extra suffering," I said.

"Or maybe it's just gearing up to hit us harder later."

We walked in comfortable silence for a moment, the fallen leaves crunching beneath our steps.

As we approached the *grove*, I spotted *Shiraz* and *Daniyal* standing near the old, overgrown clearing. But they weren't alone.

Leaning casually against a tree, arms crossed, one leg over the other, was *Agasthya.*

Before I could react, *Raghav* narrowed his eyes and muttered, *"What's he doing here?"*

At the sound of his voice, *Agasthya* tilted his head slightly and smirked. *"I saw you guys heading here. Figured it was safe enough to talk to you in person now."* He pushed off the tree, taking a slow step forward. *"Besides, I was getting tired of stalking and sending cryptic messages. Felt like a bad detective novel."*

Daniyal let out a low chuckle, lacing his words with sarcasm. *"Wow. You are so smart. Truly, a master of subtlety."*

Agasthya ignored him completely. *"So... have you guys found anything yet?"*

Shiraz crossed his arms. *"Even if we did, why would we bother telling you?"*

Agasthya sighed, his usual calm arrogance tinged with something else this time—something heavier. He took another step closer, lowering his voice.

"Look, I know you don't trust me. I don't blame you. But don't forget—I'm a target too. And I've managed to survive an entire year here. That means I know how this place works better than you do."

He let that sink in for a moment before continuing, his voice carrying an edge of urgency.

"So we have two options. Either we work together, or you keep playing this high-stakes game on your own—until you back yourself into a corner you can't escape from."

His words hung in the air, sinking into each of us.

For the first time, none of us had a quick response. Because as much as we hated to admit it—he was right.

A heavy silence settled over us. The only sound was the distant rustling of leaves and the occasional chirp of crickets. It was *Daniyal* who finally broke the tension with a sigh.

"Alright, we'll tell you." His voice was laced with reluctance. *"But don't take this to mean we trust you completely. It's just that, right now, we don't have a lot of options. So, we have to put up with whatever's left."*

Agasthya smirked, bowing slightly in an exaggerated gesture. *"And the honour is all mine, Your Majesty."*

Daniyal rolled his eyes. *"Yeah, yeah. Just shut up and listen."*

Agasthya straightened up. *"So? What's up?"*

Shiraz stepped forward, taking control of the conversation. *"Before the exams, we went through all the blueprints and floor plans. Every single image clicked by Aaron and Daniyal."* He paused for a moment, letting that sink in before continuing. *"After analysing all of them, we found something strange—there's a room beside the Records Room. But here's the catch: it only exists in the floor plans before 2020. After that? It's gone. Completely erased. The newer blueprints show nothing there, like it never existed."*

Agasthya raised an eyebrow. *"So, you guys think it's still there? Just... removed from the papers?"*

"Exactly," Shiraz confirmed.

Agasthya turned to me and *Daniyal*. *"Did you guys see any opening when you were down there? Anything that looked like it could lead to another space?"*

I shook my head. *"No. If there was something, it wasn't obvious."*

Agasthya hummed in thought, then leaned forward slightly. *"Okay. So what's next?"*

Raghav crossed his arms. *"We have to break in. Like we did last time. It's the only way to find out what's going on."*

"Actually... we can't," Shiraz said.

All eyes turned to him.

"Why not?" I asked.

Shiraz gave me a look, as if the answer should have been obvious. *"Come on, guys. Think about it. The rain's stopped. Autumn has kicked in. We don't have the excuse of bad weather anymore. If we try the same method as before, there's a much higher chance we'll get caught."* He paused, his voice carrying the weight of logic. *"And don't forget—last time, you barely made it out in twenty minutes. We can't afford to be reckless."*

His words hit harder than I expected.

Because he was right.

Up until now, we had been operating under the assumption that we could just repeat what we did before. But the circumstances had changed. No rain to mask our movements. No storm to keep security distracted. If we got caught this time, there would be no excuses, no easy way out.

CHAPTER TWENTY-TWO

THE ENEMY WE NEED

The sky had deepened into a shade of burnt orange, the last traces of daylight fading as we sat in the grove, surrounded by nothing but the rustling leaves and the weight of our own thoughts. The cold was settling in, creeping into my skin, but my mind was too occupied to care. No one spoke. We were all thinking the same thing—*where do we go from here?*

And then, Shiraz spoke. Not in his usual confident tone, but as if he had let his thoughts slip out unintentionally.

"What if we hack the security cameras?"

The words lingered in the air for a moment, hanging between us like something absurd yet strangely possible. We all turned to look at him.

Daniyal was the first to react. *"And how exactly do you plan to do that? I don't think any of us here know a damn thing about hacking. It's not something you can just 'figure out' overnight."*

I nodded. *"Exactly. Even if we had the right software, which we don't, it's not like we can just punch in some keys and take over the system."*

"I know how," Agasthya's voice cut through the conversation like a blade.

All eyes snapped toward him. There was something almost amused about the way he said it, like he was enjoying our surprise.

I frowned. *"You know how to hack?"*

A slow smirk spread across his face. *"How do you think I sent Daniyal that message and made it disappear right after he read it?"*

Raghav narrowed his eyes. *"We didn't put much thought into it before."*

Daniyal crossed his arms, unimpressed. *"And you just conveniently forgot to mention this earlier?"*

Agasthya shrugged. *"You never asked."*

I rolled my eyes. *"Fine. If you can actually do this, then the plan is simple—we search the area while you hack into the main building's security cameras."*

"Sounds good to me," Shiraz said, though there was still hesitation in his voice.

"Whoa, whoa, hold on." Agasthya raised his hands in mock surrender. *"You guys think this is as easy as buying a lollipop from a store? It's not. First, I need access to the security room to see how the cameras are operated, how the feeds are stored, and what kind of system they're running. Only then can I figure out how to replace the video feed."*

Daniyal exhaled sharply. *"So, you're saying we need to break into the security room first."*

Agasthya nodded. *"Absolutely, Your Majesty."*

Shiraz ignored his sarcastic tone and asked, *"And how do we do that?"*

Silence.

No one had an answer. Because, really, what the hell were we even trying to do? We weren't *criminals*. We weren't *hackers*. We were just students who happened to be caught in something far bigger than ourselves.

"Guys," Raghav finally spoke, rubbing his forehead, *"we still have four days before the holidays. There's no need to rush. We'll figure this out tomorrow. Right now, I can barely think straight. Exams drained me, and honestly? All I want is dinner and then sleep. Heavy sleep."*

He wasn't wrong. *Exhaustion* was pressing down on me, too. The entire day had been a mess of *stress* and *tension*, and now, sitting in the cold, it was catching up to me fast.

Agasthya let out a dramatic yawn. *"Well, looks like I've had enough of you guys for today. I'm calling it a night. See you all tomorrow... perhaps."*

With that, he turned and walked off into the night, leaving us watching his retreating figure.

The moment he was out of sight, Daniyal exhaled sharply. *"We don't trust him, right? It's not just me?"*

"No," Shiraz said. *"It's not just you."*

Raghav shifted uncomfortably. *"He knew how to hack and didn't say a word about it until now. That's not normal."*

"We don't have a choice," I muttered. *"No matter how we feel about him, right now, he's the only one who can pull this off. We just have to go with whatever we've got."*

No one liked that answer. But no one argued, either.

Without another word, we turned toward the dorms, walking into the night with a plan that was just as *uncertain* as everything else surrounding us.

CHAPTER TWENTY-THREE

TIMED TO FAIL

The morning air had a crispness to it, the kind that lingered for a few hours before the sun took over. The campus was slowly waking up, and as *Raghav* and I walked towards the *cafeteria*, the faint chatter of students echoed around us.

"I swear, that was the best sleep I've had in weeks," Raghav said, stretching his arms above his head. *"I didn't even wake up in the middle of the night. Just—out. Like a corpse."*

I chuckled. *"Yeah, same. After all the exams, it felt like my body just shut down on its own. No nightmares, no tossing and turning. Just pure, uninterrupted sleep."*

"Almost makes you forget the mess we're caught up in, doesn't it?" he said, shaking his head. *"But now, back to reality. Gym, basketball—if we even get time for that anymore."*

"I'd kill for a game right now," I said. *"Haven't played in weeks."*

"Man, my legs probably forgot how to move on a court," he sighed. *"The second this is over, we're hitting the gym and getting back into it. No excuses."*

I smirked. *"Deal. If we make it through all this without getting expelled or arrested, gym sessions are on."*

As we reached the *cafeteria*, the scent of eggs, toast, and coffee filled the air. We grabbed our plates, piled on whatever seemed edible, and found a table. Within minutes, *Shiraz* and *Daniyal* joined us.

"Morning, guys," Daniyal said, setting his tray down.

"Morning," Raghav mumbled, already halfway through his first bite.

Shiraz smirked. *"So, feeling rested enough?"*

Raghav looked up, as if he had been waiting for someone to ask. *"More than anything. Sleep feels like heaven when you actually get it after days."*

We all chuckled, the momentary lightness of the conversation almost making us forget everything else.

But I had to bring reality back in. *"So, what do we know about this security room?"*

Raghav groaned. *"You had to ask this, didn't you?"*

Daniyal leaned forward. *"Well, there's not much to know. It's just one of the rooms in the main building. A small, typical security room."*

Shiraz nodded. *"Yeah, it's not some high-security vault. I mean, for most people, it's just another part of the campus. Nothing special."*

"Which means getting near it isn't a problem," Raghav added.

"Unless they decide to check the footage and see you snooping around," Daniyal pointed out. *"Which, honestly, I doubt they would."*

"So, what's the issue?" I asked.

Shiraz sighed. *"The issue is, there's always a security guard inside. He monitors everything from there. And in the evening, there's a shift change."*

Raghav cut in. *"Which means there's no chance of sneaking in at night."*

"Exactly," Daniyal said, tapping his fork against his plate. *"No gaps in security. No easy way in."*

I leaned back, thinking. *"There must be a point where the guy leaves for a bit, right? Bathroom break, stepping out for something—he can't just sit in there all day."*

Daniyal nodded slowly. *"If we want to know that, we'll have to monitor him. See his routine."*

"Right," I said. *"If we can find even a five-minute window when he's out, Agasthya can do his thing."*

Shiraz exhaled. *"Alright, one thing sorted. Now, finish your breakfast quickly and head to class. We'll talk about our next step at lunch."*

No one argued. We needed to keep up appearances, attend lectures, act like normal students. So we finished eating, grabbed our bags, and headed for class—our minds still fixed on the task ahead.

We reached the class and after almost 6–7 hours—

The bell rang, signalling the end of the last class. Almost instantly, the lecture hall came alive with movement—chairs scraping against the floor, backpacks slung over shoulders, muffled conversations blending into a steady hum. Everyone was eager to get out, and so were we. *Raghav* and I exchanged a glance, nodded, and made our way straight to the *cafeteria*.

The midday rush had settled, leaving the cafeteria with just a few scattered groups lingering over their meals. As we stepped inside, my eyes landed on *Shiraz* and *Daniyal*, already seated at our usual table. They were oddly quiet, their plates barely touched.

Grabbing our food, we made our way over, trays in hand. *Raghav* was the first to break the silence.

"You guys are awfully quiet. What happened?"

I frowned. *"Yeah, what's wrong?"*

Daniyal didn't answer immediately. Instead, he tilted his head slightly and muttered, *"On your three o'clock."*

Both *Raghav* and I instinctively turned our heads. Standing near the *cafeteria counter* was a man—probably in his late forties, built broad like a retired cop, but with a sluggishness in his posture that suggested years of dull routine. His uniform was slightly wrinkled, a dark blue shirt tucked into black trousers, the fabric stretching at his midsection. His face was lined, with sunken eyes that carried the exhaustion of someone who had been doing the same job for far too long. A thick Mustache covered his upper lip, and his thinning hair was combed back in an effort to maintain some sense of authority. Despite his tired appearance, there was something in the way he stood—arms crossed, gaze sweeping over the room—that reminded me he wasn't just a regular staff member.

"So, he's the one, huh?" *Raghav* muttered.

"Yup," *Shiraz* confirmed, barely glancing up from his plate.

I watched as the guard approached the counter, took a plate, and, without a word, turned back toward the exit.

I frowned. *"Okay, so he comes to the cafeteria to grab lunch."*

"Not exactly," *Daniyal* corrected.

I looked at him, confused. *"What do you mean?"*

Daniyal nodded toward the exit as the guard disappeared through the doorway. *"He doesn't eat here. He just takes his lunch back to the security room."*

I exhaled sharply, my mind already working through the implications. *"But still, he comes out, right? It still takes him time to grab his lunch and get back there."*

Shiraz nodded. *"Yeah, but he was only here for five minutes. If we factor in his walk to and from the security room, that gives us roughly ten minutes total."*

Raghav let out a low whistle. *"Damn. That's not a lot of time."*

"Exactly," *Daniyal* said. *"And the real problem is, we don't even know how much time Agasthya needs to pull this off."*

I sighed, rubbing my temples. We kept finding new pieces of the puzzle, but none of them guaranteed a solution. *"I guess the only thing left to do is head*

to the grove and discuss this in detail. What do you guys say?"
They all nodded in agreement, their expressions set. No one said it out loud, but we were all thinking the same thing: We'd come far ahead in this, but there was still no guarantee that whatever we were doing was right.

CHAPTER TWENTY-FOUR

VICTORY WAS A LIE

The walk to the *grove* was quiet. No one said a word. The only sound was the crunch of fallen leaves beneath our shoes, the occasional rustle of wind through the trees. But in our heads? Chaos. Everyone was deep in thought, mapping out possible ways to pull this off.

As we reached the *grove*, we took our usual places. *Shiraz* sat on the fallen tree log, arms resting on his knees. *Raghav* leaned against it, arms crossed, staring at nothing in particular. *Daniyal* stood with his hands in his pockets, exhaling slowly. I just sat on a rock, running my fingers through my hair. We were all in the zone, waiting for someone to say something worthwhile.

Shiraz finally broke the silence. *"Okay, so where's that Mr. Whackadoodle?"*

"Yeah, haven't seen him in a while," Raghav added.

I turned to *Daniyal. "Any cryptic, creepy messages from the guy?"*

Daniyal shook his head. *"Nope. Nothing."*

Raghav sighed. *"Great. The only time we actually need him, he's nowhere."*

And right on cue, a voice rang out from behind the trees. *"What's up, nerdizzles?"*

We all turned, and there he was. *Agasthya* stepped out, grinning like he had just cracked the meaning of life. *"Looks like someone's been missing me a lot,"* he smirked, shoving his hands in his jacket pockets.

Shiraz gave him a deadpan look. *"You know, it's getting harder every day to believe there's nothing wrong with you."*

Agasthya just shrugged and cut straight to business. *"So, what have you guys cracked out yet?"*

I leaned forward slightly. *"Depends. Are ten minutes enough for you to do your stuff in the security room?"*

Agasthya's smirk widened. *"Oh, please. If that's all it took, I would've done it myself."*

Daniyal's voice was firm. *"Then how much time do you need?"*

Agasthya turned to him, mock bowing. *"Your Majesty, the peasant requires at least twenty minutes to fulfil your royal demands."*

Daniyal didn't even blink. *"Fine. We need to keep him out for at least twenty minutes."*

I exhaled, shaking my head. *"This is tougher than taking keys out of the warden's cabin."*

No one laughed. We all just stood there, the weight of the problem sinking in. The security guard wasn't some clueless guy we could just distract with small talk. He had a job, and from what we had seen, he took it seriously.

Shiraz ran a hand down his face. *"Alright, let's think. How do we get him out of that room for a full twenty minutes?"*

Silence settled again. Each of us trying to come up with something.

This wasn't impossible. But damn, it felt close.

We all sat in deep thought, the quiet only broken by the occasional shuffle of feet against the dirt. Then, *Daniyal* broke the silence. *"Guys, I think I got something."*

All eyes turned to him. I leaned in slightly. *"What is it?"*

Daniyal straightened up. *"If we want to keep him out for at least twenty minutes, we need something that creates urgency. Something that keeps him engaged the whole time, right?"*

"Yeah, so?" Shiraz asked, brows furrowed.

Daniyal continued, his voice lowering slightly. *"What if we add something to his food that causes severe stomach distress? Something that keeps him locked in the bathroom for that long?"*

Raghav exhaled, considering. *"Then we'd need an agent that can be mixed in his food without raising suspicion."*

Daniyal nodded. *"We saw him taking food earlier. What does he eat?"*

Shiraz thought for a moment. *"Nothing special. Just regular cafeteria food—dal, rice, chapati... and cola."*

A smirk crept onto my face. *"We definitely can't add anything to his food. But his cola? That's an option."*

Shiraz snapped his fingers. *"How about bisacodyl?"*

Agasthya immediately threw his hands up. *"Whoa! We're not trying to kill the guy. Take it easy."*

Raghav rolled his eyes. *"It doesn't kill anyone, you idiot. It's just a laxative. How did you even pass science?"*

Agasthya scoffed. *"Well, actually, I was a commerce student."*

Shiraz snorted. *"Huh. Figures."*

Agasthya crossed his arms. *"Hey, not everyone takes science and then switches to law like you nerds."*

Before things escalated further, I stepped in. *"We can't use bisacodyl. It's a tablet, so we'd have to crush it into powder, and even then, it takes at least three to four hours to work. We don't have that kind of time."*

Raghav exhaled through his nose. *"He's right."*

Daniyal tapped his fingers on his knee. *"What about magnesium citrate? It's mild, so even if we mix it in, it won't be noticeable. Plus, it only takes an hour to kick in."*

I considered it, then nodded. *"Yeah, that could work."*

Raghav rubbed the back of his neck. *"Great, but... how do we add it?"*

Silence fell again. That was something we hadn't figured out yet.

We stood there in silence, letting the weight of the plan settle in. Then *Raghav* broke it. *"I have something that might help, but it's a bit risky."*

Shiraz let out a dry chuckle. *"With everything we've done so far, I don't think any of us even register risk anymore. So, hit it."*

Raghav took a breath. *"Alright. Before he arrives for lunch, one of us takes a cola and adds magnesium citrate to it. Meanwhile, when he gets his food, just as he's about to leave, one of us—purely by accident—bumps into him, spilling his food and drink all over the floor. And himself. He'll have no choice but to rush to the bathroom to clean up. While he's gone, we order a fresh plate for him and replace his cola with the one we spiked earlier. He comes back, takes it, drinks it, and the rest is history."*

Silence followed.

I let the plan sit in my head for a second. It sounded smooth on paper, but in reality? One wrong move and we'd all be in deep trouble.

"Okay," I said, *"now the real question is—who among us is going to casually 'stumble' into a guy who looks like a former special force's operative?"*

All eyes turned to *Shiraz*. Even his own, as if trying to make sense of how this had happened.

"No. No way. Not happening," Shiraz said, shaking his head firmly.

"Oh, come on," Raghav nudged. *"For the team."*

"Yeah," I added. *"Didn't you just say nothing is risky anymore?"*

Shiraz exhaled sharply. *"Yeah, but I didn't know he was going to suggest this. Maybe we should improvise the plan."*

Daniyal placed a firm hand on his shoulder. *"Trust me, it's going to be fine."*

Shiraz shot him a deadpan look. *"Do you honestly believe that?"*

Daniyal didn't hesitate. "That's not the point. The point is—you're doing this. And that's it."

Shiraz groaned but eventually caved. "Fine. But if I end up with a broken nose, I'm haunting all of you."

"Noted," I said. "Then, I'll hit the medical store this evening and grab a bottle of magnesium citrate."

Daniyal turned to *Agasthya*. "And you—you better be around when this thing happens, or you and I will have some serious problems."

For once, *Agasthya* didn't have a comeback. Just a quick nod, as if he'd been put in his place.

With the plan set, we all split up. But as I walked away, I couldn't shake the unease curling in my gut.

What if this doesn't go the way we think it will?

CHAPTER TWENTY-FIVE

FOUND BUT NOT FREE

The last lecture of the day dragged on, but my mind was elsewhere. *Raghav* sat beside me, silent, lost in his own thoughts. We were both physically present in the class, nodding at the right moments, pretending to take notes—but mentally, we were already in the *cafeteria*, replaying every step of what was about to go down.

Inside my bag, the bottle of *magnesium citrate* sat hidden, like a ticking time bomb. *Raghav* had already texted *Daniyal* and *Shiraz*: *We have it. Lunch today.* That was all we needed to say.

The bell rang, snapping us back into reality. Without a second's delay, we grabbed our bags and rushed out of the classroom.

The cafeteria was filling up when we arrived. *Daniyal* and *Shiraz* were already seated at a table, looking as casual as ever. I scanned the room, my eyes instinctively searching for the guard. Nowhere in sight.

Raghav tapped my shoulder and subtly pointed to the side.

Agasthya. He was sitting at a different table, perfectly positioned with a clear view of whatever was about to go down. His presence was reassuring and unnerving at the same time.

We walked over to *Daniyal* and *Shiraz*, dropping into the empty seats. Without a word, I gave *Raghav* a quick nod. He stood up, heading toward the counter.

Daniyal leaned in slightly, his voice low. *"Where's the bottle?"*

I checked my surroundings once before unzipping my bag just enough for them to see the bottle inside. No one else noticed.

Raghav returned with a chilled glass of cola, setting it down in front of us. *"We need a cover."*

Daniyal didn't hesitate. He looked toward *Agasthya* and gave a small, almost unnoticeable signal. Across the room, *Agasthya* caught on instantly. He got up and strolled toward us, playing it cool. *Shiraz* stood as well, engaging him in a casual conversation—something about an assignment. They were creating a distraction, making sure no one paid attention to us.

That was my cue.

I slipped the bottle out, twisted the cap open just enough, and carefully poured a tiny amount of *magnesium citrate* into the cola. The drink was ice-cold, so the liquid blended in smoothly—no reaction, no fizz, no sign of tampering. Within seconds, it was done.

Agasthya gave us a slight nod before heading back to his seat. *Shiraz* sat down again like nothing had happened. We exchanged glances, the unspoken confirmation passing between us.

Now, all we had to do was wait.

A few minutes had passed. The guard was still nowhere to be seen. We sat in silence, our eyes flicking toward the entrance every now and then, waiting. *Raghav* drummed his fingers on the table. *Daniyal* checked his phone, not really reading anything. *Shiraz* exhaled slowly. I just stared at my untouched food, my mind racing.

And then—finally—the *cafeteria doors* swung open.

The guard walked in, looking as stern and unbothered as ever. As soon as he stepped inside, we all exchanged a quick glance. This was it.

We turned to *Shiraz*, giving him the nod. For a second, he hesitated. I could see the flicker of doubt in his eyes, the internal war between logic and recklessness. But then, as if flipping a switch, he stood up with quiet confidence and moved into position, weaving through the crowd without drawing any attention to himself.

The guard walked up to the counter, placed his order, and waited.

A few moments later, the cafeteria worker handed him a tray—rice, dal, some side dish, and most importantly, a chilled cup of cola. He took the tray, adjusting his grip, completely unaware that he was holding something that would soon force him out of our way.

And now, everything depended on one moment.

We kept our cool, focusing on each other, avoiding the temptation to turn and watch. If we looked too eager, someone would notice.

Then—

THUD!

A loud crash echoed across the cafeteria. Every single head turned toward the commotion. I didn't need to look—I already knew what had happened.

Shiraz had gone in hard. Too hard. He had slammed straight into the guard with full force, sending both of them crashing to the ground. The tray flew out of the guard's hands, food splattering across the floor, cola spilling everywhere—some of it soaking into the guard's shirt.

I gritted my teeth. That wasn't smooth. That was an accident.

For a second, the whole cafeteria went dead silent. Then came the murmurs, the whispers, the suppressed chuckles.

The guard got up, brushing himself off, his face twisted in irritation. *Shiraz* scrambled up right after, looking both apologetic and slightly dazed.

The guard shot him a glare. *"Next time, you better watch where you're going—or I won't forgive you so easily."*

Shiraz bowed his head slightly. *"I'm really sorry, sir. Please—let me buy you lunch. It's the least I can do."*

The guard exhaled sharply, still looking pissed. But after a moment, he gave a stiff nod. *"Fine."* Without another word, he turned and walked toward the restroom to clean up.

Shiraz wasted no time. He hurried to the counter, ordered another meal, and carried the tray back to our table. He set it down, quickly replacing the ordinary cola with our cola—the one spiked with *magnesium citrate*.

I exhaled slowly.

A few minutes later, the guard returned, grabbed his tray, and without a second thought, walked straight out of the cafeteria toward the *security room*.

We sat there for a few seconds, absorbing the moment.

It worked. It actually worked.

Daniyal glanced at me. *Shiraz*, still shaken, gave the smallest smirk. *Raghav* let out a breath he hadn't realized he was holding. From his table, *Agasthya* gave a slight nod.

No words were spoken.

Now came the next part.

We grabbed our stuff and slipped out of the cafeteria as casually as possible. No sudden movements. No unnecessary glances back. Just three students heading toward the main building like we had somewhere to be.

As we walked, *Agasthya* suddenly turned to *Shiraz* and smirked. *"If it were up to me, the Oscar would've gone to you."*

Shiraz blinked, caught off guard by the unexpected praise. *"Huh?"*

"For once, I'm impressed," Agasthya said, shrugging.

Raghav chuckled. *"Man, if Agasthya is giving compliments, we really pulled it off."*

Shiraz just shook his head. *"I wasn't acting, you idiot. I nearly broke my back."*
"Yeah, yeah, tell that to the Academy," I muttered.
Daniyal brought us back on track. *"Alright, now for the next part. Me, Aaron, and Agasthya will keep watch on the guard. No point in all of us going."*
"Exactly," I agreed. *"More people means more chances of getting noticed."*
Raghav nodded. *"Alright. We're heading to the dorms. As soon as you guys are done, message us, and we'll meet at the grove."*
We exchanged nods and split up.
Keeping our pace normal, we walked toward the main building, blending in with the crowd. Once inside, we took the stairs up to the third floor—the one with all the security and administration rooms.
The security room was on the right, third from the centre. We positioned ourselves at the staircase, pretending to be just another group of students chatting aimlessly between classes. Every now and then, one of us would steal a glance toward the hallway, checking for any signs of movement.
Minutes passed.
Then more minutes.
Thirty minutes. Nothing.
Forty-five minutes. Still nothing.
I shifted against the stair railing, growing restless. *"He should've been out by now,"* I muttered under my breath.
Daniyal exhaled. *"Yeah. Either he hasn't touched the drink, or..."* He didn't finish the sentence.
Another ten minutes passed.
An hour.
By now, doubt was creeping in. What if he didn't drink it? What if he suspected something? Or worse—what if the plan had completely failed?
Just as we were starting to question everything—
A noise.
A door creaking open.
We all instinctively glanced up.
The guard stepped out, hunched slightly, one hand clutching his stomach. His face was twisted in discomfort as he quickly walked down the corridor, heading straight for the restroom. Without a second of hesitation, he pushed the door open and disappeared inside.
The second the door swung shut behind him, *Agasthya* sprang into action. He didn't wait for a signal. He just moved.
In one swift, calculated motion, he slipped toward the *security room*,

disappearing inside before anyone in the hallway could even notice.

I clenched my jaw. Now, all we could do was wait.

And hope the guard stayed in there for at least twenty minutes.

Daniyal and I sat on the staircase, trying our best to act normal. Not too stiff, not too relaxed. Just a couple of students wasting time between classes. Five minutes had passed. The guard wasn't back. Neither was Agasthya.

I exhaled slowly, drumming my fingers against my knee. Another five minutes. Still nothing.

Every second felt *stretched*. Every movement in the corridor felt *suspicious*. We kept checking both ends of the hallway, stealing glances toward the *restroom* and the *security room*, but there was no movement.

Fifteen minutes.

Daniyal shifted beside me. *"What if something went wrong?"*

I didn't answer. I didn't want to entertain that thought.

Twenty minutes.

This was it. The point where *tension* became something real, something *suffocating*. *Why isn't he out yet?* My mind raced through the worst possibilities. Maybe the guard had recovered faster than expected. Maybe Agasthya was caught. Maybe—

Another two minutes.

Daniyal glanced at me, his jaw tight. *"I'm starting to worry."*

I didn't even need to respond. He could see it on my face.

Then—

Footsteps.

We turned our heads just as Agasthya emerged from the *security room*, walking with the same casual ease he always had.

Daniyal and I didn't waste a second. We shot up from the stairs, our hearts *hammering*, and without a word, we all moved. Not running, not walking too fast, but keeping our pace *steady, purposeful*. Daniyal pulled out his phone, typing as we walked.

We did it. Meet us at the grove.

No one spoke. No one dared to *celebrate* just yet. We navigated through the hallways, out the main doors, and across the campus until we reached the *grove*—a quiet patch of land away from prying eyes.

Raghav and Shiraz were already there, waiting. The moment they saw us, their expressions changed.

A knowing smile. A silent acknowledgment.

Agasthya exhaled and stretched his arms. *"Everything's done. Now, I just need two more days to understand the system and crack the code for replacing the video feed.”*

We all nodded. That was the final step. The one thing that would make this whole plan *foolproof.*

Raghav crossed his arms. *“And how will you tell us when it's ready?”*

Agasthya smirked. *“Easy. I'll send you a message.”*

A brief silence. Then Shiraz shook his head. *“Can't believe this all happened so easily.”*

“Me neither,” I admitted. *“This was way too smooth.”*

Daniyal exhaled. *“Don't discuss it. Just enjoy it.”*

We all chuckled, the *tension* finally easing up.

Raghav grinned. *“Alright then. Two days from now, we go back in. Until then, do whatever the hell you want.”*

Laughter. Relief.

For the first time, it felt like we had *won.* Like we had *beaten the system.*

But what none of us knew—what none of us could have known—was that our lives were *never* going to be the same after this.

CHAPTER TWENTY-SIX

THE PRICE OF TRUTH

Two days. Two whole days had passed, and not a word from *Agasthya*. No messages, no sign of him anywhere on campus. It was as if he had vanished. The holidays had officially begun today, and nearly half the students had already left for home. The campus felt empty, silent in a way that felt unnatural. I stood by the window of my dorm room, watching the dimly lit pathways below. The streetlights flickered occasionally, casting long, stretched-out shadows of the trees. The air carried a sharp bite—*autumn* was finally starting to set in.

The door creaked open behind me. *Raghav* walked in, shaking the cold off his sleeves. *"Just a tip,"* he said, kicking the door shut behind him. *"If you plan on sneaking out at night, carry a jacket. This weather's getting brutal."*

"Where were you?" I asked, turning to face him.

"Had to restock," he said, lifting a plastic bag onto the kitchen platform. *"Cup noodles, snacks, coffee... we were all out."*

I glanced at the clock. It was past 11. *"What shop is open this late?"*

"A new store opened a few blocks from the university," he said, pulling out a pack of chips. *"Open till midnight."*

"Fair enough."

He sat down on the bed, tearing open the pack. *"So,"* he said between bites, *"what were you thinking about?"*

"Nothing. Just..." I hesitated, leaning against the window. *"It's been two days."*

Raghav sighed. *"Bro, we talked about this in the afternoon. Maybe he just needs more time. I'm sure he'll contact us soon."*

"Yeah, I know," I muttered. *"It's just... I don't know if we're ready for this. Whatever we're getting into—it's big. And it's scary. Things have been quiet so far, but that's what bothers me. Quiet never lasts long."*

Raghav didn't say anything at first. He just placed the snacks aside and sat back against the wall, thinking. After a moment, he spoke. *"Tell me, "He* said, *"what choices do we have? We've come too far. The only thing we can do is move forward."*

I gave a small nod. He wasn't wrong. But before I could say anything, a knock echoed through the room.

Raghav and I exchanged a quick glance.

I walked up to the door and opened it.

Daniyal and *Shiraz* stood outside. *Daniyal* didn't waste a second. *"Agasthya texted,"* he said, breathless. *"We have to go. Now."*

There was no hesitation. *Raghav* grabbed his keys, I grabbed mine, and within seconds, we were out the door, rushing toward the *grove*.

We didn't stop running until we reached the *grove*. The air was colder here, the damp scent of soil mixing with the distant rustle of leaves. The campus already felt abandoned with the holidays, but the *grove* felt different—isolated, untouched. The shadows stretched further, the ground was softer under our feet, and every breath felt heavier in the crisp night air.

And right in the middle of it all, leaning against a tree, legs crossed, arms folded, was *Agasthya*. A bag sat by his foot, partially covered in dried leaves. He didn't say anything as we arrived—just watched.

Shiraz broke the silence. *"So? Have you done it?"*

Agasthya turned his head slightly toward us and gave a single nod. Still, he didn't speak.

Daniyal took a step forward. *"Are you saying you can actually replace the video feeds? You can hack the cameras?"*

"Yes," Agasthya said. *"It can be done. But..."*

"But what?" Raghav asked immediately.

Agasthya finally pushed off the tree, standing straight. His voice was calm but firm. *"We have to do it now."*

I blinked. *"Right now?"*

"Yes. Now."

Daniyal frowned. *"Why now?"*

"Because this is the best time," Agasthya said. *"You won't get another chance like this. It's now or never."*

The weight of his words settled in. We looked at each other. It was too sudden—too soon. We had expected some preparation, a plan, time to process what we were about to do. But now? Now we had to act.

Hesitation lingered for a moment before *Daniyal* finally exhaled and said,

"Alright. We'll do this now."

"Good," Agasthya said, crouching down and unzipping his bag. *"I'll stay here. I need to replace the feeds in real-time and monitor the system. If anything goes wrong, I'll have a better chance of fixing it from here."*

I frowned. *"And if something happens outside?"*

Shiraz straightened. *"I'll stay with him. You three go inside—we'll handle things out here."*

"You sure?" Daniyal asked.

"Yes. I'm sure."

Agasthya was already focused, pulling out a small laptop and setting things up. *"Guys,"* he said without looking up, *"be quick. Take your positions. When Shiraz texts you, that's your signal to go in."*

The three of us exchanged a final look, then nodded.

Without another word, *Daniyal*, *Raghav*, and I turned and started walking toward the *admin building*. Behind us, *Shiraz* and *Agasthya* remained in the dark.

The walk to the *admin building* felt different this time. The silence wasn't just an absence of sound—it was something more, something unnatural. The only noise came from the crunch of leaves beneath our shoes and the occasional rustle of the wind. The air had grown colder, mist creeping through the pathways, swirling around our feet as we moved. It felt as if the world itself was trying to tell us something.

As we reached the main building, I turned to *Daniyal*. *"Any message from Shiraz?"*

Daniyal pulled out his phone, checked the screen, then shook his head. *"Nope. Nothing."*

"Same here," Raghav said, stuffing his phone back into his pocket.

We peered toward the *admin building*. No guards. No staff. Not a single person in sight. The entire structure loomed over us, dark and lifeless. It looked abandoned.

Or maybe... waiting.

A strange unease settled in my chest. There was something wrong about this silence. It wasn't relief—it was a warning.

Then, a sharp ding cut through the air. *Daniyal* glanced at his phone. A single message from *Shiraz*.

"You guys are good to go. Good luck."

Daniyal inhaled sharply. *"Time to go."*

No more second thoughts. We moved, slipping through the doors and into the building.

Inside, the halls were dark and hollow, every footstep sounding louder than it should have. We didn't waste a second. The three of us hurried down the corridors, our footsteps barely making a sound on the polished floor. The *records room* was below, and we needed to get there fast.

As soon as we reached the floor, I stopped. *"Okay, the hidden room has to be somewhere here. Start searching. Check near the records room, check the corridor—walls, frames, everything. Don't leave anything out."*

Daniyal nodded. *"Alright. I'll take the records room. You two check the corridor—walls, frames, everything. Don't leave anything out."*

"Got it," Raghav and I said in unison.

We split up. I ran my hands along the walls, feeling for any ridges, any false panels. I tapped on paintings, pressed against the frames, even checked for any strange air vents or loose tiles. *Raghav* was doing the same a few feet away, his fingers running along the seams of the walls.

Fifteen minutes passed.

Nothing.

We gathered back near the *records room*. *Daniyal* exhaled, running a hand through his hair. *"Anything?"*

"Nope," Raghav muttered, shaking his head.

I clenched my jaw. *"I really hope we're not wrong about this. If we are... then this was all for nothing."*

"Come on," Raghav said. *"We can't give up now. There has to be something we're missing. That room is something they don't want people to know about. It's obviously not going to be easy to find."*

And then it hit me.

I turned sharply, my eyes scanning the hallway. What if they hid it in plain sight? Something that was always there, something no one questioned?

I took a step forward, my gaze locking onto a *fire alarm* on the wall.

Daniyal noticed me staring. *"What?"*

I pointed at it. *"What if it's right in front of us? What if they disguise it as something too obvious?"*

Raghav narrowed his eyes. *"You're thinking about the alarm?"*

"Think about it," I said. *"No one ever questions a fire alarm. It's always there, unnoticed, but still in plain sight."*

Daniyal hesitated. *"Are you sure about this?"*

Raghav exhaled. *"If the alarm goes off, we're screwed."*

I swallowed. There was only one way to find out.

I reached forward—grabbed the handle—pulled.

For a second, nothing happened. No sirens. No emergency lights.

And then—

Click.

A deep, mechanical sound rumbled beneath us. The passage lights turned a dim red, casting the entire corridor in an eerie glow. A few feet away, the tiles near the *records room* shifted. Four of them split apart in a perfect square, revealing a dark staircase spiralling downward.

The three of us stared at it, momentarily frozen. The engineering was flawless, sophisticated. The hidden room wasn't just a locked chamber—it was built to disappear entirely.

Daniyal took a breath. *"Okay... this is it."*

We looked at each other. Then, without another word, we stepped forward and descended into the unknown.

We stepped down into the darkness, our breaths steady but tense. The stairs creaked under our weight, the air thick with dust and something else—something older. Something untouched.

The moment my foot touched the floor, I realized how silent it was. There was no distant hum of electricity, no airflow—just dead, suffocating stillness.

"All good?" Daniyal's voice was hushed.

"Yeah," Raghav replied. *"Flashlights?"*

One by one, we pulled out our phones and switched on the lights. The beams cut through the darkness, illuminating the small, windowless room. It wasn't some grand hidden chamber; it was eerily similar to the *records room* above—steel shelves, metal cupboards, stacks of old boxes gathering dust. Ordinary, yet wrong.

Daniyal exhaled. *"Alright. Time to get to work. Check everything. We need to collect as much as we can."*

"Got it," Raghav said. *"Aaron and I will handle the shelves. You take the cupboards."*

Daniyal nodded and moved toward the cabinets while *Raghav* and I started on the shelves. The files were heavy, thick with paperwork, yet we worked fast, pulling everything we could. Some were labelled with batch years, others with cryptic serial numbers.

Then, I opened a file—and my stomach dropped.

"Daniyal... Raghav..."

Both of them turned to me, but the look on my face made them freeze.

"These... these aren't just regular student records." My voice barely made it past my lips. *"These are the vanished students."*

Raghav flipped open a file of his own, his breathing shallow. *"No way... No way..."*

Each file contained everything—names, parents' details, admission dates, medical histories, addresses. But there was something even worse.

"The files are mixed," Daniyal murmured. *"With the students still on record."*

It wasn't just a list of those who had disappeared. It was a *system*.

I tried to steady my hands as I flipped through the papers, but then I noticed a small section at the end of each vanished student's report. One final word printed neatly.

Connected.

Or sometimes, *Not Connected.*

The words from *Raghav's* brother's diary came back like a punch to the gut.

Daniyal clenched his jaw. *"What the hell does this mean?"*

I didn't answer. I couldn't. Because the moment I turned another page, I saw something that made my hands shake. My chest tightened, and for a second, I thought I might pass out.

No. No. No. This wasn't happening. This *couldn't* be real.

"Aaron?" Raghav's voice cut in. *"You okay?"*

Before I could answer, he spoke again—this time sharper. *"Guys. Come here. Now."*

Daniyal and I hurried over. *Raghav* was holding a report in his trembling hands. His eyes darted over the words, disbelieving.

"What is it?" Daniyal asked.

Raghav's voice came out hoarse. *"This is my brother."*

Daniyal and I exchanged a look, then leaned in. The file was complete, filled with everything about *Raghav's* brother—right down to his *current stay.*

London.

Raghav's voice cracked. *"How the hell do they know my brother's in London?"*

Daniyal didn't answer immediately. Instead, he turned to the last page. *"Check the status."*

Raghav swallowed hard, flipped to the end, and then... *"Connected."*

The word hit like a hammer.

Daniyal sucked in a breath. Without hesitation, he reached for two more files and yanked them from the shelves. One with his name. One with *Raghav's.*

Raghav grabbed his file, flipping through it, his fingers moving too fast, too shaky. Then, he stopped. *"This confirms it. We're the targets."*

Daniyal read his own file. The air felt thick, suffocating.

Then he reached the last page.

Raghav: Connected.

Daniyal: Not Connected.

For a moment, none of us spoke. We had expected to find something horrifying, something unnatural, but *this*—this was worse. It was real. It was calculated.

And yet, none of it compared to what I had just seen. The thing that made my skin crawl, my stomach twist into knots.

"Aaron?" Daniyal asked, noticing the way I hadn't moved. *"What is it?"*

I opened my mouth to say something—anything—but before I could, I heard it.

Footsteps.

From behind us.

We froze. My heart pounded so hard I could hear it in my ears. The footsteps were slow, deliberate, approaching from the staircase.

Then came the voice. Deep. Heavy. And far too calm.

"So... you finally found the place, huh?"

CHAPTER TWENTY-SEVEN

FEAR IS THE WEAPON

We stood frozen as the voice echoed through the dimly lit space behind us. A slow, deliberate sound of footsteps followed. Then—*click.*

A single bulb flickered to life, casting a weak, yellowish glow across the room.

Standing in the light was a man—tall, well-built for his age, possibly in his fifties. His hair, streaked with grey, was neatly combed back, revealing sharp, calculating eyes that seemed to strip away every layer of pretence. His suit was crisp, expensive, but not flashy—just enough to command authority without trying. There was a presence about him, something that made the air feel heavier.

He walked toward us, unhurried, like he had all the time in the world. His gaze settled on *Raghav* first.

"Raghav," he said, voice smooth yet firm. *"Son of a wealthy businessman. Comes from an educated background. Only child of your parents. Your cousin studies in London, doesn't he?"*

Raghav didn't respond, but I could see his shoulders tense.

The man's lips curled into the ghost of a smirk before he turned his attention to *Daniyal.*

"Daniyal, born in Mumbai. One of the brightest in your family. Academically successful. School topper. You've done remarkable things to make your parents proud, haven't you, my boy?"

Daniyal's fists clenched at his sides, his usual defiance flickering beneath the surface, but he didn't speak either.

And then—he turned to me.

I felt it before he even spoke. That unsettling feeling of being studied, dissected.

"And now, my favourite student." His voice dropped ever so slightly, and

I hated the way it sent a chill down my spine. *"Aaron. Born in Vapi. A sports enthusiast—basketball, tennis. Son of the owner of one of Gujarat's most successful consulting firms. And yet..."*

He clicked his tongue, shaking his head. *"Unresolved family issues. Tsk, tsk, tsk. Childhood wounds like that... they don't really heal, do they?"*

My breath hitched as he placed a firm hand on my shoulder.

And then, just as smoothly, he stepped away and stood in front of us.

Daniyal was the first to break the silence. *"Who are you?"*

I followed, voice steadier than I felt. *"And how the hell do you know all this about us?"*

The man smiled, but it wasn't reassuring. It was the kind that made your stomach turn.

"As long as you get your answers," he said, tilting his head slightly, *"does it really matter who I am?"*

Silence.

A new kind of fear settled in. The kind that wasn't loud, wasn't frantic—but deep, crawling under the skin, whispering that something was very, very wrong.

We looked at each other.

And for the first time tonight, I wasn't sure if we were in control of anything at all.

Raghav was the first to break the silence. His voice was shaky, but he fought to keep it steady.

"What are these files?" he asked, lifting one slightly. *"Some of the students listed here... they don't exist anywhere in the institute's records. I'm not even sure if they exist anywhere near it."*

The man turned toward him, his expression unreadable. Then, with slow, deliberate steps, he walked closer.

"Now, now," he mused, amusement flickering in his eyes. *"For someone trespassing in a restricted area, you certainly ask difficult questions."*

He paused, watching us like a cat watching cornered mice.

"Fine, then. You want to know what this is? I'll tell you."

He leaned in slightly. *"But ask yourselves first—are you capable of handling the truth?"*

That smirk was still there, like we had walked right into a trap we hadn't even realized was set.

We glanced at each other, an unspoken exchange passing between us.

There was no turning back now.

A silent nod.

The man caught it and smiled. *"Very well, then. Listen carefully."*

He took a step back, his voice shifting—calm, assured, almost rehearsed.

"Blackstone Academy of Law is known for producing some of the most capable and advanced minds in the country. Our graduates are at the top of their fields—dominant, unmatched. It is this reputation that makes Blackstone one of the most prestigious institutions in India."

He let that sink in before continuing.

"How do you think they achieve such excellence? What makes them stand out, year after year?"

A pause.

"We train selected students to become the best. We develop their minds and bodies to their ultimate potential. We shape them to believe that success is not just a goal—it is the only way to live."

His eyes gleamed in the dim light.

"In short, we help them become the absolute best versions of themselves."

For a moment, no one spoke. The weight of his words pressed down on the room.

Then *Daniyal's* voice cut through, sharp and cold.

"So, to put it another way—you psychologically manipulate selected students. You brainwash them into believing that nothing matters more than success."

The smirk on the man's face widened.

He let out a low chuckle.

"You really do know how to put things together, don't you?"

A slow, eerie silence followed.

We stood there, frozen.

Not just out of fear—but because something about this, about all of it, felt wrong.

I could feel the sweat trickling down the back of my neck, the air thick, suffocating.

The truth wasn't just disturbing.

It was *bizarre.*

And the worst part?

This was only the beginning.

I swallowed the lump in my throat, then spoke, building on what *Daniyal* had said.

"And those students who can't take it... the ones who realize what's being done to them, who see how their minds are being twisted, manipulated—what happens

to them?"

The man stood still, watching me.

"They run," I continued, my voice growing more certain. *"Because it becomes too much. Their minds, their bodies—they can't handle it."*

For the first time, the smirk disappeared. There was silence.

But then—slowly, like a snake uncoiling—his lips curled again.

"They," he said, tilting his head, *"are the ones who aren't worthy of this academy. They don't deserve to be the best. They are weak. Cowards."*

Raghav took a step forward, his fists clenched.

"So you are the reason my brother had to go all the way to London?" His voice was shaking, but not out of fear. *"Do you have any idea what he went through because of your so-called 'techniques'?"*

The man's expression hardened. His voice sharpened, cutting through the room like a blade.

"Your brother," he said, *"wasn't capable of this institution. He—just like you—tried to access places he shouldn't have. He thought he could report this, stop our methods. He was naive."*

A pause. Then, in a low, deliberate voice—

"And he deserved what was coming for him."

Raghav stood frozen. The anger on his face was unmistakable, but beneath it—I could see the fear, the uncertainty.

Daniyal stepped forward now, his voice firm.

"We will report all of this. Every single thing. I've recorded everything."

The man took a step back. For a second, we thought we had him.

That we had a way out of this.

Then—he laughed.

It wasn't just a laugh.

It was slow, deliberate.

Mocking.

The kind that made your skin crawl.

Then he stopped—just as suddenly as he started.

"Look around you, you fool," he said, his voice cold. *"Those files you saw? Many people before you tried the same thing."*

His eyes locked onto *Daniyal's*, unwavering.

"Tell me—have you heard of any of them?"

Silence.

"No," he answered for us, his voice sharp, crisp, final.

"Because they don't exist anymore. And if you try this... no one will believe you

either."

The smirk returned.

"And then... you'll become one of them."

The words hung in the air like a death sentence.

Then—he took a step closer, lowering his voice to a whisper.

"Tell me—do you really want me to go after your families?"

Something inside me twisted.

We stood still.

The fear that had been creeping in was now full-blown paranoia.

Because we knew, at that moment—

he wasn't bluffing.

We looked at each other.

I could hear my own heartbeat, a dull, pounding rhythm in my ears.

My breath felt short, my chest tight.

He can't do this.

This isn't possible.

I had imagined a lot of things before coming in here.

Theories.

Explanations.

But this?

Not even in my worst nightmares.

The air in the room felt heavy, suffocating.

My mind was racing, spiralling—until *Raghav's* voice cut through the silence.

"You... you can't do this," he stammered. *"Not... not our families."*

For the first time, his fear was completely visible.

There was no hiding it now.

The man tilted his head, studying *Raghav* like a predator watching its prey.

"Oh, but I can," he said smoothly. *"Tell me—do you really want to see how I do it?"*

His words sent a chill down my spine.

I couldn't stay silent anymore.

I stepped forward.

"We're not going to be threatened by your bluffs," I said, trying to keep my voice steady. *"We will stop this madness."*

The man's smirk widened.

He leaned in, close enough that I could see the amusement in his eyes.

"Oh, really?" he whispered. *"Then perhaps this will help you understand."*

He paused, letting the silence drag before speaking again.

"Tell me, Aaron—do you know where your father gets most of the people who are at high positions in his firm?"

I froze.

A pit formed in my stomach.

My eyes widened, and he noticed.

He chuckled.

"That's right," he said. *"From our academy. But you wouldn't know that, would you? You never had an interest in your father's business."*

I felt the blood drain from my face.

"Now," he continued, his voice dripping with satisfaction, *"imagine a headline: Famous businessman caught in crime—manipulates employees for financial gain."*

The words hit me like a punch to the gut.

My breathing grew unsteady.

"But... but my father has nothing to do with this," I managed to say, my voice barely above a whisper.

The man smiled.

A slow, knowing smile.

"You're right," he admitted. *"But now you understand just how much power I hold. How easily I can turn a lie into the truth."*

He let the words sink in before adding:

"Tell me—do you still want me to do something like this to you? To your friends?"

Silence.

And then—*Daniyal* stepped forward, his voice breaking.

"No... please don't," he begged. *"I'll delete the recording. Just... not our parents. Not our families."*

The man's smirk grew.

"Very well," he said. *"Delete it, and I won't do such a thing."*

Daniyal didn't hesitate.

His fingers trembled as he pulled out his phone, tapped the screen, and erased the recording.

The man watched him do it, satisfaction written all over his face.

Then, stepping back, he spoke again:

"And remember," he said, his voice calm but laced with menace, *"if you try to be too smart... don't assume I won't know about it."*

He let the threat hang in the air, his smirk deepening.

"Because I will know."

None of us moved.
None of us spoke.
He took a slow breath, then said:
"You know... I'm impressed by you three."
His tone was different now.
Calculated.
"Breaking in, finding out all of this? That's... exceptional."
A pause. Then—
"And so... I'm going to let you go."
A long silence followed.
But then—he smiled.
A smile that said everything he hadn't.
"But keep in mind... if anyone else finds out about this—"
He didn't finish the sentence.
He didn't need to.
That smile was more than enough to warn us.
"Now get out of here," he said, stepping aside. *"Before I change my mind."*
None of us wasted a second.
We turned and climbed the stairs, our breaths ragged, our steps unsteady.
We didn't speak.
We couldn't.
Fear.
Paranoia.
Grief.
It followed us up every step.
And I knew, deep down—
this wasn't over.
Not by a long shot.

CHAPTER TWENTY-EIGHT

LIVE AND LET, AGASTHYA

I watched them leave—their steps unsteady, their silence thick with fear.

It was always fascinating to observe people in moments like these—to watch their confidence drain away, replaced by uncertainty and paranoia.

They wouldn't dare dig deeper, not after this.

But of course, *I* had other plans for them.

With a composed expression, I turned and ascended the stairs.

The moment I reached the corridor, I pressed the fire alarm once more.

A blaring siren echoed through the hallway before abruptly cutting off, sealing off the hidden pathway and restoring order.

A necessary precaution.

Everything needed to return to the way it was before—as if none of this had ever happened.

Then, I turned toward the Records Room.

Inside, a man was waiting.

Not just any man—*my man.*

The one who handled matters when a firmer hand was required.

He stood at attention, silent as ever, waiting for my arrival.

And beside him, strapped to a chair with thick restraints binding his wrists and ankles, sat *Agasthya.*

The sight of him was almost amusing.

His breath was shallow, his face drenched in sweat, his eyes darting wildly around the dimly lit room.

He was terrified—and rightfully so.

He had done well—better than I had expected.

But that didn't mean he was free of consequences.

I stepped closer, tilting my head as a smirk tugged at the corner of my lips.

"You were more useful than I thought," I said, my voice smooth, almost amused.

"Well done, my boy."

Agasthya flinched as if my words were physical blows.

His fingers curled into fists against the armrests.

"Unhand me," he stammered. *"I did everything you asked—why are you doing this?"*

His voice cracked, thick with panic.

I exhaled slowly, clasping my hands behind my back as I began pacing around him.

My footsteps echoed in the room, deliberate and slow.

"You really are naive, aren't you?" I mused, shaking my head.

"Tell me something—what do you think happens next? That I let you walk away because you followed orders?"

He swallowed hard, his throat bobbing.

"Yes," he whispered. *"That's exactly what should happen. I—I held up my end. I did everything you said."*

I stopped walking, then leaned in just slightly.

My voice dropped to a whisper, just above the sound of his own breathing.

"And that's precisely why I can't let you go."

Agasthya's body tensed like a coiled spring.

I continued, my tone light, almost conversational.

"Think about it logically. If I set you free, wouldn't that make me a fool? Letting someone walk away who knows far too much about all of this?"

He shook his head frantically.

"No! I swear—I won't tell anyone. No one will ever know. Just let me go. I'll leave, I'll disappear—"

I chuckled, cutting him off.

"Oh, Agasthya," I murmured, *"I know you won't tell anyone."*

He blinked.

"Y-you do?"

I nodded slowly, watching as a flicker of relief tried to form in his panicked expression.

And then, I crushed it.

"Because I will personally make sure of it."

The way I said it—the weight of those words—made the remaining color drain from his face.

His breathing quickened, his entire body stiff with dread.

I leaned in further, lowering my voice so only he could hear.

"Here's what's going to happen," I said.

"You're going to return to your dorm, pack your things, and leave. No goodbyes. No explanations. No loose ends. And most importantly—no one should ever know where you went. As far as the academy is concerned... you never existed."

Agasthya was trembling now.

His lips parted, but no words came out at first.

"A-and if I don't?" he finally managed, his voice barely above a whisper.

I smiled. A slow, knowing smile.

Then, I leaned down beside his ear and whispered:

"Then it won't be good for you... or your family."

The moment I pulled away, he let out a slow, shaky breath.

His head hung low, his hands trembling.

He barely managed a nod.

"I swear," he mumbled, his voice raw with fear. *"I'll leave. I'll disappear. Just... don't hurt them."*

I took a step back, turning my attention to my man—the one who had been silent throughout the entire exchange.

Our eyes met.

No words were needed.

With a single nod from me, he moved forward, unfastened Agasthya's restraints, and stepped aside.

Agasthya wasted no time.

The second he was free, he bolted upright, rubbing his wrists as he stumbled toward the door.

He didn't look back.

He didn't even pause to catch his breath.

He just left.

And just like that—he was gone.

I stood there for a few seconds, staring at the door, a smirk lingering on my lips.

Exactly as planned.

As I walked away from the now-empty chair, my man stepped closer, his voice steady but cautious.

"Sir... shouldn't we keep an eye on him?"

I didn't stop walking.

There was no need.

My answer was already decided.

"No," I said calmly, adjusting the cuff of my sleeve.

"He's already exactly where we need him to be—trapped in his own fear."

He remained silent for a beat, as if waiting for me to elaborate.

I decided to indulge him.

"Right now, his mind is turning against him. He's replaying everything that happened, over and over, convincing himself that any misstep will cost him his life—or worse, his family's."

I let out a quiet chuckle.

"He'll do what's safest. He'll run. Either straight home, where he'll lock himself away and pretend none of this happened—or somewhere far, far away. Just like the others before him."

A brief moment of silence stretched between us.

Then, he nodded.

"And the others? The ones from downstairs?"

That made me stop.

Slowly, I turned toward him, studying his face.

"No," I said, my voice quiet but deliberate.

He frowned slightly, waiting for my reasoning.

I took my time.

"Right now, they are still reeling from what happened. Their fear is raw, but it hasn't settled yet. That's the thing about fear—it doesn't always break people immediately. Sometimes, it needs time to sink in. To twist. To poison the very bonds that hold them together."

I started walking again, slower this time, measuring each word carefully.

"They think they're strong as a group. That's their weakness."

I smirked.

"But fear has a way of creeping in. Soon, they'll start questioning each other. Wondering if someone slipped up. If one of them said too much. If they can really trust the person standing next to them."

I turned to my man again, locking eyes with him.

"Give it time," I said. "Let them believe they made it out. Let them think this is over."

A brief pause.

A darker smile.

"It won't be long before their own paranoia does the work for us."

"And when it does," I whispered, "we'll move in."

"And after that?" he asked quietly.

I exhaled, feeling the night air shift around me.

"After that... we move to the next stage."

He gave a short bow of acknowledgment.

"As you say, sir."

I gave one last glance at the now-empty room before stepping toward the exit.

The pieces were falling into place.

"We have a lot to plan ahead," I murmured as we disappeared into the corridor.

And then, without another word—

we left.

CHAPTER TWENTY-NINE

TRUST DIED TONIGHT

The three of us walked in silence.

The night air felt colder than before, wrapping around us like an unseen force, pressing against our skin, seeping into our bones. I could still hear the echo of *that man's voice*, calm yet laced with something sinister. I could still feel the tension of that moment—the weight of *his words*, the unshaken confidence in *his stance*, the way he made us feel like we were nothing more than pieces in a game already lost.

No one spoke, but the silence between us wasn't empty. It was heavy. It was suffocating.

I kept walking, but my mind drifted.

Drifted home.

To *Vapi.* To my father. To the home I had left behind in anger, in defiance, convinced that I didn't need him, that I didn't need his approval, his concern, his expectations.

Had I ever needed them?

I wanted to believe I didn't. I wanted to believe I had made peace with it. That *his absence* from my life—the lack of his voice, his presence—had stopped mattering. But as I walked through the darkness of this unknown, the cold whisper of uncertainty creeping in, I couldn't help but wonder...

If something happened to me today, would he care?

Would he sit at the dinner table, waiting for a call that would never come? Would he stand by the window, staring at the road, thinking I'd show up like I always did?

Or would he just move on, as if I had never been there at all?

And my mother—what about her?

I could already see her breaking apart. She had always been the one to believe in me, to see something in me that I couldn't. Even when I was reckless, stubborn, difficult—she had held on. If she lost me now, how would she bear it?

Would she ever forgive me for leaving?

Would I ever forgive myself?

I swallowed hard.

No.

No, I couldn't think like this. Not now.

I clenched my fists, pushing the thoughts away, burying them deep where they couldn't reach me. I told myself I was still here. That nothing had happened. That nothing would happen.

That *I would make sure of it.*

A sudden voice broke through the silence.

"What have we gotten ourselves into?"

Raghav's voice was low, almost breathless. His steps slowed as he spoke, like the weight of everything was finally sinking in. *"This... this isn't what I expected at all."*

Neither of us answered.

Daniyal, who had been walking slightly ahead, kept his eyes forward. His silence was different. It wasn't just shock or disbelief—it was something else. Like he was trying to piece something together, something that still wasn't making sense.

After a while, he muttered, *"I don't think we've escaped it."*

Both Raghav and I turned to him.

"What do you mean?" Raghav asked.

Daniyal exhaled sharply. *"I mean... I still feel it. Like it's not over. Like we're still in it."*

I didn't say anything, but I knew exactly what he meant.

Because there was something else.

Something too bizarre to explain.

Something I hadn't told them yet.

I wasn't sure how they would react to it.

Especially Daniyal.

The thought settled in my chest like a stone. I didn't know how to bring it up. I didn't even know if I should.

By the time we reached the grove, I still hadn't decided.

Shiraz was already there, leaning against a tree, arms crossed. The dim light of his phone screen flickered against his face, casting strange shadows. He looked up as we approached.

"Where's Agasthya?" Raghav asked first.

Shiraz shrugged. *"He left. Maybe fifteen, twenty minutes after you guys. Said something about his work being done here and that he was leaving."* He scoffed. *"Honestly? Didn't seem to care about much else."*

Forget that.

"Finally," he muttered, pushing off the tree. *"You guys took long enough."*

Shiraz frowned. *"How did it go? What did you find?"*

The three of us exchanged glances.

Raghav hesitated, then took a breath, about to say something—

But before he could, I stepped forward.

I looked straight at Shiraz.

"Tell me," I said, voice steady. *"Why did you do it?"*

Shiraz blinked, his expression shifting slightly. *"Do what?"*

"I never thought in a million years that you would do something like this."

Both Raghav and Daniyal turned to me, confusion flashing across their faces.

"What the hell are you talking about?" Daniyal asked.

I exhaled, steadying myself. *"Whatever I have to say, you're not going to like it."*

I turned to Daniyal, meeting his eyes.

"Especially you."

Silence.

Shiraz's gaze didn't waver. Daniyal narrowed his eyes. Raghav's expression tightened as he looked between us.

"What the hell is going on?" Raghav muttered.

None of them knew yet.

But they would.

And after that, there would be no turning back.

The three of them stared at me, waiting.

Waiting for me to explain what I had just said.

I leaned back against a tree, exhaling slowly, my mind racing.

If I said it—if I brought this truth to light—there would be no coming back from it.

This group, this fragile sense of unity we had managed to hold on to, would shatter. I knew that. And yet, as much as I didn't want that to happen, Daniyal deserved to know.

I closed my eyes for a brief second. Then, I looked straight at him.

"Tell me," I said, voice steady. *"According to you, Ishaan disappeared, right?*

The last message you got from him... you never heard back after that?"
Daniyal frowned but nodded. *"Yeah. That's pretty much it. Why?"*
I took a breath.
"What if I told you that he contacted someone way before that? That there was a chance—however small—that he could've escaped? That he could've made it home?" I paused, letting the words sink in before finishing, *"But someone ratted him out?"*
Silence.
They were all looking at me now.
Daniyal's face was still confused but serious, like I had just jolted him awake from a deep sleep. Raghav looked puzzled, his mind working through what I had just said.
But Shiraz...
Shiraz already knew.
He wasn't looking at me in confusion. He wasn't trying to piece things together like the others. His face had changed the second I spoke—tension crept into his features, his jaw clenched slightly. It was subtle, but it was there.
No matter how hard he tried to hide it, I could see it.
And in that moment, I knew.
I swallowed hard and said the words.
"Shiraz is the one responsible for Ishaan's disappearance."
Daniyal moved so fast I barely had time to react.
He grabbed my collar, his grip tight, his face inches from mine. *"Are you out of your goddamn mind?"* His voice was raw, shaking. *"Shiraz would never do that. He knew Ishaan as much as I did!"*
I didn't push him off. Didn't even try.
I just looked him in the eye and removed his hand from my collar—calmly, deliberately. *"I know you can't believe it,"* I said, voice even. *"Even I didn't—until I saw it with my own eyes."*
Daniyal's eyes darkened. *"Found what?"*
I took a slow breath.
"When we were looking at the reports," I said, *"I found one on Ishaan. At first, it was just standard information, nothing unusual. But at the last page... there was a sentence."*
I locked eyes with him.
"'Source of information: Shiraz.'"
The words landed heavy.

Daniyal didn't speak. Neither did Raghav.

Daniyal turned, his movements stiff, controlled, like he was forcing himself not to explode. He walked straight up to Shiraz, his voice dangerously low.

"What the hell is he talking about?" His jaw was tight, his hands clenched. *"Is this true?"*

Shiraz didn't answer immediately.

Instead, he walked forward a little, running a hand through his hair, exhaling sharply. His expression was strained, as if saying the words would physically hurt him.

Then, in a voice thick with regret, he said it.

"He's right."

Daniyal stiffened.

Shiraz swallowed. *"I ratted Ishaan out to the university."*

Daniyal snapped.

With a sharp intake of breath, he grabbed Shiraz's collar, his voice breaking as he shouted, *"Don't give me that bullshit! Don't you dare say you 'had to'—how could you do this? You're the reason he's gone! His parents are suffering in silence because of what you did!"*

Shiraz shoved him back, his own voice rising. *"I had to!"* His eyes burned. *"I didn't have a choice!"*

Raghav, who had been silent until now, finally spoke. His voice was quieter but firm.

"What choice didn't you have?"

Shiraz ran a hand over his face. He looked exhausted, defeated.

Then, he whispered, *"Because I wanted my family to live longer. Okay?"*

Silence.

The weight of his words settled between us, heavy and unmoving.

Even Daniyal—still fuming—froze.

Shiraz let out a slow, shaky breath. *"A week before his last text... I talked to Ishaan,"* he said. *"I don't know why he called me—maybe he just needed to talk to someone, maybe he trusted me. But he was different. Paranoid. Restless. He didn't say much, but..."*

His voice dropped lower.

"'For now, this is the place I'm hiding.'"

"'I can't tell anyone. It's not safe.'"

"'If something happens, don't look for me.'"

Shiraz clenched his fists. *"Two days after that, I got a call from an unknown number."*

The air felt even heavier.

"They asked for Ishaan's location." His voice was flat. *"They said if I didn't tell them, it wouldn't be good for me."*

I felt a chill crawl down my spine.

Daniyal took a step closer. *"Who were they?"*

Shiraz shook his head. *"I don't know."* His voice wavered. *"They didn't just call once. They kept calling. Kept threatening. And then—"*

He exhaled sharply.

"One day, when I was in the market, a man passed by me. Just a stranger. But as he walked past, he whispered in my ear..."

Shiraz's voice dropped.

"'Your mom is alone in the apartment.'"

"'What if the house blows up immediately?'"

I felt my breath catch.

Shiraz let out a bitter laugh, but there was no humour in it. *"And then he said, 'If you don't want that to happen, tell us where Ishaan is.'"*

No one moved.

No one breathed.

Shiraz's voice was hollow now. *"I gave them his location."* His hands curled into fists. *"And then I ran to my house."* He swallowed hard. *"It was fine. My mom was fine. Everything was normal."*

He let out a shaky breath. *"And then I got one last text."*

"'If you dare speak to anyone about this, it won't be good for you.'"

Silence.

Shiraz looked up, his eyes burning. *"That's why I didn't tell anyone, "*He said. *"That's why I kept my mouth shut. I thought if I just stayed quiet... if I pretended, I didn't know anything, I could figure out who did this. Who put me in this position."* He exhaled. *"But then Ishaan disappeared. And then we came here. And I thought maybe—just maybe—we'd find answers without digging into this again."*

His voice dropped lower.

"I was wrong."

We all stood there, frozen, absorbing everything he had just said.

Daniyal still wasn't okay. His breathing was uneven, his expression stormy. But his hands had dropped to his sides. His shoulders had slumped slightly.

Because as much as he wanted to blame Shiraz...

We had faced the same thing tonight.

The same threats. The same fear.

And suddenly, Raghav spoke.

His voice was sharp, urgent. *"Now I get it."*

We all turned to him.

He looked up, his expression unreadable.

"This makes sense now," he muttered.

"What the hell are you talking about?" Daniyal snapped.

But Raghav didn't answer.

Instead, he turned away. *"I'll be back in a minute. Stay here. Tell Shiraz what happened."*

And then, before any of us could stop him—

He ran.

We waited in silence. No one spoke. No one moved.

The weight of everything we had just uncovered hung between us, thick and suffocating. Each of us trying to piece things together, trying to make sense of a night that had already shattered any illusions we had left.

For Daniyal, it was too much.

I could see it in the way he sat there, his hands clenched into fists, his jaw tightening and loosening as if he was trying to force down whatever storm was brewing inside him. His entire world had shifted in the span of one night. And for the rest of us... the hammering thoughts in our minds weren't any kinder.

Then, finally, footsteps.

We looked up as Raghav returned—but he wasn't alone.

In his hand was *the diary*.

The diary that had haunted us for nights. *The one that had sent us down this spiral in the first place.*

No one spoke.

We just looked at each other.

Then, Raghav exhaled slowly and said, *"I think it's time I show you guys the final entry."*

Silence.

Daniyal's jaw tightened again.

The last entry. The third one.

To be honest, none of us wanted to see it.

Whatever had been written in that diary had already left us unsettled before. It had clawed its way into our thoughts, creeping into the quiet spaces of our minds, making sure we never really forgot what was in it.

But tonight was the night everything was being laid bare.

It wouldn't do to be left with one last secret.
There was no going back now.

CHAPTER THIRTY

THE LAST ENTRY

October 8th, 2022

Time: 1:37 AM

This is my last entry.

Not because I want it to be.

Because it has to be.

I have written before, desperately trying to make sense of this place, trying to stitch together the twisted pieces into something logical, something explainable. But there is nothing to explain. There is only the horror of *knowing*.

I used to believe this university was just playing a psychological game, a slow manipulation of minds.

But it is so much worse.

They don't just control you.

They *consume you.*

You don't notice it at first. The excitement, the nerves, the rush of something new—it blinds you.

But then, it begins.

Not all at once.

No, they are *patient.*

They unmake you one thought at a time.

You stop laughing.

You stop talking.

You stop fighting.

You become *less.*

Until one day, you look in the mirror and realize you are nothing but a hollow shell wearing your own face.

I have seen it happen.

I have watched students, full of life and arrogance, wither into silence.
Not because they were told to—because something inside them was *taken*.
They sit in corners, staring at nothing, breathing but not living, existing but not present.
And now, *I am one of them.*
I feel the weight of something I cannot name pressing down on my skull, burrowing into my thoughts, twisting the way I see the world.
I know I should be afraid.
I know I should run.
But the worst part?
I don't want to anymore.
Even now, as I write this, my fear is crawling beneath my skin like something alive.
I am being *watched.*
I don't need to turn around to know.
They are here.
They have always been here.
They were here when I first stepped onto this campus, and they will be here long after I am gone.
But when I turn, there's no one there.
Or maybe there is.
Maybe they just don't need to be seen anymore.
And if you are reading this—*they are watching you too.*
Burn this.
Burn it before it's too late.
Burn it before it sees you.
Before it knows you.
Because if you don't...
It will never let you go.
There is no hope in these words, no answers that will help you.
They are beyond this.
Beyond you.
If you keep this, it will haunt you.
I promise you... it will keep haunting you.
No one spoke.
The air around us had shifted, but not into silence.
The wind had thickened, howling low and constant, wrapping around us like an invisible force.

The leaves rustled, not in their usual way, but as if something unseen was moving through them.

As if the trees were whispering—*warning.*

For the first time, we weren't just feeling uneasy or paranoid.

We were *scared.*

Scared to look around.

Scared to acknowledge where we were.

Scared to stand in an open space at this time of night, as if something unseen would notice us.

The rustling grew louder.

The branches creaked like something was shifting between them.

The shadows didn't just loom—they twisted, stretched, *watching.*

Raghav closed the book slowly, his fingers gripping the cover a little too tightly.

But still, no one spoke.

Not until Shiraz broke the silence.

"How... how are you holding this to yourself?" he asked, his voice barely above a whisper. *"It's like this isn't a diary, but some kind of cursed book. Every time you open it, it comes up with something worse... something that leaves a mark on you."*

Raghav didn't respond.

He didn't need to.

We all felt it.

A few seconds passed before I found my voice.

"Why did you think it was necessary to show us this now?"

Raghav exhaled sharply, as if he had been holding his breath for too long.

"Because this is how they do it," he said. *"First, they make sure fear has rooted itself deep in your mind. Then, over time, they break you apart. Slowly. Carefully. Until you become... one of them."*

He looked up at us, his expression hollow.

"It all makes sense now, but not in the way any of us expected. This isn't just some conspiracy. It's like a horror film, where the more you uncover the truth... the more dangerous it becomes for you."

No one disagreed.

We stood there, uncertain and shaken, surrounded by shadows that felt too dense, too watchful.

The wind picked up again, whistling through the trees, shifting the leaves like unseen footsteps circling us.

The night had become colder, sharper.

None of us checked the time, but we knew it was well past midnight.

Then Daniyal spoke.

His voice was steady, but the weight of his words was undeniable.

"I'm out."

We turned to him.

"I can't do this anymore," he continued, shaking his head. *"There's no point in going further. The deeper we go, the more terrifying this gets. And honestly... I don't think this will ever end. Let them do whatever the hell they want."*

Raghav was silent for a moment. Then, with a sigh, he nodded.

"I'm with him. This is too much. We thought we were uncovering a pattern, but we were wrong. We're not solving anything—we're becoming a part of something vicious, a loop that will never end. And I don't want to end up like my brother."

Shiraz rubbed his temples.

His voice was quiet but firm.

"I guess it's time. We need to bury all of this and move on. We did everything we could, but this... this is beyond us now. And honestly, it's getting dangerous."

I listened to them.

And deep down, I knew they were right.

No one could be blamed for wanting out.

But something in me felt *different*.

The diary had broken something in us tonight, but it had also revealed something.

We were standing at the edge of something enormous, something we barely understood.

And maybe that was the worst part—understanding wouldn't save us.

It would only drag us in deeper.

The wind howled.

The trees groaned.

Somewhere in the distance, a faint, unrecognizable sound echoed—a sound I didn't want to place.

I took a breath.

"Then I think we should stop talking to each other, too."

They all looked at me.

"Pretend none of this happened. That we don't know each other. It's getting harder to trust each other now... especially after what we uncovered tonight."

No one argued.

No one could argue.
The group we had formed—the one that stood together through fear, through discoveries, through the shadows of this place—had *shattered*.
It was *over.*
One by one, they turned and walked away, their footsteps swallowed by the wind.
The trees loomed, bending slightly as if leaning in to listen.
And then, just for a second—I swore I heard *another set of footsteps.*
Not ours.
Something else.
I didn't turn back.
But what none of us knew was that this was just another part of *the loop.*
And the circle would bring us back together again.
But not in a way *any of us would survive.*

CHAPTER THIRTY-ONE

BACK INTO THE BLACK

A month had passed.

And to be honest, *a lot had changed since then.*

I barely saw Daniyal and Shiraz anymore. Sometimes we'd stumble upon each other in the hallways, in the cafeteria, or somewhere around campus. But we just moved past each other like strangers, like we had never spoken a word to one another.

As if *none of it had ever happened.*

Raghav was different.

He was my roommate, which meant we saw each other every day.

But we might as well have been living on opposite ends of the university.

We went about our own lives, *never speaking, never acknowledging what had happened.*

Something had shifted in all of us since that night.

We weren't the same people anymore.

To shake the feeling, I kept myself busy. Late-night walks, basketball, tennis—anything to exhaust my mind.

Every morning, I hit the gym.

But no matter how much I tried to drown out the thoughts, *the weight of that night never left me.*

It clung to me like a shadow, lurking in the corners of my mind.

Raghav found his own ways to cope.

He spent his time playing cricket and badminton, losing himself in the rush of the game.

Afternoons were dedicated to the library.

That was where I found myself now, flipping through notes and textbooks, trying to get ahead of things before the winter break.

Exams were right around the corner, and *I needed to focus.*

The evening sky outside had deepened into a dark blue, the last traces of an orange hue fading away.

It was almost 6:30 when I decided to pack up and head back to my dorm.

Just as I was about to close my notebook, my phone lit up with a notification.

A message from *Raghav.*

It had been a while since he texted me.

When I opened it, there wasn't much written.

Just a single line:

If you still consider me something, meet me immediately at the grove.

For a second, I just stared at the screen.

Then I let out a slow breath.

The grove.

I wasn't going back to that disgusting place.

My first instinct was to ignore it.

After everything, I had no reason to set foot there again.

But no matter how much distance had grown between us, Raghav was still my friend.

And if he was saying this, if he was reaching out after all this time, then it *meant something.*

I sighed, shoved my books into my bag, and stood up.

The walk to the grove felt heavier than I expected.

The wind was cool and calm, brushing against my skin.

The ground felt colder, the path littered with fallen leaves that had completely shed in the winter air.

Each step forward sent a ripple of unease through me.

It had been nearly a month since I last saw *that thing.*

Now, I was going back.

When I finally reached, I saw him sitting on a log, his elbows resting on his knees.

But he wasn't alone.

Leaning against a tree, arms crossed, was Daniyal.

Shiraz stood nearby, pacing back and forth, his hands tucked into his jacket.

It had been so long since I saw them together like this.

Raghav stood up as I approached. He gave me a faint smile.

"So, you decided to show up."

Daniyal and Shiraz looked at me.

"Long time no see," Shiraz muttered.

Daniyal tilted his head. *"Heard you've been keeping yourself busy."*

I shrugged. *"Just trying to stay occupied."*

Neither of them smiled.

They only nodded.

There was an unspoken tension between us, something fragile and unresolved.

I exhaled. *"Why did you call us here?"*

Raghav's gaze flickered to Daniyal and Shiraz for a moment before he finally spoke.

"My brother's back from London. He's at his parents' house."

Silence.

I should have felt something—shock, disbelief, anything.

But the truth was, *I wasn't surprised.*

Some part of me had been expecting this.

I rubbed the back of my neck and sighed. *"Well... this should shake things up."*

Silence settled over us, thick and heavy, before Daniyal finally broke it.

"Why are you telling us this?"

His voice was cautious, edged with suspicion.

"What's the motive behind it?"

Raghav exhaled, running a hand through his hair.

"When he was in London, I could barely reach him. But now that he's here, we can talk to him—find out what really happened. Maybe he can help us get out of this."

I let out a bitter laugh.

"You realize he ran away, right? He didn't escape—he was pushed. And whatever pushed him changed him forever."

"I know," Raghav admitted, his tone softer now.

"But think about it—what have we even been doing for the past month? We're avoiding each other, pretending none of this ever happened. We don't talk, we don't check in, we don't even care what's happening around us anymore. How long do you think we can keep this up?"

No one spoke.

The realization hit harder than I expected.

As much as I wanted to leave all of this behind, I couldn't deny the truth—*ignoring it wasn't the same as escaping it.*

Shiraz finally broke the silence, arms still crossed.

"Now that I think about it... this is exactly what they want, isn't it? If we keep ignoring everything, we're not escaping—we're just becoming like the ones

before us."
Another truth, thrown into the cold evening air.
I sighed. *"What's the guarantee that if we go back into this, we won't end up like them?"*
Daniyal shook his head.
"After everything that's happened, you really think there's a guarantee? There isn't. It's all risk. As long as we keep digging, we'll always be at risk. But we don't have much of a choice, do we? Either we step back into the black hole... or keep living like ghosts of ourselves."
The wind rustled through the trees, dry leaves scraping against the ground. Somewhere in the distance, birds chirped, oblivious to the weight of our conversation.
I exhaled. *"If we're going to talk to him, we do it in person. Vacation starts in a few days—we leave for Mumbai. Pack your things."*
The three of them exchanged looks before nodding in agreement.
"I'll take care of our accommodation," Raghav said.
"I'll check train tickets," I added. *"We leave in two days."*
And just like that, the decision was made.
As we turned to leave, a single thought settled in my mind, refusing to let go.
We had circled back into this mess. But this time, I wasn't sure what the cost would be.

CHAPTER THIRTY-TWO

ANOTHER RIDE, ANOTHER RECKONING

The station was quieter than I expected.

A layer of mist clung to the air, thick and damp, the kind that made everything feel heavier.

The station lights cast a dim glow over the platform, barely cutting through the fog.

It was early—*too early*—and the world still seemed half-asleep.

Our suitcases stood beside us, lined up like silent spectators.

Daniyal, Shiraz, and Raghav stood near me, their faces lit by the dull glow of their phone screens as they scrolled mindlessly, passing time.

No one spoke.

There wasn't much to say.

I exhaled, my breath visible in the cold air, and glanced down at the train tracks.

The last time I stood at a station like this, waiting for a train, *my life had changed forever.*

Nagpur.

That single journey had thrown me into something I never could've imagined.

And now, here I was again, waiting for another train.

Another journey.

Another unknown.

A distant rumble broke my thoughts.

The train emerged from the fog, its headlights cutting through the mist, growing larger, louder.

The brakes screeched against the tracks as it slowed, stopping right in front of us.

Silently, we pocketed our phones, grabbed our bags, and boarded.

Inside, the train was mostly empty.

Just a few scattered passengers, some curled up in their seats, others staring blankly at their phones.

It was too early for conversation.

We found our seats and settled in.

The moment the train pulled away from the station, exhaustion began to creep in.

The rhythmic sway of the carriage, the faint hum of the tracks—it all worked like a lullaby.

Within minutes, one by one, they drifted off.

First Shiraz, then Daniyal, then Raghav.

Their slow, steady breathing filled the space around me.

I stayed awake.

I had unfinished business.

Carefully, I stood up, stepping over Raghav's stretched-out legs.

The train rocked gently as I made my way down the corridor, past empty seats, past doors leading to other compartments.

The world outside blurred into streaks of gray and blue as the train picked up speed.

No one knew about this.

Not Daniyal, not Shiraz, not even Raghav.

And they wouldn't.

Not yet.

I reached the place I needed to be.

Took care of what needed to be done.

Then, without a word, I turned and made my way back.

By the time I reached my seat, the exhaustion finally caught up with me.

I leaned back, let my eyes close, and let the steady hum of the train pull me into sleep.

For now, the journey continued.

I woke up to the sound of the train rattling over the tracks, the muffled chatter of passengers, and the occasional cry of a chaiwala calling out his wares.

The sun had shifted far across the sky—*half the day had passed while we slept.*

It had been a long time since I'd had sleep this deep, this uninterrupted.

Maybe it was the exhaustion catching up to me, or maybe it was just the rhythmic sway of the train that made it easier to drift off.

Either way, *I felt heavier, sluggish,* like my body wasn't fully awake yet.

Daniyal stirred first, stretching his arms with a groggy yawn.

Shiraz followed, rubbing his eyes.

Raghav blinked a few times before checking his phone.

No words were exchanged—just the unspoken agreement that we all needed to shake off the sleep.

One by one, we took turns heading to the washroom, splashing cold water on our faces, letting the sting of it wake us up properly.

By the time we returned to our seats, our heads were clearer.

Phones came out again, screens lighting up our faces as we scrolled through messages, news, or whatever could pass the time.

We barely noticed how quickly it slipped away.

The train finally pulled into Mumbai Central with a low screech of metal against metal.

The city stretched beyond the station, vast and endless, pulsing with life even in the middle of the afternoon.

We grabbed our suitcases, stepped onto the platform, and just like that, *we were in Mumbai.*

The City of Dreams. The city that never sleeps.

Everything moved fast here—people weaving through the crowd, heads bent toward their phones, rickshaws honking impatiently in the distance.

No one stopped.

No one cared.

Everyone had somewhere to be, something to do.

A city that ran on ambition, on chaos, on an energy so thick you could almost feel it pressing against you.

The local trains rumbled past in the distance, so overcrowded that people clung to the doors, hanging on with nothing but sheer balance and habit.

A sight that belonged only to *Mumbai.*

Raghav was already a step ahead, booking a cab before we even left the station.

"We'll head straight to my brother's place," he said, glancing at his phone.

"Where does he stay?" Daniyal asked.

"Bandra West."

I raised an eyebrow.

Of course, he does.

Shiraz let out a low whistle.

"Bandra West, huh? Talk about casually flexing your rich family background without actually saying it."
Raghav rolled his eyes.
"Oh, shut up."
The cab arrived, a sleek black sedan that looked slightly out of place in the chaotic mess of Mumbai traffic.
We loaded our bags into the trunk and slid inside, the air-conditioning a welcome contrast to the thick humidity outside.
As we pulled away from the station, weaving through the tangled streets, one thought settled in my mind.
Mumbai.
This city had seen it all. But would it be ready for what we were about to bring into it?
The ride through Mumbai's chaotic streets felt longer than it was.
Forty-five minutes, give or take, but the weight in my chest made it feel heavier, slower.
We finally pulled up to our destination—a towering building, easily forty stories high.
Just another Mumbai thing.
Skyscrapers touching the sky, money and ambition stacked on top of each other.
Raghav paid the driver, and we stepped out, rolling our suitcases toward the entrance.
The glass doors slid open, and a cool blast of air-conditioning hit us as we stepped inside.
The lobby was modern, sleek, polished.
Everything *screamed expensive.*
We stood in silence as we waited for the elevator.
None of us said it out loud, but we all knew.
This wasn't just another visit.
The lift doors slid open, and we stepped in.
Raghav pressed the button for the 35th floor.
The smooth hum of the elevator filled the air as we ascended.
My fingers tapped against my suitcase handle, a nervous rhythm I didn't even realize I was making.
As we neared our floor, the elevator slowed, coming to a halt before the doors slid open with a soft chime.
Just to our left was the apartment entrance.

Raghav rang the doorbell.

And then, for the first time since all this began, *we hesitated.*

Because *this was different.*

This wasn't the university, with its hidden truths lurking beneath its polished walls.

This was someone who had gotten out.

Someone who had *survived*—if you could even call it that.

A few seconds passed before the door swung open.

Standing there was a man, definitely older than us, his sharp features framed by a neatly trimmed beard and hair combed back.

He wasn't muscular, but he had the kind of build that looked naturally fit.

His eyes swept over us before settling on Raghav.

Then, he smiled.

"Hey, bro. What a surprise, man."

Raghav grinned, stepping forward to hug him.

"I know. It's been a long time."

His brother let out a chuckle as he pulled away.

There was something refined about him, something that told me he wasn't just another Mumbai guy.

And when he spoke again, it became clear—*his accent had shifted,* carrying the smooth polish of a British influence.

London had left its mark on him.

"And who are these guys?" he asked, glancing at the rest of us.

Raghav gestured towards us.

"These are my friends—Daniyal, Shiraz, and Aaron."

"Nice to meet you all. Come on in."

We stepped inside, the cool air of the apartment wrapping around us as the door shut behind us.

The place was spacious, modern, filled with subtle touches of someone who had lived abroad for a while.

"Where are Uncle and Aunty?" Raghav asked, looking around.

"Mom went out to buy groceries, and Dad's at work," his brother replied.

"It's just me."

He smiled, shaking his head.

"Man, it's been a long time since we talked. Look how much you've grown."

He leaned against the back of the couch, crossing his arms.

"Tell me, how's it going? What are you up to these days?"

Raghav shifted slightly.

"I'm studying law."

His brother's smile widened.

"That's really nice. So you're in a university, then? Which one?"

And just like that, *the atmosphere changed.*

Raghav's voice dropped, almost hesitant.

"Your ex-university." A pause. *"Blackstone Academy of Law."*

His brother's expression froze.

The warmth drained from his face, replaced by something *cold, unreadable.*

For a moment, the room was silent.

Then, before he could even react, Raghav spoke again.

"We know what's going on there. We know the truth. We're stuck in the same situation you were in when you were there. And before it gets worse, we need your help."

His voice was steady, firm.

"You have to tell us what exactly happened to you—and how you got out."

His brother didn't speak right away.

His eyes flickered between us, his face unmoving, as if he was processing every word.

Then, finally, he exhaled.

"To be honest..." His voice was lower now, quieter. *"I still don't think I ever escaped."*

The words sent a chill down my spine.

"And frankly," he continued, locking eyes with Raghav, *"I'm afraid that you guys won't be able to get out of it either."*

A heavy silence filled the room.

He looked directly at his younger brother now, and his next words came out slow, deliberate.

"You should have never gone there."

His jaw tightened.

"You don't know what you've done."

We exchanged glances.

We had expected something like this.

But hearing it—*hearing it from someone who had lived through it, someone who had made it out*—made it feel *real.*

More real than it had ever been before.

CHAPTER THIRTY-THREE

THE SURVIVOR'S TRUTH

The silence in the room was *suffocating*.

Five of us sat there, waiting—no, *hoping*—for someone to break it.

But the truth was, none of us had the words.

No justifications.

No explanations.

Because if the man who had actually survived Blackstone—if Raghav's brother—had just told us, point-blank, that *we had made a huge mistake*, then what was there left to say?

Daniyal was the first to crack.

"We know we messed up," he said, his voice steady but quieter than usual. *"And that's exactly why we came to you. We were hoping you'd have something—anything—that could help."*

Raghav's brother didn't respond right away.

He just leaned back slightly, arms crossed, his gaze shifting between us.

Then, finally, he asked,

"How did you guys even find out about this?"

A pause.

"And how do you know I was involved?"

None of us answered.

Instead, Raghav reached into his bag, pulled out a small, worn diary, and set it on the table.

The reaction wasn't immediate.

No flicker of shock, no anger, not even curiosity.

His brother just raised an eyebrow at the sight of it.

Then, in a calm, almost detached voice, he asked,

"Where did you get this?"

"I came home after you left," Raghav admitted. *"I was in your room, looking around, and I stumbled upon it."*

A long beat of silence.

Then, without touching the diary, his brother slid it further away from himself, almost like it carried something *toxic.*

"Please don't tell me you read those three entries."

His voice was different now—*tighter,* like the words were physically painful to say.

Shiraz exhaled through his nose, shaking his head slightly.

"It's not just him," he said. *"We all read them."*

For the first time, a visible reaction.

A sharp inhale.

A hand dragging through his hair, fingers pressing against his scalp like he was trying to physically steady himself.

Then, he placed both hands on his head, elbows resting on his knees, his whole posture *screaming exhaustion.*

A few seconds passed.

Then, without a word, he stood up.

"Let's talk about this in my room."

No one argued.

We followed him as he led us down the hallway, stepping into his room one by one.

The moment we were all inside, he shut the door and locked it.

And just like that, *we had crossed into something deeper.*

Something we might not be able to walk back from.

The room felt smaller now, the weight of what was coming pressing in from all sides.

We sat in silence, all eyes on Raghav's brother as he leaned forward slightly, elbows resting on his knees.

"Alright," he said finally. *"I'll tell you everything I know. But you need to understand something—this isn't a movie. It's not some psychological thriller you can just close and walk away from. This is real. And whatever is happening inside that university is... extreme."*

Shiraz let out a quiet scoff, shaking his head.

"Trust us, we know exactly what you mean. We've seen things we can't unsee."

Raghav's brother rubbed his hands together, then dragged them down his face like he was trying to wipe something off—maybe the weight of memories.

"Alright. Here it is."

His voice was steady, but there was something in his eyes—*something haunted.*

"First of all, whatever you read in that diary—it's vague. Those were my thoughts when I was still trying to piece together what was happening, how they were operating. But you also need to understand that those entries were written years ago. And yet, I know one thing for certain."

He exhaled sharply.

"Whatever it is they're doing, they haven't stopped."

His words sent a chill through me.

"Now," he continued, *"tell me—how deep are you in this?"*

The four of us exchanged glances.

A long breath left me as I finally answered.

"Deeper than you think," I admitted. *"And based on our current situation... we don't even know what their next move is going to be."*

I hesitated, then added, *"Can you tell us anything about that?"*

Raghav's brother shook his head.

"I'm afraid I can't. They change their patterns depending on the students. Whatever I faced back then... it might be completely different from what you're dealing with."

"Have you guys had any interactions?"

Daniyal leaned forward, his expression dark.

"Let's just say we crossed paths with someone. Someone who didn't hesitate to threaten us—directly. Told us that if we don't stop, they'll go after our families."

A visible shudder ran through Raghav's brother.

His forehead glistened with sweat as he ran a hand over it, looking like he was reliving something—something he had tried to bury.

After a few moments, he turned sharply to Raghav.

"Who the hell told you to get into this?"

His voice was sharp, almost desperate.

Raghav swallowed.

"I didn't know there would be something like this," he said. *"Who would have thought a university would have secrets this dark?"*

Silence settled over us again.

But in that silence, something went unsaid.

A question that should have come earlier.

A question that, somehow, all of us had overlooked.

I turned to him, my voice low.

"Bro..."

He looked at me.

"Yeah?"

"How did you escape this?"

His expression changed instantly.

His face went unreadable, his eyes distant, like he was deciding whether to tell the truth or not.

The pause stretched longer than it should have.

Then, finally, he exhaled.

"There's something I never wrote in that diary," he said. *"Something I was too ashamed to put down."*

Raghav leaned in.

"Bro, you have to tell us. We're at a dead end here. Whatever it is, just say it. We won't judge. We know what you went through."

His brother gave a humourless chuckle, shaking his head.

"You say that now," he murmured. *"But wait until you hear what I have to say."*

The room felt suffocating, the weight of unspoken horrors pressing down on all of us.

Raghav's brother sat hunched forward, staring at the floor like the words he was about to say were clawing their way out of him.

When he finally spoke, his voice was quiet—haunted.

"When this was happening to me, I felt... distant. From others. From myself. Like I wasn't even a person anymore."

He swallowed hard.

"I couldn't go back to being normal. Fear, confusion, silence—they took over everything. And with time, it only got worse. It got stronger. I knew that if I didn't do something—anything—it would change me forever."

He paused, exhaling sharply, as if he was trying to force himself to keep going.

"So... one night, I went to them. I told them I'd do anything if they let me leave."

His hands clenched into fists.

"I swore I'd go far away. That I'd disappear, make sure no one ever found out about this."

He let out a bitter chuckle.

"They agreed."

For a second, no one said a word.

But the way he said it, the way his voice wavered—I knew there was more.

And when he finally continued, my stomach twisted.

"But... they had one condition."

The room seemed to shrink.

"They told me... that in exchange for my freedom, I had to bring them two students. Two students who were smart, capable, who could walk into this—blindly. I don't know what I was thinking back then. I don't know if I was even thinking at all. But I agreed. Immediately."

He let out a shaky breath, looking at his hands as if they were stained.

"I started researching. I found two students, dug up everything I could about them, and handed over their names. A few days later, they called me. Told me I was free to leave."

His voice cracked slightly.

"But if I ever spoke about this to anyone, they'd destroy everything I cared about. My family. My friends. My future."

That last word barely came out.

"That's why I ran," he admitted, almost whispering. *"That's why I flew to London."*

He rubbed a hand over his face, his voice heavy with something deeper than guilt.

"I don't know what happened to those two students. I don't even know if they're still alive. And every single night since then, I—I can't sleep. I think about what I did, what I handed them, and I just..."

His voice broke.

"I just didn't have a choice."

Shame was written all over him—on his face, in his posture, in the way his voice trembled.

None of us spoke.

We didn't need to.

The weight of his confession hung in the air, *suffocating, inescapable.*

Daniyal was the first to move.

He stood up, walked over, and placed a firm hand on his shoulder.

"It's okay, man," he said quietly. *"We know. You didn't have a choice."*

Raghav's brother shook his head, his expression unreadable again.

But this time, I knew what was behind it.

"I'll say it again," he muttered. *"The pattern is random. That means if they ever reach out to you again... it won't be like what I went through."*

He looked at each of us, his gaze dark and certain.

"It'll be something else. Something worse."

No one spoke after that.
No one moved.
The silence that followed wasn't just silence.
It was *something else entirely.*
Something cold. Something final.

CHAPTER THIRTY-FOUR

AUTHOR OF THE UNSEEN

We stepped out of his apartment into the cold night air.

The streets were quieter now, a stark contrast to the noise inside my head.

No one spoke as we exited the building.

Not a single word.

It was as if we had all been thrown into deep water, struggling to make sense of which way was up.

I pulled out my phone and booked a cab.

Raghav's house was our next stop—*his parents were away on vacation,* which meant we had the place to ourselves.

A safe space, at least for the night.

The ride was thirty minutes long, but it felt like both a moment and an eternity.

The city lights flickered past the windows, casting shifting shadows on our faces.

The silence in the cab wasn't the comfortable kind; it was the kind that pressed down on our chests, heavy with unspoken thoughts.

By the time we reached Raghav's apartment, it was already past 8 PM.

None of us had realized how much time we had spent inside his brother's home.

Time had slipped away, lost between the weight of revelations and the frustration of unanswered questions.

At the reception, Raghav picked up the spare key his parents had left for him.

We rode the elevator up to his apartment, and the moment he unlocked the door and flicked on the lights, Shiraz finally broke the silence.

"Honestly... when we went to your brother's place, I really thought we'd walk out with answers," he said, exhaling sharply. *"But now? Now we're just more confused than ever."*

Daniyal leaned against the doorframe, arms crossed.

"It's not his fault," he said. *"The university has kept things so tightly sealed—there's only so much he can tell us."*

I shook my head.

"Still... we didn't get all the answers. Frankly, I don't even know if we got any answers at all."

Raghav sighed and shut the door behind us.

"It's not just my brother," he said. *"Even if we had spoken to someone else, I doubt they'd be able to tell us more than he did."*

Shiraz let out a short, humourless laugh.

"I guess."

We all stood there for a few moments, the weight of the situation pressing down on us.

Then Raghav clapped his hands together, forcing a change in tone.

"Look, we'll figure this out—after some rest. We've had a long day, and thinking with an exhausted mind and body isn't going to help us."

I wanted to disagree.

We all did.

But he was right.

Pushing forward while running on fumes wouldn't get us anywhere.

Daniyal groaned, rubbing his temples.

"Alright... let's do it."

"Great," Raghav said.

"There are two bedrooms, each with its own bathroom. Aaron and I will take one; you and Shiraz take the other. Freshen up, and we'll meet in the living room to order some food."

No one argued.

We split up, and for the first time in what felt like days, I stood under a stream of hot water, letting it wash away the exhaustion clinging to me.

But no amount of steam could clear my mind.

The conversation at Raghav's brother's place replayed in my head like a broken tape, looping over and over.

When I stepped out of the shower, dressed in fresh clothes, I joined the others in the living room.

We ordered food, and while we ate, we let Netflix fill the silence, the flashing screen giving us an excuse to not talk.

It was strange—*just a few days ago,* we would've been making sarcastic remarks about whatever we were watching, laughing at something ridiculous on-screen.

Now, we barely spoke.

It was only after we cleaned up and turned off the TV that we returned to reality.

Daniyal leaned forward, resting his elbows on his knees.

"Let's go back to the university," he said. *"I'm sure we'll figure out something."*

Shiraz nodded.

"Yeah... it's not like we have any other choice."

Raghav ran a hand through his hair.

"Right. Let's just go back."

I stared at the floor for a moment before speaking.

"We're not going back."

All three of them turned to look at me.

Shiraz frowned.

"What do you mean?"

I lifted my gaze, my voice steady.

"We still have unfinished business."

A silence stretched between us.

The air in the room thickened.

Shiraz narrowed his eyes.

"What unfinished business?"

I met his gaze but didn't answer.

"You'll see," I said simply.

"For now, let's get some sleep. We have a plane to catch tomorrow."

Daniyal sat up straight.

"A plane? Where the hell are we going?"

I stood up and stretched, suppressing a smirk.

"You'll see," I repeated.

No one pressed further.

Maybe they were too tired, or maybe they understood that I wouldn't give them an answer yet.

Either way, the conversation ended there.

As I walked toward the bedroom, I felt something shift inside me.

This was it.

The moment I had been waiting for—the real task.

The one that had been left unfinished ever since I first stepped onto that train to Mumbai.

Tomorrow, *I would finish what I started.*

And this time, *I wasn't leaving without the truth.*

The airport buzzed with the usual chaos—travellers rushing to their gates, last-minute announcements crackling through the speakers, the rhythmic clatter of suitcase wheels rolling across polished floors.

But for me, everything was quiet.

Tuned out.

I sat still, boarding pass in hand, my mind set on what lay ahead.

Shiraz, on the other hand, was restless.

His fingers tapped against the armrest as he leaned toward me.

"Dude, mind telling us why we're flying to Dehradun?"

Daniyal chimed in.

"Yeah, what's so important there?"

Raghav sighed.

"Exactly. Yesterday, we were in Mumbai, and today, we're suddenly boarding a plane to Dehradun. What the hell is going on?"

I remained calm, focused.

They wouldn't understand yet.

Not until we got there.

"You'll see," I said, my voice steady.

"Trust me, this is our only hope of getting
real answers."

The three of them exchanged glances, frustration evident on their faces.

But they knew arguing with me was pointless.

After everything, I wasn't making decisions blindly.

If I was leading them somewhere, there was a reason.

They gave up and sat in silence, though I could feel their curiosity hanging in the air like a thick fog.

Then, the announcement came, breaking through the tension.

"Attention all passengers on Flight 6E-721 to Dehradun, this is your final boarding call. Please proceed to Gate 24 for immediate boarding. The gate will close in ten minutes. Thank you."

We got up, slinging our backpacks over our shoulders, and joined the queue.

There was no turning back now.

As we moved through the boarding gate and onto the jet bridge, the realization started sinking in.

We were actually doing this—*leaving Mumbai, leaving behind whatever safety we had,* and stepping into something unknown.

Thirty minutes later, we were settled into our seats.

The overhead compartments were shut, seatbelts clicked into place.

The usual safety announcements played, but I barely registered them.

My focus was elsewhere.

The plane began to taxi down the runway.

The engines roared to life, the vibrations beneath us growing stronger.

Then, in a sudden rush, the plane accelerated, pressing us back into our seats.

Within seconds, we were airborne, leaving Mumbai behind.

For them, this was a journey into the unknown.

For me, *this was a gamble—one that had to pay off.*

As the city lights faded beneath us and the sky stretched endless above, one thought repeated in my mind:

Whatever I've set in motion... it better be right.

And just like that, a 2-hour-and-30-minute journey had begun.

Sleep had swallowed us whole the moment the plane took off, exhaustion finally catching up.

It felt like we had closed our eyes for only a second before a voice stirred us awake.

"Sir, the flight is about to land. Please fasten your seatbelt," the air hostess said politely.

Groggy and disoriented, we buckled up as the plane began its descent.

Outside the window, the sky had dimmed to an evening hue, the lights of Dehradun flickering in the distance.

The aircraft touched down with a soft jolt, rolling down the runway before coming to a slow halt.

Seatbelts clicked open, and we joined the slow-moving crowd toward the conveyor belt, collecting our bags before heading through security.

It took almost an hour before we finally emerged through the arrival gates.

They were still confused.

I wasn't.

Without a word, I stepped outside, hailed a cab, and gave the driver an address.

"Shivalik Heights, Apartment 5C, Rajpur Road."

The others exchanged glances, but no one questioned me this time.

The moment we got into the cab, the city faded past us, Dehradun stretching out in all directions.

The Doon Valley—*nestled between the Shivalik Hills and the foothills of the Garhwal Himalayas*—was a world away from the suffocating chaos of Mumbai.

The air smelled different here, fresher, laced with the faint scent of pine and earth.

The streets were quieter, lined with old colonial houses and newer glass buildings standing side by side.

People walked at an unhurried pace, as if time moved differently in this part of the country.

But we weren't here to admire the scenery.

Fifteen minutes later, we pulled up in front of a modest apartment building.

I handed the driver some cash, and we stepped out.

The evening had settled in, a cool breeze rustling through the trees.

Streetlights flickered on, casting a warm glow over the pavement.

Inside the building, I pressed the button for the fifth floor.

The elevator doors slid open with a soft chime.

One final step.

We walked down the corridor, stopping outside a nondescript door.

My heart pounded in my chest—not from fear, but from the weight of what was about to happen.

I lifted my hand and pressed the doorbell.

A few seconds later, the door swung open.

A man stood before us.

His face was clean-shaven, his glasses perched neatly on his nose.

He wore the kind of clothes you'd expect from a retired professor—loose, unassuming.

But he didn't look old.

Early thirties at most.

I exhaled.

"Are you Rohan Mehta?"

The man studied me, then gave a small nod.

"Yes. That would be me."

Silence.

A thick, suffocating silence.

Daniyal, Raghav, and Shiraz were frozen beside me, their eyes wide with disbelief.

Yes.

That's right.
Rohan Mehta.
The journalist who vanished into thin air.
The man who wrote that article and disappeared without a trace.
The one whose name was whispered in conspiracy circles, speculated about in online forums, reduced to a footnote in news archives before being completely forgotten.
And yet—*here he was.*
Standing in front of us, *very much alive.*
A ghost, resurrected.
The others hadn't moved.
I could feel their disbelief, their silent shock pressing down like a heavy fog.
Because *this wasn't possible.*

CHAPTER THIRTY-FIVE

Survival isn't Freedom

They stood frozen, their minds struggling to catch up with what their eyes were seeing.

Raghav was the first to find his voice.

It came out strained, barely above a whisper.

"This... this isn't possible. Are you the Rohan Mehta?"

The man before us—very much alive—studied us with wary eyes.

His stance was guarded, his expression unreadable.

"Who are you?" he asked, his voice even but laced with caution. *"And what do you want?"*

Before anyone else could speak, I stepped forward.

"I'm Aaron," I said, keeping my tone steady. *"Vivaan must have told you about me."*

For a moment, there was nothing.

Then, I saw it—the flicker of recognition in his eyes.

"Aaron..." he muttered, almost to himself.

And then, with a slight nod, he said, *"Ah. So you're the one. I've been expecting you."*

He stepped aside, pushing the door open further.

"Come in."

They hesitated, exchanging glances.

But really, what choice did they have?

One by one, we stepped inside.

The air was thick with tension, the silence stretching just a bit too long.

Rohan shut the door behind us, then turned back.

His gaze was sharp, assessing.

"You made sure no one saw you?"

"Yeah," I said. *"Pretty sure. Almost no one even knows we're in Dehradun."*

Rohan gave a single, approving nod.

"Good."

Before he could say anything else, Daniyal took a step closer, his eyes locked onto Rohan as if trying to make sense of what he was seeing.

"You... you were supposed to be—"

"Dead?" Rohan cut in, a hint of amusement in his voice. *"Missing?"*

He exhaled through his nose, shaking his head.

"Well, as you can see, I'm neither. I'm right here."

Daniyal didn't respond.

None of them did.

They were still trying to wrap our heads around this.

Shiraz turned to me.

"How did you even know he was here?"

I glanced at Rohan, silently asking if I should answer.

He gave a slight nod.

"When we decided to go to Mumbai, I knew we needed someone who knew more about the university than we did," I explained.

"I had a gut feeling Raghav's brother wouldn't have the full picture. And that's when it hit me—Rohan Mehta. If there was one person who truly knew what was going on, it had to be him."

The room was dead silent.

I could feel all eyes on me, waiting.

"So, I started digging. And I found his partner. Someone who wasn't just a colleague, but a friend. His name is Vivaan."

At that, Rohan's expression softened ever so slightly.

"I reached out to him, told him everything," I continued.

"At first, he didn't say much. Just told me to give him two days. He wanted to run a background check on me—make sure we weren't a threat."

"A background check?" Daniyal echoed.

"For safety," I clarified. *"He looked into us, found nothing suspicious. And then, on the train... while you all were asleep, he sent me Rohan's location and everything else we needed to know. And the rest is history."*

Even as I finished speaking, the disbelief in the room hadn't faded.

It was as if our minds refused to process it.

But disbelief wouldn't change reality.

We were here now.

And whatever Rohan Mehta was about to tell us next...

It could either save us.

Or ruin us completely.

We settled into our seats, the weight of what had just happened still pressing down on us.

Rohan glanced at us, then asked, *"Would you guys like anything? Water? Juice?"*

"Just water is fine," Daniyal said.

Rohan nodded.

"Alright. Water it is."

As he disappeared into the kitchen, Shiraz leaned toward us, whispering,

"I wouldn't mind a glass of juice..."

Daniyal shot him a look.

"Shut up."

Raghav chuckled under his breath.

A minute later, Rohan returned, placing four glasses of water on the table before sitting down with us.

We took small sips, still adjusting to the fact that the man in front of us was supposed to be dead.

Rohan leaned back slightly.

"Vivaan told me everything," he said.

"What you guys did... takes guts. Honestly, when I first heard about it, I didn't believe it. Pulling off something like that isn't child's play."

We exchanged brief glances, offering faint smiles in response, but no one spoke.

Then Raghav cleared his throat.

"Umm... sir, if you don't mind me asking, I have a question."

Rohan looked at him.

"Go ahead."

Raghav hesitated for a second before speaking.

"Before we talk about the university, I just... I need to know—what happened to you? After the article got published?"

For a moment, Rohan didn't answer.

He lowered his gaze, staring at the tiled floor as if trying to unearth a memory he had buried long ago.

When he finally spoke, his voice was steady, but his expression unreadable.

"I faced the same thing every other student from that academy did," he said.

"After the article went public, the university went straight for the channel I

worked at. My boss told me to take it down. Said it wasn't worth the trouble."
He exhaled sharply.
"But I couldn't do that. I wouldn't do that. I had already made my choice, and removing that article would've meant betraying everything I stood for."
A tense silence settled over the room.
"So I refused," he continued.
"And I lost my job."
The words hung in the air, heavy and sharp.
"Even then, I left the article up. I thought... I hoped the truth would be enough."
He gave a humourless chuckle.
"But the academy was far more powerful than I ever imagined. Somehow, they found a way to strip me of my home. Claimed it was illegal. That it never belonged to me in the first place."
Daniyal muttered something under his breath.
Shiraz just shook his head, stunned.
"I lost everything," Rohan said.
"My job. My home. My life."
His voice hardened.
"And still, it wasn't enough for them."
He ran a hand over his face, as if brushing away the remnants of his past.
"The threats started soon after. Not just against me, but against my friends. My family. They wanted to make sure no one ever heard from me again."
A chill ran through me.
"They tried to hunt me down," he continued, his voice quieter now.
"I knew they wouldn't stop until they erased every trace of me. So I did the only thing I could."
He looked up at us.
"I vanished."
The room felt colder.
"I travelled constantly, moving from city to city, staying in places where no one would think to look for me. Remote villages. Abandoned towns. I made sure I never left a trail."
He let out a slow breath.
"Eventually, things started to quiet down. I think they assumed I was dead. So I came here, to Dehradun."
Rohan gestured vaguely around the apartment.
"With whatever savings and investments I had left, I bought this place. Started over. I work at a small café two blocks from here. It's... enough."

We sat there, trying to process the weight of everything he had just told us. Shiraz finally spoke, his voice low.

"That... that must have been hell. I'm sorry you had to go through all that, sir."

Rohan gave a faint, almost tired smile.

"It wasn't easy."

He paused, then added,

"Even now, I can't risk seeing my family. If they find out I'm alive..."

His eyes darkened.

"I won't be for much longer."

A cold silence stretched between us.

For the first time since we had arrived, *I truly understood what we were up against.*

This wasn't just about uncovering secrets anymore.

This was survival.

CHAPTER THIRTY-SIX

SCRIPTED FOR POWER

Rohan exhaled, running a hand through his hair.

"Alright, that's enough about me. Let's get back to why you're here. What do you need to know? How can I help?"

Daniyal placed his half-empty glass of water on the table with a soft clink.

"Right. We want to understand how the university operates... how it manages to do what it does. You were the first to expose it, sir. You must know more than anyone."

Rohan studied us carefully, his gaze sharp, measuring.

"I know you've uncovered the hidden rooms and passages beneath the university," he said at last.

We all exchanged glances before nodding in agreement.

"Among those hidden places," Rohan continued, *"there is one that's more important than the rest. It's where they train the selected students. Where they brainwash them."*

A cold silence followed.

The words hung in the air, *heavy and unsettling.*

Aaron cleared his throat.

"But how? How does no one know about this?"

Rohan leaned back slightly.

"Because it's designed that way. The place itself is nearly impossible to find. And even if someone stumbles upon it, they make sure no one speaks about it. Not even in whispers."

I frowned.

"But sir... brainwashing is a psychological method. There has to be some kind of source. A technique. A tool. Something. How do they do it? What makes it so powerful?"

Rohan went silent.

A strange expression crossed his face—one that sent an uneasy feeling creeping up my spine.

Then, in a slow, measured voice, he said,

"I do have an answer. But trust me when I say... it's worse than you think. If you believe it's just psychology, what I'm about to tell you will make your soul shiver."

A wave of unease passed through the room.

Daniyal and Raghav exchanged wary glances, while Shiraz shifted uncomfortably.

For a second, no one spoke.

Then Shiraz broke the silence.

"Sir... we came here for the truth. Even if it terrifies us, we need to know."

Rohan watched us for a moment, then gave a small nod.

"You have guts. I respect that."

He stood up.

"I'll tell you. No—better yet, I'll show you."

With that, he turned and walked towards his bedroom.

Without hesitation, we followed.

Rohan led us into his bedroom, the air inside feeling strangely still.

He flicked on the lights, casting a dim yellow glow over the room.

It was simple, almost *too bare,* except for a large wooden cupboard against the far wall.

Without a word, he walked over, opened it, and reached inside.

His fingers felt around for something, then he pulled out a small, unmarked key.

He turned to his desk, crouched down, and unlocked one of the drawers.

As he slid it open, I caught a glimpse of what was inside—folders, photographs, stacks of old documents.

Carefully, Rohan retrieved a few of them and laid them out on the bed.

I stepped closer.

There were photos of people—men and women in expensive suits, standing on stages, giving speeches, shaking hands with world leaders.

Others sat in grand offices, their names engraved on golden plaques.

Some faces I recognized immediately—*powerful lawyers, business tycoons, politicians.*

All alumni of Blackstone Academy of Law.

At first, none of us spoke.

We didn't understand why Rohan had kept these.

Then Raghav broke the silence.

"What... what are these pictures? And these documents? What do they have to do with any of this?"
Rohan exhaled, tapping his fingers against one of the photos.
"Oh, trust me... they have everything to do with this."
His eyes flicked to each of us.
"Tell me—what were your first impressions of the university? Before all this. Why did you choose to study there?"
I hesitated, then answered,
"Well... for starters, it's the most prestigious law academy in the country. The best of the best come from there. Just like the people in these pictures."
I gestured at the documents.
"It was a dream academy for anyone who wanted a real shot at success."
Rohan gave a sharp nod.
"Exactly."
His voice turned low, almost grim.
"Now tell me—how do you think they manage to pull this off?"
Daniyal folded his arms.
"Let me guess. The brainwashing is connected to this, isn't it?"
Rohan gave a dry chuckle.
"You're catching on."
He sat down on the edge of the bed, rubbing his temple.
"But it's not just brainwashing. It's more than that. You see, it took me a whole year to piece this together. I studied the university's history, tracked down every alumnus who became powerful, and analysed their rise to success."
He lifted a photograph of a man in a black suit, standing beside a judge.
"And do you know what's common among all of them?"
We waited.
"They don't care about morals. They don't care about ethics. They don't care about the right way to live. To them, the only thing that matters is power. And in their world, defeat is the ultimate humiliation."
A heavy silence followed.
"I started noticing this pattern," Rohan continued.
"I researched every possible psychological method, read over a hundred books. And still... I found nothing that could explain how the university does it."
He took a breath.
His voice dropped lower.
"But then, finally—I did find something."
Something in his tone made my skin prickle.

Rohan reached over and pointed at the page in Raghav's hands.

Raghav frowned.

"It's just a page with some writing..."

Rohan's expression darkened.

"It's a printed page from an ancient Greek text. The Silent Gospel of Nyx."

The name alone sent a strange chill through the room.

None of us had heard of it.

But somehow, *it didn't sound good.*

Not at all.

CHAPTER THIRTY-SEVEN

THE SILENT GOSPEL OF NYX

Before Rohan could continue, Daniyal raised a hand.

"Wait. Mythology?"

He frowned, shaking his head.

"You're saying a brainwashing technique is based on mythology? That doesn't make any sense."

Rohan exhaled, rubbing his temples as if he had expected this reaction.

"I thought so too," he admitted.

"At first, it sounded ridiculous. But the deeper I went into it, the more I realized—this matches the university's pattern perfectly."

We exchanged uncertain glances.

"Hear me out," Rohan continued.

"To some anthropologists and mythologists, this is just hogwash. They don't believe in it at all. But... there are others who claim it's real. Very real."

He picked up the page again, his fingers tightening around the edges.

"This text—The Silent Gospel of Nyx—has been whispered about for centuries."

Something about the name sent a cold wave through my body.

Rohan leaned forward, his voice steady but low.

"It's an ancient text, supposedly written in the 6th century BCE, during the rise of the Greek city-states. Some say it was created for an elite order of rulers, strategists, and warlords—people who wanted to transcend human limitations and become immortalized through dominance and success."

I felt my breathing slow.

"The text is attributed to an unnamed philosopher and military tactician. A man who claimed to be a disciple of Nyx, the primordial goddess of the night. His writings were considered so radical—so dangerous—that Athenian authorities

erased all records of his existence."
The room felt smaller.
"Some versions of the text resurfaced centuries later in Rome," Rohan went on, his eyes dark and serious.
"There were rumours that Julius Caesar himself studied its principles before his rise to power. And after his assassination, the Senate ordered all copies of the book to be burned, fearing that its teachings had corrupted him."
Silence.
I could hear the ticking of the clock on the wall, the distant hum of traffic outside.
"But it didn't die," Rohan said.
"The Gospel has always resurfaced. Whispers of it have passed through the ears of rulers, warlords, even corporate elites. And some believe..."
He paused.
"That its teachings are still shaping the world today."
I clenched my jaw.
This wasn't just psychological manipulation.
It wasn't just mind games.
It was *something else entirely.*
Raghav swallowed hard.
"So... you're saying the university is using this book to shape the minds of selected students?"
Rohan leaned back, rubbing his eyes.
"What I'm saying is—this matches the pattern perfectly."
None of us spoke.
I had thought we had seen everything.
That we had uncovered every secret, stared into the darkest parts of the university.
But this?
This was something we couldn't even begin to imagine.
Even in our nightmares.
The air in Rohan's room felt dense, like something invisible was pressing down on us.
No one spoke.
No one moved.
But Daniyal—somehow—stayed composed.
His expression didn't change, his voice steady when he finally broke the silence.

"Okay. Let's say this is true," he said.
"Then what else can you tell us about the book?"
Rohan exhaled slowly.
"Well... according to what I've learned, The Silent Gospel of Nyx isn't just some forgotten myth. It's a guide—a blueprint for achieving absolute power."
I frowned.
"A guide?"
"Yes. It doesn't preach faith or devotion like religious texts. Instead, it teaches how to rise above morality, shed weakness, and dominate at any cost. It's believed to have been written for an elite order of rulers, strategists, and warlords who wanted to transcend human limitations."
Raghav inhaled sharply.
"What do you mean?"
Rohan leaned forward.
"The book has three major stages."
His tone was different now—*like even speaking about it carried a weight of its own.*
"The first stage is called The Doctrine of Supremacy."
Morality is a cage for the weak.
Ethics and compassion slow down those destined to rule.
Success belongs to those who take it.
Mercy breeds debt; fear breeds respect.
True leaders never hesitate.
Power is not inherited—it is seized.
I felt my stomach twist.
Raghav shifted uncomfortably.
"This... this is insane."
Rohan continued, his voice steady but grave.
"The second stage is The Three Laws of Power."
The Law of the Unshakable Mind — To rule, one must be immune to guilt, hesitation, and empathy.
The Law of the Expendable — Allies are tools. The moment they lose value, they are a liability.
The Law of Absolute Will — Reality belongs to those who impose their will. The weak follow: the strong kneel—or they disappear.
I clenched my fists.
"And the final stage?"
Rohan exhaled, his expression dark.

"The last part is what makes this even more disturbing."
The Ritual of Self-Divinity.
We waited, but none of us were ready for what he was about to say.
"This final stage... teaches how to sever all attachments. To become more than human."
Destroy all moral anchors—family, love, regret.
See people only as assets or obstacles.
Immortality is achieved through dominance—those who control history never die.
A sickening dread settled in my chest.
"People who read about this claim it changes them," Rohan murmured.
"They start seeing others as pawns, not equals. Success stops feeling like a goal—it becomes a necessity. Any action, no matter how ruthless, feels justified."
I swallowed hard.
"Some say they lost all emotional connections," he continued,
"that they stopped feeling guilt. Hesitation. Remorse."
"This is complete madness," I whispered.
"All of this... just so the university can produce powerful alumni? Just so they can take credit?"
Rohan let out a bitter laugh.
"I know. But we don't have a choice. The university is too powerful. If you try to go to the police or any higher authority, they'll buy them off in seconds. No evidence. No reports. No case."
His expression turned grim.
"And if they find out we know this? They won't spare us."
The room fell into silence again.
We looked at each other, and for the first time, despite finally getting all the answers we had been searching for...
We realized we were completely trapped.
For the first time, we weren't just afraid of what the university had done.
We were afraid of what it might do next.
But we couldn't just sit here.
We had to do something.

CHAPTER THIRTY-EIGHT

BEFORE IT BREAKS

As we stepped out of Rohan's bedroom and into the dimly lit hallway, a heavy silence lingered between us.

The weight of everything we had just learned pressed down like an unseen force, thick and suffocating.

The floorboards creaked under our footsteps as we made our way back to the living room.

Shiraz, who had been unusually quiet, finally spoke up.

His voice was steady, but there was an edge to it.

"We're involved in this now, aren't we?" he asked, glancing at Rohan.

"If we try to dig deeper, if we push forward, we know exactly what we're getting ourselves into, right?"

Rohan exhaled, his gaze unreadable.

"It's a possibility," he admitted.

"But think about it—there may have been students before you who figured out pieces of this, just like you have. Maybe they didn't know the methods, maybe they didn't see the full picture... but they knew something."

His expression darkened.

"And yet, you don't hear about them, do you? You don't know their names. You don't know if they ever existed."

A chill ran down my spine.

He had a point.

A disturbing, undeniable point.

Shiraz clenched his jaw, but he didn't respond.

None of us did.

Because the alternative—acknowledging what must have happened to those students—was a thought we weren't ready to confront.

I cleared my throat.

"Then what is the way out?" I asked.

"Sir, if we figure out a way to expose them... and if that requires your help... would you stand with us?"

Rohan didn't answer immediately.

He sat down on the edge of the couch, rubbing a hand over his face, lost in thought.

Then, with a weary sigh, he said,

"I don't know, Aaron. The last time I tried to fight this... it didn't end well for me."

I refused to let that be his final answer.

"Sir," I pressed, stepping closer.

"If we figure this out, if we pull this off, you could go back to the life you left behind. The life that mattered to you the most."

Rohan's fingers curled slightly, as if the thought of his past life still had a grip on him.

But instead of answering, he looked at me with something close to regret.

"And what if you fail?" he murmured.

"Then what happens?"

The question hung in the air, heavy and unshakable.

Daniyal stepped in, his voice unwavering.

"If we fail... if we get exposed during the confrontation, we promise you—no matter what, we won't let your life get affected. At least not this one."

Rohan looked up at us then, scanning each of our faces, as if trying to measure whether we truly understood the risk we were taking.

And for a long, tense moment, he said nothing.

Then, finally, he let out a slow breath and leaned back.

"...Alright," he said.

"I'll be a part of this. I'll help you."

Relief washed over me, but it was short-lived.

"But remember this," Rohan continued, his voice dropping lower.

"It's not just my life on the line. It's all of yours. And not just you—but your closest ones, too."

He leaned forward, eyes locked onto us.

"You've got guts. I'll give you that. But courage alone won't save you. If you're going to do this, you need to plan everything down to the last detail. No mistakes. No reckless moves. Understood?"

We exchanged glances, the weight of his words settling in.

Then, as one, we nodded.

"Don't worry, sir," Raghav said.
"We'll make sure of it."
Rohan didn't say anything, but after a moment, he gave a small nod—just a faint, tired smile ghosting across his face.
Without another word, we stood.
Rohan walked us to the door, pausing just before opening it.
For a second, I thought he was going to say something else.
Some final warning.
Some last bit of advice.
But he didn't.
He just opened the door.
And as we stepped out into the night, the cold air hitting my skin, I realized something.
There was no turning back now.
We didn't talk.
There was nothing left to say—not right now.
The moment we stepped out of Rohan's place, we booked a cab and headed straight to our hotel.
The drive was silent, the city lights blurring past as my mind replayed every word spoken in that room.
By the time we arrived, exhaustion pressed down on me, but my thoughts wouldn't slow.
We filled out the formalities at the reception without a word, moving like ghosts through the lobby.
Even dinner felt mechanical.
We ate just enough to keep ourselves going, our minds elsewhere.
An hour later, we finally made it to our rooms.
The air inside was cool, sterile, a stark contrast to the weight I carried in my chest.
Without a second thought, I grabbed my towel and stepped into the shower.
The moment the water hit my skin, a deep breath escaped me.
Steam curled around me, rising in soft waves, condensing against the glass.
Droplets cascaded down my back, tracing over the tense muscles that had been wound tight all day.
I ran my hands through my hair, letting the water wash away the remnants of exhaustion, but it couldn't rinse away the thoughts.
Rohan's words played in my head like a loop.
There may have been students before you who figured things out... yet, you don't

hear about them, do you?

I exhaled sharply, pressing my hands against the cold tiles.

What if we ended up like them?

What if we were already too deep?

The steam thickened, wrapping around me like a suffocating fog.

I closed my eyes, willing myself to push the thoughts aside.

Fear had no place here—not now.

Not when we were this close to something bigger than ourselves.

The water cooled slightly, snapping me back.

With one last rinse, I stepped out, running a towel through my slick hair.

The mirror was fogged, my own reflection barely visible—almost like a reminder that I was losing myself to something I still didn't fully understand.

By the time I returned to the room, the others had settled in.

No one looked ready to sleep.

We sat in a quiet circle, the weight of the night still hanging over us.

Raghav broke the silence first.

"So... we're flying back to Nagpur tomorrow, huh?"

Shiraz leaned back against the headboard, sighing.

"A shame, really. We came all the way here and didn't even get to see the city."

Daniyal scoffed.

"We don't have time to think about that. We've got much bigger problems."

I nodded.

"I agree. And I'm afraid we can't come up with a foolproof plan right away. There's too much to consider. Like Rohan said—there can't be any mistakes. One wrong move, and we're caught. And if that happens..."

I hesitated.

"God knows what they'll do to us."

Raghav let out a humourless chuckle.

"Well, there goes the Dehradun vibe Shiraz was trying to build up."

"Touche," Shiraz muttered.

Daniyal shot him a tired, unimpressed look, raising an eyebrow as he shook his head in disappointment.

I sighed, rubbing my face.

"Sleep. All of you. We're in the endgame now."

No one argued.

One by one, they pulled their blankets over themselves, letting the exhaustion take over.

I lay down, staring at the ceiling, listening to the slow, steady rhythm of my friends' breathing as sleep pulled them under.
Tomorrow, we'd be back in Nagpur.
Back in the heart of it all.
And the real battle would begin.

CHAPTER THIRTY-NINE

THE QUITE SIEGE

The morning sun stretched across Dehradun, casting a golden hue over the misty hills.

The air was crisp, carrying the scent of pine and damp earth, a stark contrast to the weight on our minds.

The roads, lined with towering deodar trees, shimmered in the soft light as the city stirred awake.

Birds flitted between branches, their calls distant, almost lost beneath the hum of early morning traffic.

The sight should have been calming, but to us, *it was nothing more than the backdrop to an impending war.*

We checked out of the hotel in silence.

No unnecessary words, no distractions.

As soon as we stepped outside, we hailed a cab straight to the airport.

The journey was quiet, each of us lost in our own thoughts.

The occasional honk of a passing vehicle barely registered.

Even the grandeur of the mountains slipping away behind us felt insignificant.

By the time we reached the airport, the terminal was buzzing with travellers.

Announcements echoed through the speakers, yet we moved mechanically—checking in, passing security, and making our way to the boarding gate.

The minutes blurred.

Soon, we were walking down the jet bridge, stepping onto the plane that would take us back to Nagpur.

I settled into my seat, glancing at the others.

No one spoke.

No one even closed their eyes.

Sleep had no place here.

My thoughts spiralled, trying to weave together a plan—something airtight, something that would ensure we weren't walking into our own graves.

Expose them. But how?

Maybe we could gather concrete proof—record conversations, steal documents.

No.

They would have countermeasures in place.

The university had survived for too long without slipping up.

There was no way they'd leave behind evidence that easy to obtain.

Maybe we could go public—leak the truth to the media, force them into the spotlight.

But that required credibility.

Who would believe a handful of students over an institution backed by power and influence?

Maybe we could find someone higher up, someone outside their grasp who could intervene.

But if the university had the means to silence its own students, what were the chances they didn't have a grip on officials too?

Each idea felt weaker than the last, crumbling before it even had the chance to form.

I clenched my fists.

There had to be a way. We just hadn't found it yet.

The hours slipped by unnoticed.

Before we knew it, the seatbelt sign blinked on, and the captain's voice crackled through the speakers, announcing our descent.

Nagpur loomed below, sprawling and sunlit, oblivious to the storm that was about to unfold within its walls.

Touchdown.

We moved through the airport in silence, grabbing our luggage, weaving through the crowds until the exit doors slid open before us.

A hot gust of wind greeted me.

The moment my feet hit the pavement, I took a slow, deep breath.

Nagpur.

We were back.

There were still ten days left before the holidays got over.

Ten days to decide everything.

Our fate. The university's fate.
A gamble with only two outcomes—*victory or destruction.*
Wasting no time, we hailed a taxi.
The city blurred past us as we drove through familiar roads, the weight in my chest growing heavier with every kilometre.
Thirty minutes later, we arrived at the university gates.
The sight of it—so still, so deceptively normal—sent a shiver down my spine.
Daniyal handed the driver the fare and turned to us.
"You know what to do. Go to your dorms. Meet at the grove in an hour."
We nodded.
No further words were needed.
One hour.
And then, the real war would begin.
Raghav and I dropped our bags in the room without a word.
We didn't even sit down.
The air inside the dorm felt heavy, like a reminder of how much had changed since we left.
Without discussing it, we stepped back out and headed toward the cafeteria to grab a quick bite.
The hallways were eerily silent.
No echo of footsteps, no laughter.
It felt like walking through the ruins of a once-bustling world.
The university still had ten days of holidays left.
Most students had returned home, their lives temporarily suspended for family, for freedom.
But us?
We were knee-deep in something we didn't sign up for—something bigger, darker.
I glanced at Raghav, who looked around too, a frown settling on his face.
We were both wondering the same thing: *What if none of this had happened?*
What would our lives look like right now?
Probably carefree.
Probably happy.
But there was no time for 'what ifs' anymore.
We walked into the cafeteria, picked up something quick—half-eaten sandwiches, two cups of watered-down coffee—and headed out again.
The food didn't matter.

Our minds were elsewhere.

The walk to the Grove felt longer than usual.

Not because of the distance, but because of the thoughts clouding our heads.

Plans.

Theories.

Possibilities.

Every idea I had felt like a dead end.

I tried thinking about how we could expose them—go public, leak documents, use hidden cameras—but every path led to the same brutal conclusion: *They'd find us. Silence us.*

How do you fight something that doesn't play by any rules?

When we reached the Grove, it was deserted—just like we expected.

Even so, it looked different in winter.

The leaves had thinned out, the trees looked lean and bony, almost like skeletons rising from the frost-covered ground.

The sky above was pale and steel-blue, and the cold had settled into everything: the benches, the bark, the earth.

The wind wasn't strong, but it was just sharp enough to sting.

We took our usual places in silence, as if drawn to them by instinct.

I stared out at the horizon, the bare branches swaying slightly, like they were whispering secrets we couldn't quite hear.

Even thinking hurt at this point.

A few minutes passed.

No words.

No ideas.

Just the soft rustle of wind and the occasional crunch of dead leaves.

Then Daniyal and Shiraz arrived.

Even they didn't say anything—just sat down in their usual spots like actors falling into place for a play none of us remembered auditioning for.

For a while, nobody broke the silence.

And then Raghav let out a frustrated sigh, throwing a pebble toward a patch of dry grass.

"This is insane," he muttered.

"We've been thinking for days—weeks—and yet we've got nothing. If it keeps going like this, then everything we've uncovered so far? It's worthless. Absolutely worthless."

Daniyal looked up slowly.

"I might have something," he said, hesitantly.

Shiraz leaned forward.

"But?"

Daniyal hesitated again.

His jaw clenched slightly. *"But... it doesn't just involve us."*

CHAPTER FORTY

THE CALL UNMADE

"What do you mean it doesn't just involve us anymore?" I asked, narrowing my eyes at Daniyal.

He didn't answer immediately. Instead, he looked out toward the trees—bare, still, and breathless—as if weighing the consequences of his own thoughts before giving them shape.

"Think about it, Aaron," he finally said. "Everything we've done so far—it was about us. About our questions. Our suspicions. We chased ghosts, uncovered lies, dug through the dirt of this place... but it was all to make sense of it ourselves."

He paused, his voice low but firm. "What we're about to do now... it's bigger than any of that. This isn't just about uncovering secrets anymore. This is about shaking the very roots of an institution that's far more powerful than we realize."

Shiraz crossed his arms. "I get that, but that's the whole point. They're untouchable. So far, we haven't seen anyone—anyone—with even half the power to take them on. Where exactly are you going to find that?"

Daniyal turned toward us, a strange fire in his eyes. "There is one. Every state has its own intelligence unit. Maharashtra has the MBI—Maharashtra Bureau of Intelligence. They're the only people I know who can't be bought, bribed, or bullied by institutions like this. If we're serious about bringing the truth out... we need a power bigger than Blackstone itself. And that's them."

There was a brief silence.

Then Raghav leaned back, looking half-sceptical, half-stunned. "Okay, I'm not saying your ideas are always extreme, but this one? It's borderline insane. Even if we entertain the possibility, we'd have to confirm whether involving them is even doable. And for that... we'd need Rohan."

"Exactly," I said, already pulling my phone out. "Let's talk to him before we run with this. If there's anyone who'd know how deep this can go, it's him."

I stared at the phone screen for a moment, hovering over his contact's name.

My thumb hesitated, just for a second, and then I hit the call button.

This wasn't just another step forward.

This... was a leap into something far more dangerous than we'd ever imagined.

The phone rang.

We had it on speaker, all of us hunched in a tight circle around it like we were waiting to hear from a prophet.

One ring. Two. Three.

Each second of silence stretched longer than the last. And just when I thought he wouldn't pick up—

Click.

"Hello?"

A familiar voice. Calm, alert, a little groggy, maybe. It was Rohan.

"Sir, this is Aaron," I said, straightening up a little.

"Yes, Aaron. Tell me."

"Actually... it's something Daniyal thought of. We didn't want to move forward without you knowing."

"Alright. Let's hear it."

So, we laid it out. Everything.

Daniyal took the lead, explaining the MBI angle, how this had gone beyond us, beyond the walls of the university. We were out of options, we needed a power greater than theirs, and the state intelligence bureau felt like the only card left to play.

When the explanation ended, no one said anything for a few seconds.

Then Rohan's voice came through again, low and contemplative.

"Well... he's not wrong."

A beat of silence.

"If you look at it practically, they're probably your only shot at surviving this clean. You'll definitely need someone like them on your side now."

Shiraz jumped in. "But that's the thing, sir—we don't even know how to reach out to people like that. How do we even begin?"

Rohan let out a dry chuckle. "Boys... even I can't help you there. Getting in touch with someone inside the state's intelligence wing isn't like ordering a cup of coffee. These people don't exactly advertise themselves."

Another silence. This time heavier.

Then he spoke again.

"Aaron, Vivaan told me that your father runs one of the biggest consultancy firms in Gujarat. A pretty influential man, if I remember correctly."

I felt my stomach drop before he even finished the sentence.

"Yeah," I muttered. "He is. Quite powerful."

"Then contact him. I'm sure he can get you connected. You just have to figure out how to bring it up."

I hesitated. My throat went dry.

"I don't know if I can, sir. We... haven't really spoken in a long time. And to be honest, I don't think we've ever had the best father-son dynamic."

Rohan paused, then spoke, slower this time. Softer. Like he knew exactly where I was coming from.

"Hmm. Been there."

He let those words hang in the air before continuing.

"Listen to me, Aaron. I know it's not easy. But sometimes, moments like these... they're not just about fixing a problem in front of you—they're a chance to heal what's been broken behind you too. I know you think he doesn't care. That maybe he's never cared. But just try talking to him. You might be surprised by what you find."

I didn't say anything right away. My heart was pounding a little harder than usual.

"Okay," I said finally. "I'll try."

"Good. Call me when you have something solid. I'll be waiting."

Click.

The line went dead.

I stared at the screen, but I wasn't really seeing it. I was back in Vapi. I was standing in our living room, tense and bitter, throwing words at him like daggers. I remembered his face—angry, disappointed, silent. The last conversation we'd had was less of a conversation and more of a battle.

And now I had to call him. Ask him for help.

Not for myself. But for something far bigger.

I swallowed hard.

Maybe Rohan was right. Maybe this wasn't just about the university anymore.

Maybe it was about fixing the boy I used to be.

Either way, I knew what I had to do.

And it started with a phone call I'd been avoiding for years.

CHAPTER FORTY-ONE

AT LAST, HEARD

The screen was still lit, the call log glowing faintly in my hand.

Rohan's number stared back at me like an unanswered question—*no, like a wound I hadn't let heal.*

I didn't move.

The wind rustled through the grove, making the branches above us whisper like they knew something I didn't.

Daniyal, Shiraz, and Raghav were all watching me now—waiting, hoping, maybe even praying I'd do what needed to be done.

But I just stood there.

The weight of the phone felt unnatural in my hand, like it didn't belong to me anymore.

Like it had become something else—a bridge I wasn't ready to cross.

"Bro," Raghav said, his voice breaking through the silence, gentle but impatient. *"What are you waiting for? Call him."*

I didn't reply.

I couldn't.

My throat felt like it had been sewn shut.

I kept staring at the screen like the numbers might rearrange themselves and disappear, freeing me from the choice.

But they didn't.

"I... I can't," I said finally, my voice barely audible. *"I can't. I'm not ready."*

Shiraz took a step closer.

"Aaron, you have to," he said firmly. *"This isn't about just you anymore. This is bigger than your past. It's our only chance. You know that."*

I clenched the phone tighter, my fingers trembling now.

And then—without warning—I snapped.

"I SAID I CAN'T!" I shouted, the words bursting out of me like they'd been

caged for years. *"I'll do it when I'm ready!"*
The silence that followed was deafening.
No one said anything.
They didn't have to.
I wasn't angry—I was breaking.
And they saw that.
Before anyone could stop me, I turned and ran.
I didn't think.
I didn't look back.
I didn't care where they were or what they were saying.
I just ran.
Through the grove, past the trees, across the path we'd walked together only minutes ago—my feet pounding the earth like I was trying to outrun everything that had ever hurt me.
The words.
The silence.
The look in my father's eyes that night in Vapi.
The memory of walking out, thinking I'd never need him again.
I didn't stop until I reached the dorm.
And even then, I didn't breathe.
Because this wasn't just about making a call.
It was about facing someone I'd spent my whole life trying not to become.
And I wasn't ready for that.
Not yet.
Raghav came back to the dorm a few minutes after I did.
I heard the door click softly behind him, and for a second, I thought he might say something.
He didn't.
He walked past me, calm as ever, and dropped onto his bed without a word.
The mattress creaked under his weight, followed by the faint tapping of his fingers as he started scrolling through his phone.
No sighs.
No glances.
No questions.
He knew.
He knew that right now, anything he said would only scrape at a wound that was still bleeding.
So, he gave me the silence I didn't know I needed.

The hours that followed passed like a blur, slow and strangely hollow.

We didn't talk.

We didn't even make eye contact.

Just existed in the same space, orbiting around each other like two planets caught in the same lonely gravity.

I flipped through pages of a book I wasn't reading.

He watched reels he probably wasn't watching.

Every few minutes, I'd check the time without registering the numbers.

The sky outside turned from gold to grey to black.

Eventually, I stood up and left the room without a word, heading down to the cafeteria.

We didn't go together this time.

I didn't ask him, and he didn't ask me.

Dinner was quiet.

A few scattered students lingered in the hall, murmuring over trays and half-finished conversations.

The clatter of spoons and trays echoed louder than usual.

I ate alone, the food tasteless, my thoughts louder than everything else.

By the time I came back to the dorm, Raghav was still out.

I sat by the window, the night pressing up against the glass.

Somewhere in the trees beyond, I imagined Daniyal and Shiraz still sitting there, wondering what the hell had gotten into me.

I didn't blame them.

I barely understood it myself.

Minutes passed.

Maybe more.

Then the door creaked open.

Raghav walked in, holding a brown tray with whatever was left of his dinner.

He didn't look surprised to see me sitting in the dark.

He didn't say anything either.

Just placed his tray down, sat, and ate in silence.

I got up, grabbed my hoodie from the hook behind the door, and slipped it on.

The fabric was cool against my skin—*familiar, grounding.*

"I'm going out for a walk," I said, my voice quiet, almost distant.

Then I opened the door and stepped out, leaving the room—and everything in it—behind for a while.

The cold night curled around me like a second skin.

My breath fogged the air in front of me as I walked without purpose, the silence louder than anything.

Lights along the path fought against the creeping mist, casting halos through the thickening fog.

But I didn't see any of it.

I wasn't walking.

I was drifting.

And then, without realizing, my feet had brought me back to the grove.

Of course. It had to be here.

Like the universe wasn't done with me yet—like it was standing here, waiting, arms crossed, reminding me there was still something I hadn't faced.

I stood in the middle of it all, staring into the nothingness, then pulled out my phone.

One touch.

His name was still there in the log.

A name I hadn't called in months.

I stared at it for a moment—just stared—then tapped.

It started ringing.

I didn't even know what I was going to say.

All the things I'd rehearsed in my head over the past few weeks—gone.

All I had now were fractured thoughts and the kind of fear that sits heavy in your gut.

Then—his voice.

"Hello?"

I almost froze.

Almost.

"Hey, Dad. Are you busy?"

"I'm always busy. What is it? What happened?"

Still sharp.

Still distant.

I swallowed, then said, *"I need your help."*

Silence.

A scoff.

"My help? You've made it very clear you don't need me. What happened to all that pride, huh? That bold little speech of yours?"

I clenched my teeth.

"Yeah. I remember what I said. And I meant it. But right now... I need to put all

that aside."

He didn't say anything.

So I kept going.

"Because something's happened. Something bigger than me, bigger than us. And I don't know who else to go to. I'm asking you because I don't have anyone else."

I paused, took a breath, then said the words like I was pulling them out of my own throat.

"I need you to get me in touch with someone from the State Department of Intelligence."

"What?" he snapped. *"Are you insane?"*

"No. I'm not." My voice cracked a little.

"I know how this sounds. But I'm telling you, I'm not playing games. I'm not being reckless. I'm not being dramatic. This is serious. And the only way out of this mess—this madness—is through someone like them."

"Are you in trouble?" he asked, tone shifting.

I almost laughed.

"Trouble? No, Dad. I'm in the middle of something I can't even begin to explain."

"And I know—I know—how I've come across to you my whole life. A rebel. A disappointment. The kid who had the world handed to him and still walked away. But I'm telling you... this isn't about me."

My hands were shaking.

I didn't even realize it until the phone nearly slipped from my grip.

"I don't care if you don't respect me. I don't care if you never understood my choices. But right now, for just one goddamn moment, I need you to listen to me—not as a businessman, not as the man who built everything I walked away from—but as my father. Please. I'm asking you... as your son."

There was silence.

Then I said the words that hurt more than I thought they would.

"I know I've never been the son you wanted. I know that when you look at me, you see a failure—a waste. You gave me everything, and I gave it all up. That's on me. And I'm not here to fix all of that with one phone call. But I'm standing here, asking for your help, because I don't know where else to turn."

The silence on the other end was heavy.

Like even he didn't know how to respond.

"And I don't want someone from Gujarat," I added. *"It has to be Maharashtra. Please. That part is important."*

He didn't speak.

I almost thought he hung up.

But then I heard a long breath.

A pause.

And finally—

"...Okay. Give me a day. I'll see what I can do."

I blinked, stunned.

"Really?"

"Yeah," he said quietly. *"Really."*

Just as I was about to thank him and hang up, his voice stopped me.

"Wait."

I stayed silent.

"The holidays are going on. Why aren't you home, Aaron? Is it because of me?"

His voice was softer now.

Hesitant.

"Is it because I told you not to come back?"

Still, I said nothing.

He continued, almost in a whisper,

"I know I was harsh. I know I pushed you away. But you need to understand—I did what I did because I thought I was building something for you. I created an empire... your empire. And when you rejected it, yeah, I was angry. But now? I get it. You're chasing something real. And you're stronger than I thought."

A lump rose in my throat.

"I was wrong," he said.

"You're not a disappointment. You never were. You're my son, Aaron. My greatest achievement. And if you ever change your mind, if you ever want to turn that dream into a firm—my offer still stands. It's all yours. Just... come home sometimes. If not for me, at least for your mother. She misses you. More than either of us can say."

My lips parted, but nothing came out.

"I'll call you tomorrow," he said.

"I have a meeting. Goodbye."

And then—he was gone.

I didn't move.

Didn't breathe.

Didn't even blink.

I just stood there, phone still in my hand, heart pounding like a drum left out in the rain.

My legs gave way, and I leaned back against the tree behind me, looking up at the fog-covered stars like they might make sense of the storm inside my chest.

That voice.

Those words.

All my life, I'd waited to hear something like that.

And I didn't even know how much I needed them until they were spoken.

THE FUSE IS LIT

I was still leaning against the tree in the grove, the cool bark pressing into my back as the weight of the night sank in.

My mind was a storm—one I couldn't quite silence.

Everything felt heavier now.

I had come here to breathe, but instead, I was drowning in thoughts I couldn't untangle.

Then came a voice from behind me, calm yet piercing.

"It's a different feeling, isn't it? Hearing the one thing you've always wanted to hear."

I spun around, suddenly alert—but then, just as quickly, I felt the tension melt away.

Daniyal.

He stepped closer, hands tucked casually in his pockets, as if he'd just wandered over by accident.

"How did you find me?" I asked, still surprised.

He gave a half-smirk.

"I had a feeling you'd be here."

I raised an eyebrow.

That wasn't an answer—and he knew it.

He sighed.

"Alright, alright. Raghav told me you went out for a walk. This seemed like the kind of place you'd end up."

Fair enough.

He joined me without another word, resting against the same tree, the silence settling comfortably between us for a moment.

"So.. how did it go?" he asked quietly, eyes fixed ahead.

I didn't answer right away.

How did it go?
I wasn't sure I had the words yet.
"Let's just say... it wasn't what I expected."
He glanced sideways at me.
"Yeah, I can tell from your face."
Then a beat passed.
"Will he help us?"
I nodded slowly.
"He said to wait till tomorrow. He'll see what he can do."
Daniyal let out a breath.
"So we wait."
"Yeah. We wait."
There was something oddly comforting in that—in not having to chase.
Not just yet.
Daniyal pushed himself off the tree, dusting his hands.
"Alright. Ready to head back?"
"Yeah," I said, voice low.
We started walking.
Back under the scattered lights of the campus, the silence between us wasn't awkward.
It was a shared pause.
Like we both knew the gravity of what came next.
As we reached the dormitory block, Daniyal gave me a small nod and split off toward his room.
I walked alone to mine.
When I opened the door, the room was dark except for the faint glow of the streetlight bleeding through the curtain.
Raghav was already asleep, one leg kicked over the blanket, breathing softly.
I didn't say anything.
Just slipped off my shoes, climbed into bed, and stared at the ceiling for a while.
Tomorrow, I thought.
We wait.
Then, finally—
Sleep found me.
I slept better than I had in days.
The kind of sleep where everything goes still—no thoughts, no dreams, just silence.

But like all good things, it ended far too soon.

My alarm blared into the calmness like a slap, dragging me out of the peaceful void.

8:00 AM.

Too early.

But I didn't mind.

Not today.

There was still a lingering lightness in my chest—something left over from last night.

Not hope exactly, but something close enough.

The feeling hadn't faded.

And I wasn't ready to let it go just yet.

Raghav, unsurprisingly, was still dead to the world.

That guy could probably sleep through an earthquake.

I didn't bother waking him.

Instead, I got dressed, laced up my shoes, and slipped out into the morning air.

The gym was quiet.

A few regulars were scattered around, lost in their own routines.

I worked up a decent sweat before heading out for a run.

The breeze was cool, the sky a muted grey, and the campus was still half-asleep—exactly how I liked it.

After the run, I ended up shooting hoops with a couple of students who, like me, hadn't gone home for the break.

We didn't talk much—just passed, dribbled, and let the rhythm of the game do the talking.

For a moment, it felt like normal life.

No secrets.

No university conspiracies.

Just the thud of the ball against the court.

By the time I was done, two hours had passed.

I headed to the cafeteria, ordered a solid breakfast for myself, and asked for an extra plate—one I knew I'd have to personally deliver if I wanted it eaten.

When I got back to the room, sure enough, Raghav was still curled up like a hibernating bear.

I placed the plate on his desk, stood over him, and nudged his shoulder.

Nothing.

I shook him harder.

Still nothing.

Finally, I yanked his blanket off.

"Wake up, you idiot—it's 10:30!"

He groaned like I'd committed a war crime.

"Ugh... what?"

"Breakfast is on your desk. Get up and eat before I throw it out."

That got his attention.

He blinked at me through half-closed eyes, then sat up, groggy but grateful.

"You're a lifesaver, man. I knew I could count on you."

We sat in the quiet as he dug into his food.

I told him everything—what happened last night, what was said, what wasn't.

I didn't dramatize it.

I just laid it all out.

Raghav wiped his mouth with the back of his hand and looked at me.

"So... we just wait now?"

I nodded.

"Yeah. Just wait."

Funny how that word used to feel like a delay.

Now, it felt like a fuse.

After breakfast, the day drifted by in slow motion.

Raghav and I were slouched in the dorm, phones in hand, laptops open, switching between games, random YouTube videos, and completely pointless scrolling.

The kind of lazy afternoon that feels both relaxing and slightly suffocating.

A few hours passed like that—barely a word exchanged between us—until Raghav suddenly paused and blurted out,

"Bro... tell me something. Do you ever feel like having a girlfriend?"

I paused the game, raised an eyebrow, and glanced over at him.

"What?"

"I mean, c'mon," he shrugged.

"We're in university, man. People expect that kinda thing, don't they?"

I leaned back, letting the controller drop on my lap.

"Honestly? I never really thought about it. Since the moment we stepped foot here, we've been drowning in this mess. There hasn't exactly been time for romance."

He nodded, eyes still on his screen.

"Yeah, same. But don't you think we should? Like, doesn't it ever cross your

mind?"
I thought for a second, then shook my head.
"Right now, my life is a ticking bomb. I can't afford distractions—not even good ones. So no, I'm good. What about you?"
"Pretty much the same," he said.
"Stuck in the same storm as you."
He paused, then gave me a sideways glance.
"But hey... did you ever have a girlfriend? Like, before all this?"
I chuckled quietly.
"Not exactly a girlfriend. But yeah... there was someone."
Raghav perked up immediately.
"Oh ho? Do tell."
"We were more like friends, really. I had a crush on her. She probably had no idea. I never told her. And before I got the chance... she moved to Bangalore for her studies, and I ended up here."
He clicked his tongue.
"Man, that sucks."
"Nah," I smiled faintly.
"Even if I had told her, it wouldn't have worked out. Life had other plans. It's all good."
I leaned forward, resting my elbows on my knees.
"Okay, now you. Don't pretend like you haven't had anyone."
Raghav grinned—the kind of grin that screamed confidence overload.
"Hell yeah. Of course, I have."
"Seriously?"
"Yup. We were together for about a year and a half. She was amazing—smart, fun, everything. But long distance eventually did its thing, and we broke up."
I gave him a nod of respect.
"Sorry it didn't work out."
"Don't be. It made sense at the time. We ended on good terms. She's doing great. And honestly, I still think she was one of the best things that happened to me."
Just as I was about to respond, my phone buzzed.
Dad.
I picked up.
"Yes, Dad?"
His voice came through firm, as always.
"Aaron, I've found someone who might be able to help. He's a senior officer with the MBI. I'm sending you his contact details."

My grip tightened.

"Okay..."

"Listen carefully. If he doesn't find your situation serious enough, it could backfire. So be clear. Be calm. And most importantly—don't ruin your reputation. Or mine."

"I understand. Thank you, Dad. I promise, once all of this is over... I'll come home."

There was a pause, then a softer tone from him.

"That's what I like to hear. Good luck."

"Thanks. Bye."

The moment the call ended, I shot a message to Daniyal and Shiraz.

Evening. Grove. Urgent. Things are about to get serious.

Because they were.

And we needed to be ready.

CHAPTER FORTY-THREE

SILENCE IS A WARNING

As the sky turned a deep amber with the setting sun, Raghav and I walked briskly toward the grove.

Neither of us spoke.

There was no need.

We both knew the weight of what we were about to do.

We weren't just digging into shadows anymore.

We were dragging giants into the light.

By the time we reached the grove, Shiraz and Daniyal were already there, standing like sentinels in the growing darkness.

Shiraz looked at me, his face unreadable.

"You got the number?"

I nodded and held up my phone.

"Great," Daniyal said.

"Before we call, let's get our story straight. No fumbling. We explain everything—clearly, precisely. One mistake and this entire thing blows up in our face."

Shiraz folded his arms, scanning the dying light around us.

"Yeah. One wrong word... and we're finished."

We huddled in close, hammering out the details—who says what, when, how.

No gaps.

No contradictions.

Then, with a final breath—

I dialled.

The phone rang once.

Twice.

Then a voice cut through—sharp, cold, and unsparing, the kind that demanded instant respect.

"Hello?"

I cleared my throat, my heart pounding harder than it should have.

"Good evening, sir. My name is Aaron. My father gave me your contact and—"

The voice interrupted, slicing clean through my words.

"Your father spoke to us. He didn't mention specifics. If I don't find this worth my time... you're the one who's going to regret it. Understand?"

"Yes, sir," I said quickly.

"But I assure you—this is something only your department can handle."

"Go on. I'm listening."

So I started.

From the beginning.

The invitation.

The early days.

The subtle oddities that turned into glaring red flags.

The confrontation.

The chase.

The records.

The blueprints.

Every thread we'd unravelled.

Then Raghav picked up seamlessly, connecting the dots, laying down the pieces.

Shiraz followed, outlining the psychological tactics, the coded language, the buried whispers of a forbidden text.

And finally, Daniyal tied it all together—the silence from those in power, the walls closing in, and the man who had helped us behind the scenes.

Rohan Mehta.

By the time we finished, nearly an hour had bled away into the dying evening.

The other side of the line stayed silent.

Then, finally—

The voice returned.

Calm.

Measured.

Heavy.

"Rohan Mehta. You're talking about the one who disappeared without a trace?"

"Yes, sir," I said.

"That Rohan Mehta."

A long pause.

"Hmm. Alright. Send me his contact information. I want to verify it myself. And the photos of the blueprints—everything you've collected. I'm sending you a number. Send it all there. Understood?"

"Yes, sir."

"And one more thing," he added.

"Keep this classified. No one else knows—not your classmates, not even your professors. We'll contact you again tonight. Make sure you pick up."

"Understood."

I hesitated—just a second—before speaking again.

"Sir, one last thing. More of a request."

"What is it?"

"If possible... don't inform our parents. We don't want them dragged into this. I hope you understand."

Another pause.

Then, softer—almost human:

"I respect that. Don't worry—I won't involve them. But from now on, follow every instruction given. Exactly. No deviations. Got it?"

"Got it, sir. We're on it."

Click.

The line went dead.

A few seconds later, a message came in with the number.

Without wasting time, Daniyal and I forwarded Rohan's contact, along with every document, every blueprint photo we had collected.

Meanwhile, Shiraz and Raghav called Rohan directly, warning him about the verification call.

Everything moved fast.

Sharp.

Precise.

No mistakes.

When it was all done, we just stood there for a moment, the four of us frozen in place.

We'd done it.

We'd opened the door.

But none of us knew what was waiting on the other side.

Daniyal exhaled first, breaking the silence.

"Let's go to my room. We wait there till the call comes tonight."

We nodded.

No further words.
But as we walked away from the grove, the same thought weighed on all of
us—
We might've just triggered something we can't take back.
And when the night calls back—
we'd better be ready.

CHAPTER FORTY-FOUR

AN HOUR TO BURN

The four of us sat in near-total silence inside Shiraz and Daniyal's dorm room.

No words.

No movement.

Just breathing. And thinking. And fear.

The phone lay on the desk between us, a sleeping grenade.

Every few minutes, it lit up with useless notifications, each *ping* jolting our nerves tighter, sharper—like we were waiting for a sniper's bullet.

Four hours had passed.

Nothing.

Another fifteen minutes crawled by.

Still nothing.

Then thirty more.

Still nothing.

And then—

At 11:03 PM—the phone rang.

Same number.

Same chill stabbing through my chest.

I reached out, my hand cold and clammy, glancing at the others.

Raghav, Shiraz, Daniyal—they gave reluctant nods.

I picked it up.

Speaker mode on.

"Hello?" came the voice.

Sharp.

Direct.

The same man from before.

"Yes, sir. It's Aaron."

"Where are the others?"

"They're here with me, sir. You're on speaker."

"Good. Patch Rohan Mehta into this call. Now."

No hesitation.

No questions.

I did it.

A few tense beats.

Then Rohan's voice chimed in—shaky, but present.

"I'm here."

The officer's voice returned.

Steady as a drawn blade.

"I've gone through everything. Your files. Your story. The photos. I've spoken to Rohan as well."

Pause.

"What you boys pulled off... took guts. That much I'll admit."

A flicker of pride.

Quickly crushed.

"But you're still underestimating how deep this goes. This university isn't just powerful... it's protected."

"Sir," Daniyal cut in, unable to stop himself, *"with all due respect—we've shown you everything. The blueprints, the books, the survivors—"*

"Exactly," Rohan interrupted. *"Isn't that enough?"*

Silence for a beat.

Then the officer said, almost pitying,

"You're thinking like students."

"Not like survivors."

The words hit like a slap across the face.

"If we act now, they'll erase everything. Witnesses. Evidence. Maybe even you."

The words hung in the air.

Heavy.

Icy.

I heard Shiraz mutter something under his breath.

Rohan added, grimly,

"They almost erased me. You think they'll hesitate with you?"

Another pause.

Then Raghav's voice, steady despite the storm inside him.

"So what do we do, sir?"

The line went dead silent.

You could hear the wind scraping against the window.
Then the officer spoke—
Slow.
Final.
"There are two paths ahead of you."
The room stopped breathing.
"First," he said, *"you go all in. You let them think they've won. You surrender. You pretend the ambition, the greed—it's real. You become one of them."*
I felt the blood leave my face.
"You embed yourself in their ranks. Play the part. Record everything. Every move. Every whisper. That will be your proof."
The words felt poisonous, yet strangely hypnotic.
"But know this—" he added coldly,
"—if they sense even a flicker of betrayal... they will end you."
Raghav gritted his teeth.
Shiraz's fists curled into the bedsheet.
"And the second option?" Shiraz asked, voice rough.
The officer didn't hesitate.
"You take what you have... and you negotiate. You show them you know enough to be dangerous. You offer them your silence in exchange for your freedom."
A blade hidden behind the offer.
"You'll save yourselves."
"But you'll have to live knowing you left others behind."
I felt like something sharp had lodged itself between my ribs.
"You can't bring the system down from the outside," the officer finished.
"Not with what you have. Either you burn it from within... or you survive by walking away."
The finality in his voice felt like the tolling of a bell.
No turning back.
No rescues.
No do-overs.
Just consequences.
I looked around.
Daniyal—silent, staring at the ground.
Raghav—seething, but trapped.
Shiraz—jaw clenched so tight, I thought he might shatter.
And me?
I didn't know if what I felt was bravery or pure, desperate stupidity.

Then the officer spoke one last time.

"You have one hour. Call me back with your decision."

Click.

The call ended.

The room collapsed into a deeper silence.

Only the low hum of the ceiling fan remained—buzzing like an insect trapped in a jar.

Rohan's voice—gentler, softer—broke the stillness.

"You, okay?"

No one answered.

He sighed.

"I've been where you are. I wanted to blow it wide open too. I wanted to watch them burn. But it's not that simple."

"You're all braver than I ever was," he added.

Shiraz, for once, spoke up.

"Don't say that. You survived. That matters."

"Barely," Rohan said.

"But you? You have a chance to finish what I started. Just... make sure whatever choice you make—you can live with it."

Then the line dropped.

Leaving behind only silence.

And the clock ticking mercilessly down.

One hour.

That's all we had left to decide what kind of men we were going to be.

CHAPTER FORTY-FIVE

HEART VS MIND

The moment the call ended, and *Rohan* stayed on the line, *silence* took over. That kind of silence that doesn't offer peace—just a *boiling storm* held under a thin sheet of calm.

I sat there, trying to breathe, trying to not let the weight of those two options crush whatever little resolve I had left. My hands were clammy, and I could see *Dan's* leg bouncing in that nervous rhythm of his. The kind he does before a big exam or when we know something irreversible is about to happen.

Shiraz was the first to speak.

"We choose the first option."

His voice was hard. Not loud. Not dramatic. Just sharp enough to cut through the room.

Raghav looked at him, then nodded, his eyes burning with a strange mix of *grief* and *purpose*.

"Yeah. We go in. We play the part. We gather evidence from inside. We take them down from the core. No shortcuts. No compromises."

Daniyal let out a tired scoff.

"You're joking, right? You want to walk straight into the mouth of the beast, willingly? Have you two lost your minds?"

Shiraz turned to him with ice in his stare.

"We've seen what this place does to people. We've seen what it did to Ishan. Don't you dare tell me I've lost my mind."

The mention of *Ishan* shut *Dan* up for a second. His throat moved as if he was trying to swallow down something bitter.

I didn't speak right away. I was listening. I was watching. But more than anything, I was calculating. My mind, unfortunately, was too wired for logic to ignore what it knew.

"Listen," I said finally. "I get it. I do. The first option—it sounds heroic. Noble. But it's not just about what's noble. It's about what's effective. Going in... recording... gathering evidence from inside... It sounds great on paper, but you heard the man—there's a chance they wipe us out. Erase us. And then what? Nothing changes. Everything goes back to silence."

Raghav's jaw clenched. "My brother was in there, Aaron. He can't be a casualty in your calculated risk. He has a right to have justice. And if that means I risk myself, then so be it."

I stared at him. I knew where that fire came from. But I couldn't let emotion bulldoze strategy.

"And what if you die before you serve justice? What if you're caught the moment you 'join'? Do you honestly believe these people don't anticipate that move? We aren't James Bond, Raghav. We're students with a few screenshots and a dissident on a burner phone."

"Better to die trying than live knowing we chose to do nothing," Shiraz spat back.

Dan leaned forward, his voice low but firm.

"No. Better to live, stay in the game, and make real moves. You think sacrificing ourselves helps anyone? You think martyrs bring down empires alone? This isn't some goddamn freedom struggle from the history books. It's modern warfare. PR battles. Legal traps. We expose them through whatever little leverage we have and we survive to finish the job."

"And who do we save with that plan, Dan?" Raghav fired back. "Half the people stay trapped. And we sleep knowing we sold them out to protect ourselves."

"We didn't sell them out," I snapped, my voice louder than I intended. "We chose to fight smart, not suicidal. You want justice? So do I. But not if it means becoming another headline that's buried before the weekends. We play their game, yes. But we twist the rules from the outside. That's how we win."

Shiraz laughed bitterly. "And what if winning means giving up our souls? Our principles? Then we're no better than them."

"No," I said, standing up, pacing. "We're better because we're still fighting. Still breathing. Still capable of changing things—even if not everything. You think going in undercover will fix all of it in one stroke? You're wrong. It'll bury us. Quietly."

The room spiralled into arguments. Tempers flared. Chairs screeched. Words were thrown like knives—some sharp, some reckless.

Rohan never interrupted. He just listened.

For what felt like an eternity, we debated. Morality versus realism. Bravery versus strategy. Heart versus mind. Every line blurred until it felt like none of us were entirely right... or wrong.

Eventually, the fire started to burn low—not because it was over, but because we were tired. *Burnt out.*

Dan finally exhaled and rubbed his eyes. *"We go with option two."*

I nodded. Not because I loved it. But because it was the only thing that kept our feet on the ground.

Shiraz looked away. *Raghav* sat down, his eyes wet but proud.

"We might be choosing this now," he said quietly, *"but don't expect me to call this a win."*

Shiraz added, almost to himself, *"The noble fight isn't always the logical one. But that doesn't make it less noble."*

And for the first time, I had no clever reply.

We had all agreed. But it felt more like *surrender* than *victory.*

Forty minutes.

That's how long we screamed, argued, pleaded, broke down, and clawed at each other with words that would never be forgotten. It was only when *silence* finally reclaimed the room that I checked my phone and noticed the time.

Forty damn minutes.

And *Rohan* was still on the line.

"Looks like a decision has been made," he said quietly.

Raghav shot up from his chair, his voice laced with fury and disbelief.

"Why the hell didn't you say something? You've been through this. Don't you think you should've intervened?"

There was a pause. And then *Rohan* replied, his voice low and calm—too calm.

"See... whatever I say, trust me, it won't make this better. And honestly... there are no right decisions here. No perfect options. What this fight carries isn't clarity—it carries consequences. You will lose something, no matter which road you take. Because this fight... it was never fair to begin with."

He took a breath. I imagined him rubbing his eyes somewhere in a dark room, staring at the walls of a life that was never truly his again.

"Your hands are tied. And they... they've always had the upper hand."

Silence again. But this time it wasn't stormy. It was the kind that followed *funerals.*

I looked at all of them—*Shiraz, still burning; Raghav, barely holding together; Daniyal, pacing in his head like he always did when planning the next move.* And I? I felt the weight of *reality* settle in my spine.

I tapped to reconnect the officer.

"Sir," I said when he answered. *"We've made our decision, we are going with the second option"*

A breath passed on the other side. Then his voice, respectful and composed. *"I understand. All the best, guys. Make sure this is the most effective negotiation you've ever made. Go prepared. Be prepared. You're very brave—and I truly, truly respect that."*

Rohan added softly, *"So do I."*

Shiraz looked up. *"Sir... if it's not too much of a trouble... may we know your name?"*

There was a brief pause, then the voice returned—calm, human, maybe even a little proud.

"You can call me Vinay."

I nodded, a faint smile on my lips, though it felt like it belonged to someone else.

"Good to know, sir."

"Hmm..." he murmured, then asked, *"Tell me—how will you find him?"*

I looked at all of them. Then at the storm outside the window, and back at the phone.

"Don't worry, sir," I said quietly. *"I know how to find him."*

Dan looked at me, then turned to the others.

"You are thinking what I'm thinking?"

Raghav nodded grimly. *"I think we're all thinking the same thing."*

Shiraz pulled his hoodie back over his head and stood. *"Then it ends tonight."*

I held the phone again.

"We'll give you a call as soon as we end it. But if we don't... understand something went south."

There was a deep breath on the other end. Then *Vinay* replied, with steel in his voice.

"If anything happens, I'll make sure a team storms the university. Immediately. No matter the consequences."

We ended the call.

The room didn't feel like a dorm anymore. It felt like the eye of a storm. *A quiet battlefield before the first shot.*

We each knew what we had to do. There was no turning back now. We had one night to prepare.

And one final shot to end it.

I stood up, grabbed my bag, and looked into the dim light above our heads.

The calm was starting to rot. And in that rotting calm, I knew one thing: Tonight, someone's truth would die—either ours or theirs.

CHAPTER FORTY-SIX

WELCOME TO THE ABYSS

The room was *eerily silent* as we prepared ourselves — not just for a meeting, but possibly for a *reckoning*.

Each of us moved in mechanical rhythm, packing the bare essentials, loading our pockets with whatever courage we had left. It wasn't preparation; it felt more like suiting up for war, the kind where survival was written in probability, not in certainty.

Shiraz reached into the depths of his old duffel bag, pulling out a small, battered pen drive.

He held it up between two fingers like it weighed more than it should.

"When Agasthya left," Shiraz said, his voice low, almost reverent, *"he gave me this. Told me if we ever needed to do it again... this would be the key. Full access to the security feeds. All I had to do was connect it."*

Without waiting for a reply, he jammed the pen drive into the laptop.

The screen flickered violently for a second. Lines of alien code streamed down like digital rain, completely incomprehensible. None of us spoke — what was there to say? We simply watched the screen like it was pronouncing our verdict.

Finally, *Shiraz* hovered over a blinking cursor and hit *Enter*.

The screen turned black... then flashed a single line:

Access Granted.

A sharp, collective breath filled the room. For a brief moment, it felt as if the entire universe had gone silent, watching us.

"I guess that's it," Shiraz said, forcing a smile that didn't reach his eyes.

"Good," Daniyal muttered, adjusting his jacket. *"Now all that's left... is to go back there. One last time."*

Shiraz paused, his hand still lingering near the laptop. His jaw tightened.

"Think about it once more, guys," he said, turning to us. His voice cracked slightly, not from fear — but from belief. *"We can save them all. We don't have to be selfish. We can still choose the first option."*

Raghav immediately backed him up, stepping forward with eyes that burned with conviction.

"Exactly. Let's do it the right way," Raghav said fiercely. *"It's not about us anymore. It's about them. About everyone who suffered."*

I closed my eyes for a moment, feeling the storm swirl inside me. Their words weren't wrong. They were noble.

But *nobility didn't guarantee survival.*

I opened my eyes slowly and met theirs.

"Guys," I said, my voice firm, steady. *"We discussed this. Please. Let's not make it complicated now. If we splinter again, even for a second, we lose everything."*

Daniyal nodded sharply. *"He's right. We can only pull this off if we're united. No doubts. No divisions."*

For a moment, *Raghav* and *Shiraz* stood frozen, trapped between heart and mind. I could see it written all over them — the desire to scream, to fight, to drag us back to the more righteous path.

But righteousness didn't matter if we were dead.

Finally, *Shiraz* gave a slight, reluctant nod. *Raghav*, too, though his fists were clenched so tightly his knuckles went pale.

No words were exchanged after that.

Shiraz closed the door to the dorm room with a soft, heavy click — a sound that felt almost like a coffin being sealed shut.

We began walking toward the exit of the hostel. The halls stretched before us like a tunnel to the unknown.

Outside, the night had turned bitterly cold.

The air was thick with fog, curling and slithering around the lamps like ghostly fingers.

The earth was dry, cracked under our boots, but the cold still bit into our bones.

It was the perfect weather for *betrayal.*

The perfect night to make a *deal with the devil.*

And as we stepped out into the mist, I realized — we were already halfway there.

The four of us walked through the sleeping campus in a perfect line, our footsteps almost mechanical, synchronized as if we were a single organism moving toward its final act.

For the first time, all of us were heading to the *Admin Building* together.

It was a strange comfort — a small flicker of *solidarity* — but even that couldn't mask the grim reality: walking in together was guaranteed.

Walking out together?

That was still very much up for debate.

Because the man we were about to summon — *him* — wasn't just a person.

He was a *force of nature*.

A phantom stitched together from *nightmares* and *fear*, and the scars he left on our minds — on *Daniyal's, Raghav's, and mine* — still hadn't healed.

Would never heal.

Shiraz hadn't met him yet.

But deep down, I knew — once he did, he would understand why fear wasn't just a reaction around this man.

It was a *religion*.

In the room, we had promised each other: no backing out. No fear. No hesitation.

But promises are easy when you're wrapped in the safety of walls.

Out here, in the dead of night, with every step toward the *Admin Building*, words meant less, and reality weighed more.

My mind flickered traitorously — to *home*.

To the life I had left behind in *Vapi*.

The life that, until tonight, I had assumed I would eventually return to.

For the first time in weeks, I wondered if I'd ever see it again.

Nobody spoke.

There was nothing to say that hadn't already been screamed inside our own heads.

Finally, the looming skeleton of the *Admin Building* emerged from the mist — dark, cold, and ancient, like it had been waiting for us all along.

We stopped at the threshold.

I looked at them — *Daniyal, Raghav, Shiraz* — and they looked back.

No words.

Just a nod.

And then we stepped inside.

The air inside was heavier, charged, as if the building itself knew what was about to unfold.

We made our way downstairs, moving deeper, step after step, toward *Level*

R — toward the hidden world that normal students never even dreamed existed beneath their feet.

When we reached the cold landing of *Level R*, I signaled *Raghav*.

He nodded, his hand trembling just slightly — a detail no one acknowledged — and reached out to pull the alarm.

Immediately, the corridor drowned in *red emergency lights.*

The world became a living nightmare, bathed in blood and warning.

Right on cue, the tiles near the *Records Room* started to rumble and shift, grinding away to reveal the hidden staircase spiralling down into the abyss.

For me, for *Daniyal*, for *Raghav* — it was almost routine now.

But *Shiraz...*

I glanced at him — his mouth slightly open, eyes wide in disbelief, exactly like we were the first time we had seen this impossible place.

There was no time for wonder.

Without hesitation, we began descending the hidden stairs — one after another, the red lights pulsing above like a heartbeat counting down to our fate.

Every step downward felt like a *pact* being signed.

And then we hit bottom.

The base of the staircase opened up into the dark, cavernous chamber — the place where it would all happen.

Where our fate would be decided.

There was no need for words anymore.

No pep talks.

No strategies.

All that was left to do...

was *wait.*

In the thick silence, standing there on the brink of everything, I realized:

There are moments in life when you are not walking into a fight. You are walking into your own *reckoning.*

And tonight...

reckoning had a name.

The minutes dragged like hours.

We scattered slowly around the massive underground hall, pretending to browse the old shelves, the broken cabinets, the dust-laden files.

Somewhere inside these yellowed pages were the blueprints of secrets so horrific they had already changed us — twisted us.

Each document we touched was a reminder of why we were standing here.

Of why there was no going back.

The heavy silence around us was broken only by the faint hum of the emergency lights, flickering with mechanical exhaustion.

Then —

a voice.

Sharp as a blade.

Calm as death.

"Looks like the last time I let you three walk away, you weren't satisfied,"

"Perhaps you came back... for more."

I froze.

I didn't have to turn around to know.

He was here.

I heard the deliberate, slow click of shoes against stone — a rhythm too calculated, too theatrical to be anything but intentional.

When I turned, I saw him — emerging from the shadows, descending the hidden staircase with a composure that was almost *inhuman.*

He was wearing a *charcoal grey three-piece suit* — razor-sharp, perfectly tailored — that made him look like a man carved out of *ambition* and *cruelty* itself.

His black shirt underneath, no tie, gave him a predatory elegance.

Cuffs gleaming faintly.

Every move, every glance, screamed one thing:

You are already losing.

There was a faint smirk playing on his lips as he approached — the kind of smile a wolf gives before it tears the throat out of a lamb.

His cold eyes scanned us with surgical precision — and then landed on *Shiraz.*

"Ah," he said, voice smooth, almost friendly,

"Looks like Shiraz wanted to meet me too. How are you, my guy?"

We didn't react to him knowing *Shiraz's* name.

It was almost expected.

If he had known the three of us this intimately, of course he had files on *Shiraz* as well.

Nothing about him was casual.

Nothing was accidental.

Daniyal, standing firm despite the tension practically bleeding off him, shot back:

"We didn't exactly want to see your ugly face again..."

"But we didn't have a choice, did we?"
The man's smile widened — thin, dangerous.
He walked — no, glided — towards *Daniyal*, closing the space between them with a casual menace.
When he was close enough that the air between them seemed to shiver, he leaned in and whispered just loud enough for all of us to hear:
"I like that you're trying to act like a man..."
"But don't you forget how the last time went."
He tilted his head slightly, mockingly, eyes glittering like knives.
"I still remember the promises I made."
"I can still make those things happen."
Then, moving with terrifying grace, he shifted sideways — and leaned toward *Raghav*.
There was a different tone now — softer, crueller.
He whispered into *Raghav's* ear, barely audible but heavy as a death sentence:
"And if I get mad..."
"It won't be good for you."
"Or your family."
Raghav's fists clenched instinctively, but I could see it — the slight tremor in his arm, the tightening of his jaw.
No matter how much we had promised each other back in the dorm room — no fear, no backing out — facing him like this, so up close, it was a battle just to stay standing.
He had come prepared to break us again.
And he was doing it without even raising his voice.
I swallowed the lump of anger and fear clawing at my throat.
He still had the upper hand.
And if we didn't turn things around — right now — everything we had fought for would die before it even began.
The four of us stood there, hearts hammering in our ears, facing the man who had mastered the art of *psychological war*.
The *reckoning* had begun.
And this time, there would be *no mercy*.

CHAPTER FORTY-SEVEN

VICTORY WITHOUT GLORY

We stood frozen, a wall of four against a force that felt almost inhuman.

In front of us, he stood—dressed in a perfectly tailored black suit that caught the dim red lighting like it was woven from night itself. His posture was effortless, casual even, yet it radiated a dominance so suffocating it felt like standing at the edge of a cliff in a hurricane.

None of us spoke.

Maybe because words would have sounded too small against the magnitude of what we were facing.

The man noticed our silence. A slow, knowing smile curled on his face, the kind of smile that was built on certainty—the certainty that he already owned this room.

He stepped back lightly, almost as if he was giving us space to breathe, though we all knew it was just another one of his games.

"Well," he said, his voice slicing through the silence like a blade, "looks like you understood quickly."

He laughed softly under his breath, the sound dry and venomous.

"Now, now... I don't care if you came here again to dig out some dirt on whatever you think the university is doing. Whatever you're doing here," he circled around us slowly, hands in his pockets, eyes gleaming with a savage amusement, "is useless."

The weight of his presence was unbearable, like iron chains slowly tightening around our lungs.

"You can't beat it," he said simply. "You never could."

He stopped just beside me, his breath cold against my ear.

"So, I'm giving you a chance," he continued, stepping back to address all of us. "Join me. Trust me when I say..." —he smiled— "I'll make you the best corporate leaders the world has ever seen. Titans. No one will ever even come close to what you will build."

For a moment, a silence followed, and for a split second, I felt how tempting it sounded—the power, the freedom, the untouchable success.

But that thought was ripped apart when Raghav spoke, his voice sharp, breaking the air cleanly:

"You don't make leaders," Raghav said, teeth clenched, fire in his voice. "You make slaves. You brainwash them into following your orders and worshipping your empire."

The man's smile didn't fade. If anything, it widened.

"So?" he said casually. "What's wrong with that?"

He pivoted, speaking like a man giving a lecture to a room full of idiots.

"Understand this, kid. The world only cares about one thing—results.

The better the results, the higher your emergence. The more you control the outcomes... the more you control the world."

He took a few slow steps, like a wolf circling prey.

"The more power you have... the less anyone can touch you."

Shiraz stepped forward then, his voice cutting in with raw defiance.

"And what about emotions?" Shiraz snapped. "The emotions you erase. You strip people of everything real—turning them into hollow machines who care about nothing but winning."

For the first time, the man's mask cracked. His face hardened, and he turned sharply.

"Emotions," he spat the word like it disgusted him, "are for the weak.

Emotions are parasites. They distract you, weaken you, chain you to mediocrity. I erase them because I help people become something bigger. Something unstoppable."

He paused. His eyes—dead, bottomless—swept over all of us.

"Now listen carefully," he said, voice suddenly low, calm, more terrifying than before.

"You have two choices: join me... or face what's coming for you."

He looked at us, his gaze heavy, loaded, final.

"And if you think about forcing my hand..." he leaned in closer, his voice now a whisper of death,

"You know what I'm capable of. Or..." —he smiled, almost kindly— "do I need to remind you again?"

I could feel Raghav's fists clenching beside me. Daniyal was breathing hard through his nose. Shiraz looked like he was ready to explode.

As for me...

I knew one thing.

He still held the upper hand.

And if we didn't turn the tables right now, everything we had prepared, everything we had fought for, would be obliterated.

It was now or never.

And failure... wasn't an option.

I didn't wait for anyone.

I stepped forward, matching his cold, poisonous calm, forcing my voice to be steady, dominant.

"Well then," I said, ice dripping from every word,

"What are you waiting for?

Do it.

Make us disappear. Torture our families. Burn everything we have."

I leaned in slightly.

"But remember... once you start, the carnage that follows won't be ours to carry."

He smiled.

A slow, almost pitying smile.

"And what exactly," he asked, tilting his head,

"Is this carnage you're so confident about?"

Before I could answer, Daniyal took over, stepping in, voice sharp as broken glass.

"Do we look like fools to you?" he said.

"You think we didn't come prepared?"

The man's expression didn't move.

But I saw it—the slight tightening around his jaw.

"We know about the Silent Gospel of Nyx," Daniyal continued, voice low and lethal.

"The ancient book you use. The key to total manipulation."

For the first time, a flicker—barely a blink—ran across the man's face.

A glitch in the system.

But he hid it fast.

Shiraz moved in like a second wave.

"Not just that.

The MBI knows we're here.

They know you're here too.

And if something happens to us..."
He smiled darkly.
"Let's just say it'll get very messy, very fast."
Raghav, steady and fearless, stepped up beside him.
"So..." he said, raising his voice just slightly,
"Still think you can play your old games on us?"
The man stayed still, like a statue made of something much darker than stone.
And then... he laughed.
A deep, hollow laugh that bounced off the empty walls.
"You really think," he said between fits of laughter,
"Some garbage agency like the MBI can stop me?"
He shook his head, almost pityingly.
"There is nothing in this world that can stop me," he said, voice dropping like a blade.
"I can make you disappear.
I can make the MBI disappear.
I've erased people. Erased entire histories. Entire bloodlines.
What makes you think you're any different?"
The air around us turned colder.
But Shiraz didn't hesitate.
"Exactly," he shot back.
"You can erase us. You can cover it up like you always do."
He stepped forward, voice rising with precision:
"But you can't stop the investigation that follows.
Because we planted enough proof. Enough trails. Enough dirt."
"And when that blows open," Raghav added, eyes gleaming,
"You will lose all the bright students who once wanted to study here, because of this news many geniuses will avoid this university."
The man's face hardened, but he stayed silent.
And that's when Raghav went for the kill.
Instead of pushing harder, he softened his tone—controlled, composed, strategic.
"Look," Raghav said, almost conversationally,
"Instead of wasting your energy and resources trying to vanish the investigation...
fighting fires you can't fully put out...
why don't we meet halfway?"

He paused just enough to let the weight of the words settle.
"Let's say... a compromise.
What do you say?"
A beat.
A silence so sharp it could slice skin.
The man stared at us—long and hard.
Calculating.
Measuring.
And then, after what felt like a century, he smiled again.
But this time... it was different.
Quiet.
Acknowledging.
"You boys," he said, voice low,
"Are the most impressive students I've seen in a long, long time."
He looked at each of us like a king regarding worthy enemies.
"You have my respect for that."
There was a long pause before he added, slower:
"But mark my words...
If this turns the other way... if you overstep even once...
I won't be cooperating anymore."
He leaned in ever so slightly.
"So choose your next words very, very carefully."
I could feel it.
The shift.
The tides turning.
We had clawed our way to a fighting chance.
And now...
We had to make sure we didn't lose it.
The room felt like a pressure cooker about to blow.
The man stood there, arms behind his back, an executioner waiting for the
condemned to beg.
I took a breath that burned my lungs and spoke, calm but cutting,
"Here's how this ends."
He said nothing — just studied me like he was studying a lab rat.
"First," I began, "you agree to leave our batch alone.
No more targeting, no more psychological games.
Do whatever you want when the next batch comes in,
but for this batch...

it's over."
The man raised an eyebrow, amused, like a tiger humouring a mouse.
"Second," I pressed, stepping closer, "you will not, under any circumstance,
target the four of us again — me, Daniyal, Shiraz, Raghav.
We are done being your pawns."
Still he didn't move. Still that slight, irritating smile.
"And third," I said, "Rohan Mehta.
When he comes back...
you leave him alone.
No surveillance.
No intimidation.
Nothing."
He tilted his head slightly, his smile sharpening into something colder.
"And what do you offer me in return?" he said, voice dripping mockery.
Raghav stepped forward, voice iron.
"We keep your secrets.
We tell the MBI to stand down.
We act like Blackstone Academy is just another boring law university."
"And Rohan?" the man asked, voice soft but lethal.
"No articles.
No exposés.
No interviews," Shiraz said immediately.
"Nothing that puts a spotlight on you."
The man finally chuckled — a deep, cruel sound.
"You boys think you're negotiating from a position of strength," he said,
voice low and oily.
"But you're not.
You're cattle negotiating with the butcher."
I clenched my fists, nails digging into my palms.
Daniyal, unfazed, said,
"Maybe.
But even cattle can gore a butcher if pushed hard enough."
The man's smile froze for just a moment.
"You know," he said slowly, "I could make you all disappear right now.
No questions asked.
No investigation loud enough to matter."
His hand twitched slightly — like he was considering it.
The room grew colder.

Every second stretched like a noose tightening around our necks.
He stepped closer, his voice a whisper now.
"What makes you think you're untouchable?"
Raghav didn't blink.
"Because if you take us out," he said,
"there's a chain reaction waiting."
The man scoffed. "Chain reaction?"
I spoke up, tone flat.
"We've left trails.
Information.
Instructions.
If anything happens to us...
people far more dangerous than the MBI come knocking."
The man stared at me, eyes boring into mine, trying to find a lie.
There wasn't one.
We had made sure of that.
A long, burning silence.
Then, suddenly — he laughed.
Sharp. Bitter. Real.
"You little rats," he said, almost admiringly.
"You think you've trapped me."
"No," I said.
"We're just offering you the cleaner way out."
Another silence.
He walked in slow circles, thinking.
Each step echoed louder than the last.
"You ask for a lot," he said.
"Protection for yourselves, freedom for Mehta... and in return, I get... what?
Silence?"
"Not silence," Shiraz said.
"Survival."
"Longevity," Daniyal added.
"Control," Raghav finished.
The man's expression tightened — not fear, but calculation.
He was weighing futures.
We were offering him a messy survival, not a glorious one.
But survival, nonetheless.
And he knew it.

Minutes passed.
Agonizing.
Finally, he stopped pacing.
Faced us.
Neutral. Cold.
The kind of cold that kills.
"I'll agree," he said slowly, "but on my own terms."
He pointed a finger at us, like passing sentence.
"You get your batch protected.
You get your freedom.
Mehta gets to live his sad, meaningless life.
But understand this..."
He stepped so close I could smell the faint scent of leather and cigarettes.
"...I will continue.
With the next batch.
And the one after.
And after.
This university belongs to me.
My methods.
My rules.
You are nothing but a minor inconvenience."
We didn't argue.
Because he was right.
We hadn't killed the monster.
We had just convinced it to spare us.
The man tilted his head, mocking, but after a long breath... he nodded once.
"Deal," he said, his voice a death sentence wrapped in velvet.
He offered his hand — an executioner's handshake.
One by one, we shook it.
A pact made not in trust, but necessity.
As we turned to leave, he called after us:
"You think you've won," he said softly, almost kindly.
"But you've only bought yourselves time."
We didn't look back.
We couldn't.
Because even though we had saved ourselves...
we knew — deep down —
the price would be paid by others.

We had survived.
But the machine was still alive.
And its hunger was endless.

CHAPTER FORTY-EIGHT

WE LEFT PIECES BEHIND

We walked through the long, echoing hallways of *Level R*, our steps almost mechanical.

The stairway to the ground floor loomed ahead — and we took it, each step falling heavier than the last.

No one said anything.

No high-fives.

No smiles.

Just a hollow, stretched-out *silence* between us.

I tried to search for some feeling of triumph inside me — anything at all — but there was none.

It didn't feel like a *win*.

It felt... *unfinished*.

Inside my head, thoughts raced like *storms* breaking over each other.

How many did we save? *Fifteen? Maybe twenty? Twenty-five, at most?*

And what about the hundreds after us?

The ones who would walk through these very gates, clueless, only to fall into the same trap?

We couldn't save them.

We could do *nothing* for them.

I barely noticed when we stepped out of the *administrative building*.

I didn't turn towards the dormitories like instinct would have commanded me.

Instead, without thinking, my feet carried me towards the *main building* — the heart of this place.

The others followed.

Like silent ghosts.

Like they weren't thinking straight either.

My mind kept spinning:

Who was that man?

What was his real name?

When did all this begin?

Does he really rely only on the Silent Gospel of Nyx... or are there even darker methods in play?

But the worst question — the one that drilled deepest —

Were we ever truly in control... or was this "compromise" exactly what he wanted from the beginning?

Before I could untangle any of it, we reached the rooftop of the main building.

The view stretched out —

The entire university below us.

Pristine. Calm. Ordinary.

A shell that hid more *rot* inside than anyone could imagine.

We stood there for a while, breathing in the cold night air.

None of us spoke, until *Daniyal* finally broke the silence.

"Why the hell are we here?" he asked.

I turned my head slowly, the words falling from my lips without much thought.

"I don't feel like going to the dorm," I said. *"Let's just... stay here."*

The others nodded without argument, like they felt the same unspoken weight.

We all lay down on the concrete rooftop, staring up at the black sky pricked with stars.

The night swallowed us whole.

Then my phone buzzed in my pocket.

A conference call.

I picked it up, put it on speaker.

Vinay Sir's voice crackled through.

"You boys, okay?"

"We're fine, sir," Raghav replied, voice low and steady.

"We did what we had to do," Shiraz added.

There was a pause.

Then another voice — *Rohan.*

"So... what were the terms?" he asked carefully.

Daniyal sat up slightly and explained everything —
Every brutal detail.
Every condition.
How *Rohan* could finally come back home.
How we would have to bury everything deep inside us.
How we could never, ever speak of it again.
Rohan's voice cracked through the phone.
"Thank you... Thank you. I'll never forget this."
There was a long silence.
Then *Vinay Sir's* voice came back, heavy with emotion.
"You boys did something big today," he said.
"Something most people wouldn't even comprehend. Take care of yourselves."
The call ended.
The silence returned, thicker than before.
We lay there, the sky rolling above us, each of us hosting a *silent war* inside
our own heads.
Time passed.
Hours, maybe.
None of us slept.
Not even for a moment.
Finally — a pale gold streak tore across the horizon.
Dawn.
I pulled myself up and walked towards the edge of the rooftop, feeling the
cold bite against my skin.
I looked out at the early morning, a quiet world still asleep, ignorant of the
battle fought inside its borders.
I let the words slip out.
"Looks like we won."
Raghav appeared next to me, his arms crossed.
"Did we?" he asked, almost whispering.
Daniyal came up on my other side, gazing outwards with hollow eyes.
"Well... we fought."
Shiraz joined us, standing firm in the line.
"Did we?" he echoed.
The four of us stood at the edge, shoulder to shoulder, staring into a sunrise
that should have felt like a beginning —
But only felt like the end of something we could never truly fix.
The wind brushed against us.

The university lay silent beneath our feet.

The university lay silent beneath our feet.

About The Author

Murtaza Vapiwala is a law student and a storyteller with a deep interest in psychological thrillers, mystery, and layered narratives. Drawing inspiration from the intersection of legal systems and the fragility of the human mind, he crafts stories that blend suspense, philosophy, and emotion.

Doctrine of the Hollow is his debut novel — a haunting tale of identity, silence, and unseen control set against the backdrop of an elite academic institution. With this book, Murtaza brings to life a world where fear wears the face of reason, and memory can't always be trusted.

When he isn't writing, Murtaza is exploring law, philosophy, cinema, and the kind of questions that don't always have answers.

He can be reached at:

Email: murtazayv07@gmail.com

Instagram: murtaza_stark28